"THE BEST BOOK IN THE GENRE SINCE *THE EXORCIST*!"

—*The Evening Argus*

A JOURNEY TO THE VERY LIMITS OF
BELIEF . . .
AND ONE TERRIFYING STEP BEYOND!

POSSESSION
by
Peter James

"Scary enough to send the heebie-jeebie squad into your living room."

—*The Sacramento Union*

"Solidly entertaining . . . a Gothic occult web strung with madness."

—*Kirkus Reviews*

"If you want to save your fingernails, wear gloves to read *Possession*—but do read it!"

—*Inside Books*

"Chilling . . . the sort of book that could knock Stephen King off the best seller lists."

—*The Times* (London)

Books by Peter James

Possession
Billionaire
Atom Bomb Angel
Dead Letter Drop

POSSESSION

Peter James

A DELL BOOK

Published by
Dell Publishing
a division of
Bantam Doubleday Dell Publishing Group, Inc.
666 Fifth Avenue
New York, New York 10103

ISBN: 0-440-20463-1

Reprinted by arrangement with Doubleday

Printed in the United States of America

Published simultaneously in Canada

October 1989

10 9 8 7 6 5 4 3 2 1

OPM

To Georgina

Acknowledgments

A very special thank-you is owed to my agent, Jon Thurley, whose faith, encouragement and advice have been a constant source of strength. And to Joanna Goldsworthy and the team at Victor Gollancz for immensely constructive input, and for having the belief and the courage to take the ball. . . .

A mention is long overdue to David Summerscale, who taught me English at Charterhouse and who, probably unknowingly, gave me the confidence to start writing.

Many people have helped me with my research, both directly and indirectly, and it is to them that much of the authenticity of this book is due. The list is long, and so many have given much more than I ever asked for: especially Canon Dominic Walker, O.G.S.; the Reverend David Gutsell; the Reverend Jim Mynors; the staff of the College of Psychic Studies; the Reverend Gerald Shaw, Hospital Chaplain, Broadmoor; Dr. Duncan Stewart; Tim Parker of St. Cuthman's Wines; Peter Hall of Breaky Bottom; Renée-Jean Wilkin; Peter Lee; Jim Sitford; my secretary, Peggy Fletcher; and my wife, Georgina, who gave me tireless patience and encouragement.

For life is but a dream, whose shapes return, some frequently, some seldom, some by night and some by day.

—JAMES THOMSON

POSSESSION

1

Fabian lay cocooned in the rich warm softness of the bedding, and stared out through the open curtains. Shafts of red speared the dawn sky, pink, bloody.

He rolled over and studied the sleeping girl beside him. Then he slipped out of bed and walked naked through the tangle of clothes on the floor to the window. He stared out at the morning mist, and at the thick coils of smoke from the last of the winter prunings in the vineyards. Like the aftermath of a battle, he thought, and shuddered suddenly, his thin sinewy body covered in goose pimples.

The air was good, filled with dew and the strange animal smells of the girl that were all over him; he scratched himself, then stared once more out of the window, uneasily.

"Fabian?" There was a gentle rap on the door, followed by a clumsy thump.

"Two minutes." He felt the strain on his throat as he tried to shout and whisper at the same time. The girl stirred slightly, rustling like a leaf in a breeze, and was silent again.

He pulled on his jeans, collarless shirt and pullover, stuffed the rest of his clothes into his bag and sloshed some cold water on his face. He dried it off, took half a step toward the girl then stopped, picked up his bag and went out of the room, closing the heavy door silently behind him.

Otto, Charles and Henry were already outside, waiting. Otto, tall, with his hooked nose that overhung his mouth, his black hair raked sharply back from his pockmarked face, his herringbone coat hanging from his gangly frame, looked like a huge bird of prey. Charles stood beside him, rubbing his hands, bleary eyed, with his usual baffled expression, as if the morning had crept up and caught him unawares. "God, I feel bozoed," he said, yawning. Henry leaned against the car, hands sunk deep in his coat pockets, his eyes closed.

"I'm sorry, I overslept," said Fabian, unlocking the rear hatch of the Volkswagen and pulling out the scraper.

"Any chance of a coffee before we go?" said Charles.

"Let's get some en route," said Fabian, dragging the rubber scraper through the heavy dew on the windows. It was still almost dark out here. He stared at the black, threatening silhouettes of the tall pines, and at the cold gray walls of the château. He glanced up at the windows, and tried to spot the one with the open curtains; he thought he saw a face there and looked away. "I'll drive the first leg."

Charles and Henry squeezed through into the rear seat, and Otto sank down in the passenger seat. Fabian switched on the ignition. The engine turned over noisily, clattering, popping, caught for an instant, then died.

"Ace," said Charles. "Going to be an absolutely ace morning."

"Yrr, ace," said Henry, closing his eyes. "Wake me up in Calais."

"I would prefer to be heading south rather than north," said Otto, toying with his seat belt. "Bloody thing; I can never remember how it goes."

The engine clattered, then fired again, rasping furiously.

"Sorry that we're dragging you away, Fabian," said Charles.

Fabian shrugged, leaned forward and switched on the lights.

"Is she a good screw?" said Otto.

Fabian smiled, and said nothing. He never discussed women.

The girl stood by the window, a flat, drained expression on her face as she watched the red Volkswagen drive off into the mist. She touched her left arm gently; it hurt like hell. She walked over and sat in front of the dressing table and stared in the mirror. She flinched, then stared again closely at the purple bruises on her breasts, at the gouge down her left cheek, at the swelling around her right eye and at her puffy lip, cracked and stained with dried blood. She stared for a long time, straight into her own eyes, unable to avert her gaze, then gently lowered her fingers between her legs and winced in pain at the touch. *"Salaud,"* she said.

"What ferry do you think we'll make?" said Charles.

"If the road's this empty, we should be at Calais around four."

"You're a jammy bastard, Fabian, aren't you."

"Jammy?"

"Yes, jammy."

DIJON . . . MACON . . . LYONS . . . PARIS . . .
The jumble of autoroute signs flashed past as Fabian accelerated hard around the flyover, feeling the tires bite into the tarmac, the tightness of the steering wheel, the crisp roar of the warmed-up engine, the pure thrill of an open, empty road. As the curve straightened out on to the autoroute approach, he flattened the accelerator and the Volkswagen leapt forward. Sometimes it seemed to him the car could take off, be free of the road and fly, fly straight up into the stars. He watched the curve of the rev

counter needle, flicked up through the gears each time the
needle touched the red sector, until he was in fifth, staring
at the speedometer, his foot still hard on the floor. One
hundred and twenty-five miles an hour. One hundred and
thirty.

"What are your plans this term?" said Fabian above
the roar of the engine and the wind.

Otto and Charles looked at each other, not sure to
whom the remark was addressed. Otto pushed in the
lighter and shook a crumpled Marlboro out of a dented
pack.

"I don't make plans," said Otto. "I never make
plans."

"How are your parents?" said Charles.

"Mine?" said Fabian.

"Yes."

"OK." He hesitated uncomfortably. "Still apart.
How's your mother?" He raised his arm and wound the
roof back, letting in a blast of fridge-cold air and a roar
which drowned Charles's reply. He stared at the sun to the
right, a low red ball rising above the hills of Burgundy, the
sun that would warm the grapes that would be made into
wines, great whites, great reds, blood red. In twenty years'
time he might open a bottle of Clos de Vougeot and lean
over to someone and say, "I saw the sun that went into
that bottle; I was there."

The sense of doom enveloped him again; the ball of
sun seemed too close suddenly. He wanted to open his
window and push it farther away. A shaft of light played
for an instant down the dashboard, ran down it, vibrant,
lively, like fresh blood, he thought.

"I'm going to try and play cricket this term," said
Charles.

"Cricket," said Otto, staring at him oddly.

"Cambridge might be my last chance to play."

"Did you say cricket?" shouted Fabian.

"Yes," Charles shouted back.

Fabian saw a cluster of red lights in the distance; there was still not enough daylight to make things out clearly. Several vehicles, bunched together: an amber indicator flashed; something was moving out into the middle lane. He pulled the Volkswagen over into the fast lane, eased his foot slightly on the accelerator and flashed his lights. "I didn't know you played."

"I was in the First Eleven at Winchester."

"First Eleven Wankers." Fabian grinned, turning around for an instant.

"What?"

"Wankers!"

"Fabian!"

Fabian heard Otto's voice, strange, garbled, cut short, and sensed him flinch, tighten up. He stared back at the road.

There were headlights coming straight at them. Big, blinding lights, towering above them, coming the wrong way in the fast lane.

"Truck!" he shouted. "Christ!"

His foot dived for the brake pedal, but he knew there was no point, knew he was too late. Through the glare of the yellow lights he saw the last two digits of the registration plate: 75. Paris, he thought to himself.

Then suddenly he was above the Volkswagen, looking down: Through the open roof he could see Otto, Charles and Henry jerking around like puppets. He watched, fascinated, everything in slow motion now, as the Volkswagen began to crumple against the front of the truck, then he realized it wasn't a truck at all, but another car, a Citroën, one of the large old models, upright, high off the ground.

First the nose buckled, then the roof twisted, then the windscreen seemed to turn to feathers, hundreds of thousands of feathers all floating around; things were flying through the air now, shapes, large and small. The rear doors of the Citroën opened, one inward, one outward, and the Citroën seemed to turn sideways. The back seat was filled with parcels, which began to rise up, slowly, and break open as they hit the roof; little men, white, brown, black, all furry, with their arms opened, gyrated through the air together in a strange ritualized dance. Teddy bears, he realized, as they fell and bounced, then fell.

There was a smell of gasoline; a tremendous powerful smell. Everything was obscured for a moment in a shimmer, as though a layer of frosted glass had been slipped beneath him, then there was a strange dull boom, like a tire bursting, followed by an intense searing heat. The bears burned first, then the paint on the cars started to blister.

Fabian began to vibrate in the heat, shaking uncontrollably. He tried to move, but could not; all around was shimmering now, and it moved in closer, tighter. "No," he said suddenly. "No!" He looked wildly around, struggled again. "Carrie!" he shouted. "Carrie!"

Then, suddenly, he was free of the heat, racing again down the autoroute. The light was brilliant white—the sun must have come up fast, he thought—as he gripped the wheel, felt the car accelerating. There was no need to change gear; the car was accelerating by itself, free of the road now, gliding just above the surface. The road markings had gone, the road signs, everything. He was flying now; he could fly to the stars! He pulled the wheel back, but the car would not climb, and instead flew on silently through the light, toward a vanishing point in the white mist of the horizon. He passed a wrecked car smoldering by the side of the road, then a coach on its side, a truck, its cab torn in half, two cars interlocked like fighting beetles, rusted, abandoned, another car, burning, figures dimly visible through the flames, the light ahead getting more brilliant each second. He looked around. Otto's seat was empty. "Where's Otto?"

"Must have fallen out," said Charles.

"He's just lit a cigarette. Where's the cigarette?"

"Probably taken it with him."

Charles's voice sounded strange, a long way off. Fabian looked over his shoulder. He thought Charles and Henry were there, but was not sure.

"Did we hit that car, Charles?"

"I don't know. I think so."

The brilliant light was hurting his eyes. Fabian leaned forward and fumbled for his sunglasses. Ahead he saw shadows in the white mist, shapes moving. "Tollbooth," he said. "I need some money."

"No," said Charles. "No, I don't think we need any money."

Fabian felt the car lift up, then drop away from him, found himself suspended in the white light; it was warm, and he sank back in it, and saw figures coming toward him.

Then he remembered again, and began to shake. "Carrie!" He tried to shout at the figures, but nothing came out. "Carrie! You must let me. You must!"

The figures were standing around him now, smiling, kind, pleased to see him.

2

Alex watched the waiter pour an inch of Chambertin into her husband's glass, retreat and stand stiffly beside him. David held the glass up to the dim light, swirled it around in his hand, hurtling the wine around the wall of the glass, and then examined the tears of glycerol after the wine had dropped down. He sniffed deeply, frowned, drained the glass into his mouth, sluiced it noisily around then began to chew it as if it were a tough piece of steak. Don't send it back, please God don't send it back, she said to herself; I can't bear it when you send it back.

To her relief he gave a single nod to the waiter and the ordeal was over.

"Chambertin '71," said David proudly, as if he had made it himself.

"Ah," she said, trying to look enthusiastic, trying to pretend for his sake that she really could appreciate a good burgundy, that she could tell a burgundy from a claret, which she never could and doubted she ever would. "Thank you, that's a treat."

"You sound very formal tonight," he said. "It's like taking a maiden aunt out to tea."

"I'm sorry, I'll try and be less formal." She stared at his hands, which had become so coarse, his stubby fingers red, almost raw, with the black grime under the nails, and at the battered tweed suit and the frayed woolen shirt; was

it part of his new image, or did he genuinely not care
anymore? She stared at his face, tanned, relaxed, even
turned a little leathery from the outdoor life, his hair rag-
ged, almost bushy now, like the thick tangle of his beard.
He raised his glass and pointed it at her.

"Cheers."

She raised hers and the glasses clinked.

"Know why people touch glasses?" he said.

"No."

"You can see wine, touch it, smell it, taste it. But you
can't hear it! So we touch glasses; it completes the five
senses."

"Ever the advertising man. It's still in your blood."
She smiled, and pulled out a cigarette. "What about telepathy? Can you communicate with wine?"

"I communicate with it all the time. I even talk to my
vines."

"Do they talk back?"

"They're not great conversationalists. I thought you'd
given up smoking."

"I have."

"That's what London does for you. Eats you up;
screws you up. You do things you've given up, and you
don't do things you've promised yourself."

"I do."

He nodded with a reluctant grin. "Yes. Perhaps you
do."

Alex smiled and raised her eyebrows.

"You're looking very pretty."

She blushed. She had never been very good at taking
compliments. "Thank you," she said stiffly.

"There you go. The maiden aunt again."

"What do you want me to say?"

He shrugged and sniffed his wine. "Have you heard
from Fabian?"

"Not for a few days. He'll be back tomorrow evening."

"When does he go back to Cambridge?"

"At the weekend." Alex saw her husband's face drop. "What's the matter?"

"I was hoping he might come down this weekend. We're doing some planting."

Alex brushed some long strands of blond hair off her face. David noticed the petulance in the motion. Fabian was a touchy subject. "You know, darling," he said, "it's silly, this separation—surely we could—?"

He felt the wall, even before she replied.

Alex fumbled with her cigarette, rolled it around, then tapped it several times in the ashtray.

"I've been thinking a lot about things, David." The cigarette fell on to the pink tablecloth and she picked it up again quickly and rubbed the mark on the cloth with her finger. "I want a divorce."

David swirled the wine in his glass, carelessly this time, so that some spilled over and ran down his hand. "Do you have somebody?"

"No."

She swept away a few more hairs, too quickly, he thought, trying to read the truth in the blush of her face and the blue eyes that were staring down at the tablecloth. God, she looked lovely. The confidence of her success and the toughness that had come with it had changed her, but nicely; changed her into a fine midway stage between prettiness and handsomeness.

"Would it bother you if I stayed up here tonight?"

She shook her head. "No, David, I don't want you to stay up here."

"It is my house."

"Our house."

He drank some wine, then sniffed it again testily, disappointed. "I'll go down to Sussex."

He dropped her off on the King's Road, at the top of the cul-de-sac. "I'll call you," he said.

She nodded, and bit her lip, fighting back the sadness. "That would be nice."

She slammed the door of the grimy Land Rover and turned away, hurrying down the terrace, past the smart front doors of the Regency town houses, squeezing her eyes against the rain and her tears. She threw her coat on to the stand, then walked into the drawing room and paced around restlessly. She looked at her watch. Eleven-thirty. She felt too churned-up to sleep.

She opened the door under the stairs and walked down the steep narrow staircase into the basement, through the light trap and into the familiar smells of developer and fixer in her darkroom. She closed the door behind her with a click that sounded like a pistol shot. She felt acutely aware suddenly of the silence in the room and wondered, for a moment, was noise carried in light? Did you cut out noise when you cut out light? She listened to her own sounds, her breathing, the rustle of her blouse, and for an instant she felt like an intruder in her own room.

She snapped on the light box, unpegged a roll of negatives from the drying line and laid it on the box. She looked closely at one of the frames; a fat black tubular object with two heads stared back.

Alex cut the roll into four strips, and laid them in the contact printer. She switched on the red safety light, took a sheet of bromide paper out of the box and fed it into the printer. "One thousand and one, one thousand and two, one thousand and three." She counted to fifteen, then snapped the light off and dropped the sheet into the shallow plastic developer tray. She up-ended the tray and rocked it sharply, sending the sheet down to the far end with a loud clack.

She watched the image on one frame, white on white, then a smudge of silvery gray appeared. Next came the perforated holes, then the outlines of the two ovals, one lower than the other. What was it? Something long, sus-

pended between the ovals, began to take shape, and then
she realized. "Bastard!" she said, grinning. Some of the
hairs began to appear, then the phallus itself, fat, limp, the
skin at the head saggy, the small slit in the front, like an
ugly grinning reptile. What did it belong to, she wondered.
An elephant? It wasn't human. Couldn't have been.

She shook her head, smiling, pulled the sheet out of
the developer and dropped it into the fixing bath. She
rocked the bath gently for a few seconds, then looked at
her watch and waited another forty seconds. She pulled
the sheet out and dropped it in the wash, checking her
watch again. She tidied up, then looked at her watch again,
impatiently. When the five minutes were up, she lifted the
sheet out and pegged it on the drying line. Thirty-six phal-
luses stared at her, all the same, taken each time from a
slightly different angle.

Idiot, she thought, as she went upstairs. Idiot. She
grinned.

She woke with a start in the large bed and wondered if
she'd overslept. She reached over and picked up her watch.
Six-fifteen. Relieved, she sank back on to the pillow and
closed her eyes. In the distance she heard a truck thunder
down the King's Road. Then she heard the click of a door;
it sounded like her front door. She listened intently, but
realized she must have imagined it, and closed her eyes.
Another hour of sleep. She needed it. Her lungs felt sore
and there was a sharp throbbing pain in her head. She
always smoked too much and drank too much when she
saw David. Separating wasn't easy; sometimes it seemed
harder than staying together.

A shadow passed in front of her eyes in the dark room
and she felt cold suddenly. She opened her eyes and saw
Fabian standing over her bed, could see him clearly in spite
of the dark.

"Darling!" she said.

"Hi, Mum."

She stared up at him; he looked worried, agitated.

"I wasn't expecting you back until tonight, darling."

"I'll get some rest now, I'm very tired."

"You must have driven through the night."

Fabian smiled. "Go back to sleep, Mum."

"I'll see you later," she said, and closed her eyes, waiting for the click of her door closing. But she heard no click. "Fabian, darling, close the door," she called out. Then she opened her eyes and looked at the door and saw it was closed. She smiled, confused, and lapsed back into a doze.

It seemed only seconds later that she heard the shrill cry of an insect in trouble, urgent, insistent, growing louder. She fumbled for her clock, wanting to stop it before it woke Fabian. Her hand groped about on the bedside table, found keys, a book, a glass of water, the hard scaly cover of her Filofax. The shrill insistent beep continued; she lay back for a moment and waited for it to stop, then remembered it would not; the wonderful solar clock that would never switch off by itself, programmed to beep, if necessary, until the end of time. It became, instantly, yet another reason to dislike David. What a damned stupid Christmas present to give; cruel, masochistic. He had bought it because it amused him; wines and gadgets. For a man who had turned his back on urban civilization, he was too damned fond of gadgets.

She pulled on her track suit and padded out into the corridor, quietly, not wanting to wake Fabian, pleased he was back, making a mental note to cancel a meeting that evening so they could do something together, maybe go out and see a film and have some Chinese afterward. He was at a nice age now, in his second year at Cambridge, beginning to see clearly how the world worked, yet still filled with the enthusiasm of youth; he was a good companion, a mate.

She pounded her two-mile route up to the Fulham Road and around the Brompton Cemetery, then scooped

the papers and the milk from the doorstep and went back
indoors. It struck her as mildly odd that Fabian had not
left his usual trail of junk all over the hallway. She hadn't
noticed his car outside either, but maybe he'd had to park
on another street. She went back upstairs, quietly, to
shower and dress.

She wondered whether to wake him up before she left,
but went to the kitchen instead and scribbled a note. "Back
at seven, darling. If you're free we could go to the cinema.
Love, Mum." Then she looked at her watch and flew.

By the time she reached the Poland Street car park
her mood had changed to a sense of gloom. She nodded
mechanically at the attendant as she drove up the ramp.
Something wasn't right, and she couldn't place it; she felt
depressed, flat, and blamed David. Something in Fabian's
expression had unsettled her, as if he had a secret he was
keeping from her, as if there was a conspiracy and she was
the only one not to know.

3

Alex stared in disbelief as her secretary laid a third stack of Jiffy bags on her desk.

"All this is today's, Julie?" She picked up one of the packages and looked dubiously at the label. "Ms. Alex Hightower, Hightower Literary Agency" was spelled out in huge jittery letters. "Hope he hasn't handwritten the manuscript."

"Philip Main called a few minutes ago. Asked whether you had deciphered the message. He may have been joking, but I wasn't quite sure."

Alex thought of the negatives she had developed and grinned. "I'll call him back after I've opened the mail."

"In about two weeks."

Alex picked up her paper knife and searched, bewildered, for a gap in the Scotch tape.

"A Walter Fletcher rang—wanted to know if you've read his manuscript yet."

"Doesn't ring a bell."

"He was complaining bitterly that you'd had it for almost a week."

Alex stared at the shelves beside her desk, piled high with manuscripts of novels, plays, film scripts. "Walter Fletcher? What was the title?"

"The Development of Tribal Dances in the Middle Ages."

"You're joking!" Alex sipped her coffee. "Did you tell him we don't handle that sort of thing?"

"I tried to. He seems fairly convinced it's going to be big."

Alex ripped open the bag and pulled out a shapeless mass of dog-eared papers, several inches thick, and loosely bound with elastic bands. "This one's yours," she said, passing it straight to her secretary, who flinched under the weight.

Julie put it down on the desk and stared at the first page, a barely decipherable code of misspellings, crossings out and red underlining. "He appears to have typed this without a ribbon."

"Look on the bright side," said Alex. "At least it's typed."

The intercom buzzed and she picked up her phone.

"Philip Main for you."

Alex hesitated for a moment. "OK." She pushed the button. "You're mad," she said. "Completely mad."

She listened to the usual sniff, followed by the clearing of the throat that always sounded like a grunt, followed by the long hiss as he drew deeply on the inevitable Marlboro that he poked in and out of his mustache with his nicotine-stained forefinger and thumb. "Did you understand it?" His deep, quiet voice was tinged with a boyish excitement.

"Understand it? What was I meant to understand?"

Sniff; grunt; hiss. "It's a whole new form of communication; a new language. We're evolving from dialogue; it's a random communication mutated into celluloid. Nobody bothers talking anymore, that's too trite; we make films, shoot pictures, pass them around. Dialogue is too dominating—you don't get a chance to develop your thoughts if you're listening to dialogue—but you develop someone's pictures and they talk to you—part of their soul goes into them."

Alex looked up at her secretary and tapped her head.

"So, thirty-six photographs of an animal's genitals were meant to communicate something to me."

Grunt. Hiss. "Yes."

"All it communicated to me was that it was far too small." She heard a giggle from Julie.

"Organs of the Species."

"Organs of the Species?"

"It's the title; I've got the title."

"Of what?"

"A new book; we're going to write it together." Grunt. Hiss. "Your passion for photography. My obsession with the sex organs."

"Philip, I have a lot of work to do. Friday's my worst day."

"Let me buy you lunch next week."

"I have a very busy week."

"How about dinner?"

"I think lunch would be better."

"You don't trust me." He sounded offended.

"Tuesday. I could do a short lunch on Tuesday."

"I'll pick you up at one. All right?"

"Fine. Bye."

Alex shook her head and put the phone down.

"Philip Main?" said Julie.

Alex nodded, and smiled. "Mad. Completely mad, but the book he's writing could be brilliant—the bizz—if he ever finishes it."

"Will anyone be able to understand it?"

"No, so it should win a few awards."

The intercom buzzed again.

"Yes?" said Alex.

"There's a policeman down here, Mrs. Hightower."

"A policeman?" Her instinctive reaction was guilt, and she raked through her mind, trying to remember if she had any parking tickets outstanding. Or had she been reported for reckless driving? Surely not. "What does he want?"

"He'd like to have a word with you." There seemed to be an insistency in her receptionist's voice; perhaps she, too, was intimidated by policemen?

"Maybe he's written a book?" said Julie.

Alex shrugged. "Ask him to come up."

He came through the door with his cap in his hand, looked down at the ground, at his immaculately polished shoes, then up, aiming his eyes at a level just below the top of Alex's desk. He was young, she realized with a shock; she had expected someone old, but he was as young as her son. He had a flat boxer's nose, but soft, kindly blue eyes, shy eyes. "Mrs. Hightower?" he said, expectantly, to both women.

"Yes," said Alex.

He looked nervously at Julie, then at Alex, put his hands behind his back and swayed slightly from side to side. "Do you think I could have a word with you alone?"

"It's all right, officer—my secretary works with me all the time."

He looked at Julie then at Alex. "I think it would be better if I could speak to you on your own."

Alex nodded at Julie. She went out of the room and closed the door behind her.

"Mrs. Hightower—I'm Constable Harper, from the Metropolitan Police." He blinked furiously.

Alex watched him quizzically; he was making her feel uncomfortable.

"You have a son, I believe—Fabian?"

"Yes?" She felt cold, stared past him, out through the horizontal venetian slats at the gray rooftops beyond, saw the rain sliding down the window leaving trails like snails. Her mind started racing.

The policeman unbuttoned the top button of his tunic, then did it up again; he dropped his hat on the floor, and knelt down to pick it up, then composed himself. "He owns a red Volkswagen GTI?"

Alex nodded. What the hell had he done this time? The police had come before, eighteen months ago, when someone had reported him for reckless driving. She nodded blankly as the policeman read out the registration number.

"He's been traveling in France?"

"Yes. Been skiing with some friends—and then he went to Burgundy to a party—a twenty-first—the daughter of a friend of my husband's."

The policeman's eyes were wide, staring, and his mouth was twitching as if an electric current were running through it. Alex looked away from him again, and stared at her face in the word processor screen at the side of her desk. She looked old suddenly, she thought incongruously, old.

"We've had a phone call from the police—*gendarmerie*—er—police, in Mâcon. I'm afraid there's been an accident." The words began to float around her, as if each was contained in a watery bubble; she saw them, heard them again, repeatedly, in different sequences. Taken. Hospital. Arrival. To. On. Found. Was. But. Be. To. Arrival. Dead. She felt one of her knees hit something hard, then again. She stared at the policeman's face, saw two faces, then four.

"Would you like a cup of tea?"

Who had said that, she wondered, suddenly. Him? Her? She spoke mechanically, positively, tried to be courteous; tried not to make the man feel like an idiot, in spite of her mounting anger. "I'm very sorry," she said. "There has been a mistake; a very terrible mistake. My son is at home, asleep in bed, he arrived back safely this morning."

4

Constable Harper departed in a flurry of staccato apologies and twitches. Alex sat down, staring at the spots of rain on the window, and dialed her home phone number.

She heard the click as it answered, and a dull roar. Over the roar, she heard the voice of her cleaning lady. "Hold on, you don't go no away please." There was a clunk, the roar stopped and her voice came on again, clearer. "Very sorry; go turn off 'oover. Missy Eyetoya 'ouse."

"Mimsa, it's Mrs. Hightower speaking."

"Missy Eyetoya no here; you telephone please at office."

Alex waited patiently, and then repeated herself, slowly, louder.

"Allo Missy Eyetoya." There was a pause as if Mimsa was looking something up in a phrase book. "How you you?" she said positively, slowly, triumphantly.

"Fine, may I speak to Fabian please."

"Misser Fibbian? He no here."

"He's asleep in bed."

"No, he no sleeping. I just clean his room. You say he come back tonight; I just clean room for him."

Alex hung up, grabbed her coat and went out into the

corridor. She put her head through Julie's office door. "I'll be back in an hour."

Julie looked at her anxiously. "Is everything all right?"

"Yes, it's fine," she snapped.

She double-parked in the street, ran to the house and up the steps. There was a drowning roar from the vacuum cleaner and a strong smell of polish. She walked through and saw Mimsa, arched like a chicken, vacuuming the drawing room. She ran up the stairs and along the corridor to Fabian's bedroom, paused outside and knocked gently. She opened the door. The bed was neatly made and there were no suitcases, nor any mess lying on the floor. It smelled clean, freshly aired, unused.

She looked around the room, up at the strange gaunt portrait of her son. He stared back down, sternly, arrogantly, hand slipped inside his jacket like Napoleon. The eyes were all wrong; they looked cold, cruel, not those warm eyes that were full of life that was the real him. Fabian had given it to her last year as a birthday present, but it had unsettled her; she had tried it on a few different walls, and eventually hung it in his own room. She felt a shiver as she looked at it now.

She went up and looked in the spare room, then the bathroom; but there was no sign of Fabian having returned. She went to her bedroom, picked up the phone and dialed her husband.

"Can I call you back?" he said. "I'm right in the middle of something urgent."

"So am I," she said, conscious of sounding more hysterical than she had intended. "Is Fabian with you?"

"No," he said, impatiently. "He was going to that twenty-first at the Arboisses' last night. He wouldn't be back in England yet."

"David, something very strange is happening."

"Look—I'll call you back in half an hour. Are you at the office?"

"No. I'm at home."

Alex was conscious of the sound of hooting outside. It was getting increasingly impatient. She hung up and ran down the stairs. Mimsa jumped in shock as she saw her. "Missy Eyetoya, oh you give me fright!" Alex dashed outside. "Sorry," she shouted at a small, thin-lipped man in a large BMW who glared and shook his head. She jumped into her Mercedes, moved down the road, then reversed into the space the BMW had left. She went back into the house.

"You did not see Fabian, Mimsa?"

Mimsa shook her head; the whole top half of her stooped body shook as though it were attached to her legs by a fulcrum: "Don't see no Misser Fabbian. Don't been back yet."

Alex went through into the drawing room and sat down on a sofa, looking around at the apricot walls, thinking, suddenly, how pretty the room looked, and then, suddenly, how strange it felt being at home on a weekday morning. She stared at the bowl of red roses on the table by the door, and smiled. They had arrived by Interflora on her birthday, three days ago. The card from Fabian was still tucked in with them. Red roses; his favorite flowers. He always gave her red roses. She closed her eyes and heard the vacuum rev up again to a crescendo and then undulate, as Mimsa pushed the machine backward and forward over the carpet, relentlessly.

He had come into her room this morning; she had seen him; surely to God she had seen him?

She heard the front door ring and ignored it; probably the milkman; Mimsa could deal with it.

"Missy Eyetoya." She opened her eyes and saw Mimsa looking agitated. "Policeman here." Mimsa's eyes were wide open, bulging; she jerked over her shoulder with her thumb.

"That's all right, Mimsa, show him in."

Mimsa stared at her, and Alex smiled reassuringly, nodding.

A moment later, Constable Harper was standing awkwardly in the doorway, cap in hand, and mouth twitching like a rabbit. "Sorry to bother you again," he said.

Alex swept some hair from her face and pointed to a chair. He sat down and placed his cap on his knees. "Nice house."

Alex nodded and smiled. "Thank you."

"We seem to have a problem." He turned the cap over a couple of times. "I don't know quite how to say this. There is a young man in hospital in Mâcon, who was in the —er—the accident, Mr. Otto—" He pulled out his notebook and looked at it. "Mr. Otto von Essenberg. He says that the other three in the car were a Mr. Charles Heathfield, a Mr. Henry Heathfield and Mr. Fabian Hightower. Obviously he's still in a state of shock."

"Charles and Henry Heathfield?"

"Yes."

She nodded.

"Do you know them?"

"Yes. Their parents live in Hong Kong. Charles is at Cambridge with Fabian. Henry's his younger brother. Are they all right?"

Harper paled, looked at the ground and shook his head. "I understand that"—he shook his head—"that they were killed." He looked back at Alex, and turned the cap over again. "You said you saw your son this morning."

Alex nodded bleakly.

"I'm sorry, this is very difficult." He looked away from her again. "Where exactly did you see him?"

"He came into my bedroom."

"What time would that have been?"

"About six. I think I looked at the clock, I'm not sure."

He wrote carefully in his notebook. His hand was shaking. "About six?"

"Yes."

"Here?"

"Yes."

"But he's not here now?"

"No." She sensed an inevitability dawning on her and she bit her lip.

"Do you know where he's gone?"

She shook her head. It was getting harder to speak.

"Did he say anything?"

Alex nodded. "He said 'Hi, Mum.' I told him I was surprised to see him back so soon; he said he was tired and was going to get some sleep. He was in his room this morning when I left."

"You saw him again?"

Alex stared directly into the policeman's eyes. "No, I didn't see him; the door was shut, and I didn't want to wake him."

"Then you went to the office?"

She nodded.

He made another note. "What time did you leave?"

"About quarter to nine."

"And what times does your cleaning lady come?"

"About nine-fifteen."

"Was she on time this morning?"

"I'll ask her." Alex went out of the room. "Mimsa!" she called. Mimsa, intent on her vacuuming, did not hear. Alex tapped her on the shoulder. "Mimsa!"

The cleaning woman jumped. "The second fright you give me today. We don't got no Ajax. You forgot?"

Alex nodded. "Sorry, I'll try to remember."

"The winnow cleaner no come. He lazy bassard."

"Mimsa—what time did you get here this morning? It's very important."

"This morning, I early. Five to nine. I catch earlier bus—I don' normally catch it, 'cos have to make husban' breakfast; he no have breakfast this morning—got to go to the doctor for the tests, so I catch early; I go early too if OK?"

"Fine." Alex nodded and went back into the drawing room. "She was here at five to nine."

"Only ten minutes after you left?"

Alex nodded.

"Forgive me, this may sound a little rude—do you think you might have imagined your son coming home—dreamt it perhaps?"

The phone rang; she listened for a second to the shrill echoing of the bell, the very normality of it calming her down. She picked up the receiver. "Hello?"

"Hi, darling, sorry about that."

She wished her husband would stop calling her darling; she wasn't his darling anymore; why did he keep having to pretend that everything was all right between them?

"I was right in the middle of a crucial experiment—I've got a catalyst that I think is going to enable me to produce a Chardonnay to rival Chablis; and it'll be cheaper. Can you imagine a really good British Chablis?"

"Sounds very exciting," she said flatly.

"I'm talking about Premier Cru Chablis, at least! Did you sleep OK last night?"

"Yes," she said, surprised. "Fine. Did you get down all right?"

"Yes, no problems—can you hold on a second?"

Alex heard voices shouting in the background.

"Listen, darling, I've got to get back to the lab—there's a slight problem—it's turning brown. Actually I had a weird dream—well, I didn't think it was a dream but it must have been. I was woken up by it, about six this morning; I could have sworn that Fabian came into my bedroom. He said 'Hi, Dad,' then disappeared. I looked all over the house for him when I woke up, I was so convinced I'd seen him. This country life can't be doing me much good after all—I must be cracking up!"

5

She stared at the light oak coffin, with its brass handles, and the red roses that lay on top of it; at the shafts of sunlight playing through the stained glass window; at the kindly face of the clergyman at the lectern. "Now we see through a glass darkly," he read, calmly, serenely.

They were picking up the coffin now; they picked it up easily. Her son was in that; she wondered what he looked like. They hadn't let David see him when he'd gone to France. Too badly burned to identify, they had said. She felt David's hand tugging now. Do I have to stand, she thought, panicking suddenly. Do I have to walk down the aisle, in front of those staring faces? Then she remembered they were friends, all friends, and she followed her husband, lamely, through the haze of tears she was trying to hold back, outside and into the black Daimler.

The cortège stopped in front of the neat red-brick crematorium; they got out into the sunlight and stood silently watching the pallbearers unload the coffin. Two men took the roses off around the corner, and the others carried the coffin into the building and set it down in front of the dark blue curtains. Alex walked up to the coffin and laid a single red rose on the lid. She spoke quietly, with her head bowed. "Goodbye, darling."

She walked back and sat in the front pew beside David. She knelt and closed her eyes, trying to find some prayers, but could think of nothing; she heard the building filling with people and the soft organ music. She tried to listen to the words of the commital service, but could hear nothing, nothing but the sudden click and hum of the blue curtains sliding apart and the coffin starting to move slowly through them.

She felt uncomfortable at the wake, standing in the crush of people in her house, and drained a glass of champagne straight down. A bottle popped loudly near her ear, frothing and spraying, and she was swept backward helplessly in the retreating surge of people, like being carried on a huge wave, she thought.

"I'm sorry, Alex," said a woman in a black veil whom she did not recognize.

"He was a nice chap," said Alex. "They never take the shits, do they?" She fumbled for her cigarettes. Through the crowd she saw Sandy making toward her, her hair a mad cauldron of tangled jet-black strands held vaguely together with what looked like knitting needles. Instinctively she turned away; Sandy's theatrical emotions were more than she could cope with right now. She saw Otto's sharp bird-of-prey face staring down at her, hideously lacerated, a mass of welts and sticking plasters. "Thank you for coming, Otto," she said.

He nodded, gave a half-smile that turned into a cruel grin. "Fabian asked me to," he said.

Alex stared at him, but he turned away from her, back to his conversation.

She closed the door on the last of the guests, took another drag on her cigarette and another long pull on the glass. She was feeling better, from the buzz of the drink, from the cheer of the friends and family who had been around. Only David still lingered, lurking in the entrance to the kitchen, leaning against the wall, glass in his hand. "Would you like me to stay?" he said.

"No, David."

"I don't think you should be alone tonight."

"I really would prefer to be on my own. Please, I have to get over this my way."

"Why don't you come down to Lewes?"

"I'll be OK here."

David shrugged. "I suppose you blame me."

"Blame you?"

"For buying him the car."

"No. Accidents happen; I don't think it would have made any difference, whatever the car."

"If he had been going a bit slower?"

Alex smiled and shook her head.

David picked up a bottle and poured into his glass; only a dribble came out. He looked at the label. "Veuve Clicquot."

"Fabian's favorite; he always thought it was a smart champagne."

"The widow Clicquot." He paused, looked awkwardly at Alex and blushed. He sniffed the wine. "Could have done with a bit more bottle age."

"I'm sorry," said Alex. "Perhaps if you'd asked him he might have waited a couple of years before he died." She walked past him into the kitchen and switched on the kettle. David followed her and put his arm gently around her.

"You know," he said, "it's incredible we should have both had the same dream about him, at the same time. I've been thinking about that."

"It must have been about the time he died," said Alex.

"Most extraordinary coincidence."

Alex opened the jar of Nescafé and spooned some into two cups. "Still taking sugar?"

"One spoon."

"You think it was coincidence?" she said, testily.

David held the glass up to the light and examined the color carefully. "You know I'm sure this used to be a deeper yellow. I wonder if they've cut the aging time down —or perhaps I'm mistaken. The bouquet's fine."

Alex glared at him. "You think it was coincidence?"

"Coincidence?" he said blankly. "Ah, yes, well, of course." He caught the look in her eyes. "Oh, come on now, Alex, you think it was something else?"

She shrugged. "It was very strange; it was just so real."

"We'll have to let Cambridge know," he said, changing the subject.

"I hadn't thought about that."

"I'll call them tomorrow. I'd better write to Charles and Henry's parents too."

They sat opposite each other and drank their coffee. "How's your Chardonnay?" said Alex.

David smiled. "One step forward, two steps back; can't get it to stabilize. How's the agency?"

"Busy."

"Got any blockbusters on the stocks?"

"An anthology of Urdu war chants."

"Is that what the world's been waiting for?"

"I doubt it."

He raised his eyebrows. "I'm thinking of writing a book on wine."

"Good subject," she said. "I've only had sixty-four manuscripts on wine land on my desk this year."

David stood up. "You know what they say, sixty-fifth time lucky."

Alex smiled. "Give me a call when you get home."

"You want me to?"

"I want to know you've arrived safely." She kissed him and closed the door, and suddenly felt very alone.

The hallway was dark, with its somber black and white tiles and high ceiling, and she switched on the light. She walked into the drawing room, with its thick pallor of smoke and perfume and the vinous acidity of the champagne, parted the net curtains and looked through the bay

window at the street; the color had drained out of the clear
sky and it was now a darkening wash. She thought again of
Otto's strange words, "Fabian asked me to." Something
moved behind her suddenly. She sensed it, and felt fear,
stronger than any fear she had ever felt before; she was
cold and her skin was prickling, bristling with cold needles. She felt the room closing in on her and she wanted to
tap on the window, shout for help, but she was paralyzed.
She saw a shadow moving out of the corner of her eye,
rising from a chair behind her.

"Oh darling, excuse me, I must have dozed off," said
the shadow.

She stared, transfixed, as she suddenly realized it was
Sandy.

"Quite overcome by the emotion of it all—I'm on
these tranquilizers, you see, and they just don't go with
booze." She yawned, and stretched. "Has everyone gone?"

"Yes," Alex said, weakly. She switched on a table
lamp, and felt comforted by the warm glow as the color
came back to the room. "You gave me a fright."

"I'm sorry, darling." Sandy blinked, then prodded her
haystack of black hair with her fingers, and adjusted a
couple of the knitting needles.

"Like some coffee?" said Alex, relieved, and grateful
now for the company, even, she thought, Sandy's.

"I'd love some. What are you doing tonight?"

"Nothing."

"What—you're going to be here on your own?"

Alex nodded. "I want to be alone."

"You can't, darling, not tonight."

"I have been every other night; I don't mind it."

They walked through to the kitchen. Alex suddenly
found herself acutely aware of the objects that were in the
house, as if she had entered a museum. She saw the stern
portrait of David's great-grandfather in his cavalry uni-
form. "Fabian has his eyes," David used to boast proudly,
and she had always demurred; there was no point in disil-

lusioning him, no point in spoiling the pretense. Only she knew that Fabian had inherited nothing of David's, not one single gene; it was her secret, and she had kept it for twenty-two years.

"Dreadful," said Sandy. "The whole thing. There were two other boys also who . . . ?"

Alex nodded. "Brothers. Charles and Henry Heathfield."

"Shocking. So shocking. What a terrible thing. A truck on the wrong side of the motorway, wasn't it?"

"A car," said Alex.

Sandy frowned. "I was certain it said truck in the paper."

"It did. They got it wrong."

"A drunk Frenchman?"

Alex nodded.

"How can anyone drive down the wrong side of a highway? However drunk they are?"

The kettle clicked.

"Do you know anything about him, darling?"

"No, not really," said Alex. "Apparently he had a row with his wife. Been drinking all night, his business was going bust. Soft toys, or something." She shrugged. "David knows more about it."

"Dreadful."

Alex carried the cups through into the drawing room, and they sat down. Her head was beginning to ache, and she closed her eyes.

"I think you should see a medium, darling," said Sandy, staring down at the swirling coffee, trying to dissolve the last of the grains.

"A medium?"

"Yes."

"No, Sandy, that's not for me; I'm afraid I don't believe in that sort of stuff."

"I think you do."

"You think I do?" she said, incredulous.

"You're a Christian; so you believe in life everlasting."

"I'm not sure that I do." Alex stared at the nervous mess of a woman sitting opposite, who was now trying to push a cigarette into the end of a long thin holder and was having a harder time than if she were trying to thread a needle. The girl she had known since schooldays, mad, cranky, but kind; a girl who had been through three divorces, who had been a drug addict, an alcoholic, a Christian Scientist, a vegan, who had meditated under the Maharishi Yogi and tried virtually every other religion under the sun, who had made just about every kind of a mess of her life it was possible to make; this girl was trying to give her some advice.

"David told me that Fabian came to see him the morning he died, and he came to see you too."

"We both had the same dream."

"Dream?" She shook her head. "That wasn't a dream, darling, he came to see you; very common occurrence."

"What do you mean?"

Sandy stared at her, her thin tortured face that had once been so pretty but was now looking so jaded, and her huge blue eyes, like forgotten ponds, she thought. "We all have spirit guides, darling, keeping a watch on us, but they're not around all the time. If someone dies suddenly, when the guides aren't expecting it, they can lose contact and the person's spirit can wander around, lost. That may have happened to Fabian; that's why you both saw him; he was trying to get his bearings."

Alex sipped her coffee and stared at her friend with a mixture of contempt and pity.

"You think I'm an old crank, darling, don't you, someone who's made a mess of their life? Well, maybe I have in your terms, but I've had lots of other lives, some extremely happy ones, and I've been sent back this time in order to learn to cope better with rough times. I'm an old spirit, darling, I'm toughened to it all; you're not, I can tell, you're a young spirit, and you must accept my help, that's one of the things I'm here for, to help others."

Alex shook her head. She felt tired, suddenly, hemmed in, as if the room were full of people; she wanted to get away, go out of the front door, walk about outside. "Maybe the dream was telepathy," she said. "That's possible, isn't it?"

"It's possible, darling—plenty of that in the spirit world, but why should it be? We don't know much more about telepathy than we do about spirits. I think he came to you because he needed help."

"What sort of help?"

"He may be all right now, darling; he may have been reunited with his guides, they may have taken him off. But if they haven't, then he could just be wandering around, lost."

"How long would he do that?"

"Time has a different perspective on the other side, darling; it could be forever. You owe it to him to make sure he is all right, and try to help him if he isn't."

"How?"

"By seeing a medium; a medium will know. If you do that, darling, then at least you will know you have done everything you can. I can put you in touch with an excellent one." She paused and dragged hard on her cigarette holder; she blew the smoke out then flapped it away with her hand. "You don't believe what I'm saying, do you, darling?"

"No," said Alex, shaking her head. "No, I'm sorry, I don't."

6

Alex woke suddenly, afraid, sensing a light pulsating in the room. She felt her hair prickling, did not dare open her eyes, but instead, squeezed them even tighter shut, so she could not open them accidentally; she waited. Something was in the room, she could feel it.

She saw the stark wood coffin, the red rose; her face suddenly began to feel hot; she smelled gas fumes, then heat; her face was burning. Her breathing began to get out of control; she was panting, her knees were crashing together under the bedclothes. Her eyes sprang wide open. She sensed a green pulsating light. The light turned from a blur into sharp focus. Four zeros. On, off, on, off. The burning subsided and she felt only cold, and then the fear began to subside too.

She watched the dial on the alarm clock, the four zeros blinking on, off. Midnight, she thought. She looked around the room, saw the shapes, the familiar shapes. She'd been afraid of the dark when she was a child, always slept with the light on; but that fear had gone a long time ago, long before she'd married. The zeros blinked.

She snapped on the bedside light; the room seemed normal, everything seemed normal, sounded normal. She heard a truck in the distance, sloshing down the King's Road; it sounded as though it had been raining. She picked up her watch. Five o'clock, but the four zeros continued to blink. Then she remembered that had happened once before to her previous clock in a power cut; it had automatically reset itself to zero. She fumbled with it, trying to remember how to reset it, staring with tired, strained eyes at the blinking lights, and shivering in the cold. It was almost unbearably cold.

She got out of bed and walked to the window, parted the heavy curtains and put a hand outside. The air there was warm and mild; she held her hand out, puzzled. She saw steam from her breath and let out a small shriek of surprise, felt the hair prickling again down her neck. She stared out through the curtains once more, at the parked cars, at the glow of the street lamp; it was calm out there, normal. She pulled the curtains apart slightly and let the orange light into the room. A floorboard creaked under her foot and she jumped. Then she climbed back into bed, pulled the covers up and closed her eyes, but still she felt cold, bitterly cold, and the cold made her feel afraid. She picked up the telephone, listened to the hum as it pierced the silence, then she punched out the numbers that she knew by heart, and waited.

It rang, once, twice, *please be there,* three times, four times. "Oh please be there," she whispered.

"Yurlo?" She listened to the grunt, filled with relief and felt warm again.

"David?" She was whispering still.

There was another bewildered grunt.

"I'm sorry to wake you, David."

"Alex?"

"Are you awake?"

"Yrrr."

"You didn't call me."

"Didn't call you?" He still sounded half asleep.

"You were going to call me when you got home. I was worried."

"Wassertime?"

"Just after five."

There was a pause, and she heard the rustling of sheets.

"I didn't think you really wanted me to."

She felt his voice, warm, smiling, comforting; it was like talking to a teddy bear. "I was worried about you," she said.

"I'm OK. How are you feeling?"

"Not great. How about you?"

"I feel bloody awful. It's so lousy. I keep thinking about that other driver, the bastard."

"Don't."

"If he'd survived, I would have killed him."

"Don't."

"I'm sorry."

"I feel so bad about Otto and those Heathfield boys."

"At least Otto's alive," he said.

"It must be pretty difficult for him, you know, to accept that he's survived."

"I should never have bought Fabian that car."

"That's not your fault; you were always so kind to him."

"I should have got him something slower."

"I don't think it would have made any difference. Listen, go back to sleep, I'm sorry I woke you."

"It's OK; I'm wide awake now."

"Go back to sleep. I'll call you later."

"I love you," he said.

She stared at the receiver and smiled sadly, then hung up, slowly, gently, and lay back on the pillows. She loved him too, she knew, missed his big warm body, missed his tenderness; why the hell had they parted? She felt tired suddenly, tired and warm and cheered up, and fell into a heavy sleep, and dreamed dreams of Fabian, light and airy, then suddenly menacing and confused; he held her hand and laughed and then taunted her like a child, except he wasn't a child anymore, but a grown man, older suddenly, so old she could see wrinkles in his face. She awoke shivering, afraid to open her eyes in the dark room. Then she slept again and did not dream.

When the alarm went at seven, she ignored it, and when she looked at the clock again, it was ten to eight. Back to normality today, she knew; it was over. There was the scattering of the ashes, but she needed time to think about that, to think where Fabian would have liked them. The last ten days had been a haze, a blur, waiting for the French bureaucracy, trying to get the body released, brought back to England. David had been over to France, taken care of all the arrangements, and had made no demands on her. He had been marvelous. Now she had to get on with her life again, try to concentrate on her work. At least she had that; staff, partners, clients. She couldn't fall apart on them, had to prove to them that she could do it, had to prove it to David; most of all had to prove it to herself.

She toyed around with her wardrobe, trying to decide what to wear. Fabian had always been particular about what she wore, far more so than David. The right colors, the right shape, the right names—God, he had been an unbearable clothes snob at times. She smiled, half-cheered, a damp, tearful smile, and rummaged through a drawer full of silk scarves, all of them Cornelia James, and most of them bought by Fabian. Which ones? She tried to remember, pulling various scarves out and letting them gently drop back in, like cascading waterfalls, she thought. She draped a turquoise and gray one carefully around her neck, and tied it so the Cornelia James signature was clearly showing. Are you pleased, darling, she thought. Do I look OK?

She gulped down half the cup of coffee, left the rest which was too hot, grabbed her coat and hurried to the front door. The bell rang just as she reached it, and she opened it almost before the bell had stopped ringing. The woman looked up at her in surprise and stepped back, a buxom, peroxided blonde, neatly but dramatically dressed in black and white, who looked as if she had come from a casting agency for film extras and spoke through tiny rosebud lips that were too small for the expanse of her face. "Mrs. Hightower?" She spoke in a definite, precise voice as if she had been having elocution lessons to shed her East London accent.

"Yes?" Alex hesitated, on the defensive, wondering what she was trying to sell. She looked too dolled up to be a Jehovah's Witness, and anyway they normally came in pairs.

"I'm Iris Tremayne. Sandy suggested I pop around— she said you went out early and this was the best time to catch you."

The woman stared straight into Alex's eyes, and she found it unsettling, found it hard to disconnect from her gaze. She wondered for a moment whether she was selling Tupperware, or Avon cosmetics; yes, cosmetics looked likely, except that she didn't have a sample case. "Actually, I'm rather late for the office." Alex spoke pleasantly, trying to be polite.

"No, of course, if this isn't convenient I fully understand, but I thought I'd better come round right away. In case you wanted news about your son."

Alex realized suddenly who she was. "No," she said. "Thank you, but I don't want any news about my son."

"I'm very sorry to hear about what happened."

"Thank you."

"Sandy's very worried about him."

"Is she?" said Alex, conscious that her tone was becoming belligerent.

"If you'd like to have a sitting, I'd be very pleased. There'd be no charge; Sandy is a good friend."

"Mrs. Tremayne," said Alex coldly, "my son is dead. Nothing you or anyone else can do can change that; I'm afraid I'm just not a believer in"—she paused—"in whatever you call it—the spirit world."

"I think he wants to talk to you."

There was a sincerity in the woman's expression, a sincerity ingrained deep beneath the makeup, beneath the dramatic hair, a sincerity and a naïveté, Alex thought. You poor deluded fool, she wanted to say, but did not. "Thank you," she said. "But I have to go now."

Alex nodded to her receptionist, avoided catching her eye, and went upstairs to her office.

Julie looked up from her typewriter as she walked past her office, and smiled gently. "Good morning. I'll let you catch up with your post," she said. "Do you want me to cancel any of your appointments this week?"

"No, Julie, we canceled enough last week. The show goes on." Alex closed her door and stared at the bewildering stack of mail on her desk. She looked at the wooden calendar which Julie adjusted every day. April twenty-first. The last ten days had disappeared as if she had been in a hole in time.

She slit open a Jiffy bag and pulled out a neatly typed and bound manuscript. *Lives Foreseen—My Powers and Others'*. She flipped open the cover and turned to the first chapter; the first page always determined whether she would read it herself, or pass it to Julie.

"I always used to see a hand in the dark, beckoning. When I saw that hand, I knew someone would die. The first time was when I was seven, and the next day, my sister was run over by a tractor. That was the first time I became aware of my powers of clairvoyance."

She turned back to the cover, then buzzed Julie. "Does an author called Stanley Hill ring a bell?"

"No."

"I think we may have had something from him before."

"Do you want me to look it up for you?"

"No, I'll do it." Alex switched on her VDT screen and saw three words, clearly, in the center, in bright green letters; HELP ME, MOTHER.

She felt as if cold water were being flushed through her veins. The words faded and the screen went blank. The cold turned to hot, her forehead was burning and she felt sweat running down her face. She switched the unit off, then on again, but this time there was nothing but the word MENU and the list of functions.

Fearfully, she tapped a couple of keys, the menu disappeared and was replaced by the words CLIENT FILE. She moved her shaking hands across the keyboard, tried to tap the search key, but pressed the wrong key and the machine bleeped angrily at her.

"Are you OK, Alex?"

She watched Julie put down the cup of coffee almost as if in slow motion, and she was conscious of the sound of her own words when she spoke.

"Yes, I'm fine."

"You look as white as a sheet."

"I'm very tired. I haven't been sleeping too well."

"Maybe you should take some pills—you know, just until you get over the worst—"

Alex smiled. "I am over the worst."

"I think you've been very brave."

Alex felt her eyes watering, and squeezed them tightly shut; but the emotion welled up inside her until she could not contain it, and she felt the tears flooding out through her eyelids. She felt a hand squeeze hers and squeezed back hard, opened her eyes and saw Julie's pretty face staring kindly; she noticed that Julie had changed her hairstyle; it had been cropped short and she realized she had not commented. "I'm sorry," she said. "I like your hair."

"Thanks."

"You needn't worry, I'm not going to crack up on you all."

"We know that." Julie handed Alex a handkerchief.

"It's OK, I've got one." She blew her nose. "When people call, tell them not to ask me how I am, all right?"

Julie nodded.

"Tell them also not to mention Fabian; it would be much easier for me."

"Yes, of course."

Alex looked fearfully at the word processor. She saw the imprint of the words in her mind. Clear. Unmistakable. "I can't remember how this thing works—I want to find the name of an author—this chap."

Julie tapped the keyboard, and a moment later the words STANLEY HILL appeared.

"Submitted a manuscript to us in 1982, called *Star Gazer to the Stars.*"

"A modest title," said Alex. "Why did we reject it?"

Julie leaned closer to the screen. "Not enough meat."

"There are dozens of other agents—why did he send us his next one?"

"You must have written him a very nice letter."

"I doubt it," said Alex.

"Do you want me to read this one?"

"No, send it straight back; tell him we're not interested in this sort of stuff."

"It sells well," said Julie. "Look at Doris Stokes."

"I don't care if it sells a million; I don't want to handle it."

She watched Julie take the manuscript and walk out of the room, then stared again at the screen. She switched it off. Help Me, Mother. The words went around in her mind. She switched on the machine again and the words stared back at her, calmly, unflickering:

HELP ME, MOTHER.

7

"You look very preoccupied."

Alex waved away the smoke with her hand. "You keep disappearing."

Philip Main pushed the Marlboro cigarette through the hair of his walrus mustache, emitted a long slow grunt which had a rasp to it like a moped racing down a distant lane, and released another explosion of smoke. "In the cosmic sense?"

"No." Alex smiled. "In the physical sense."

"Hrrr," he said thoughtfully.

She waved her hand again. "The smoke, you're getting worse."

"Ah," he said in his soft low voice, shrugging his shoulders apologetically. "A chap's few pleasures; still, this is only a transient inconvenience, for a few more thousand years, five, six maybe at the most—an insignificant time."

"Before?"

"Before we have evolved enough to stay on our own all of the time; no need to meet; all communication will be by telepathy and unexposed film; the thrill of exposure, that will replace all of today's social contact—the pleasures and"—he held up his cigarette—"and the inconveniences."

She stared, smiling, at his elongated frame, shoulders

hunched in his battered tweed jacket, and up at his gaunt fiery face, with the mustache that hung down like a statement. In his forties, he still looked more like an overgrown student revolutionary than a scientist with three respected, if controversial, books to his name. "How's the book coming?"

He lowered his head and stared at her as if she were a goldfish in a bowl. "Proof; there is proof." He raised his wineglass, drank and lowered it again, leaving his mustache looking like a damp rug.

"What proof?"

"You'll see. You'll be stunned, girl, stunned." His face changed as he spoke, becoming animated.

"Good," she said, feeling rather lost.

"Irrefutable proof that Darwin was right."

"You've been able to recreate the origins of the universe in a repeatable laboratory experiment?"

"There's a little bit of fine tuning, but yes, good Lord yes, I've seen it done. DNA, girl, out of two bits of dust."

"And where did the dust come from?"

"Thin air, girl," he said, triumphantly. "Thin air!"

A waiter presented her Dover sole for inspection and then began to fillet it.

The tone of Main's voice suddenly became gentle. "Has your husband been around the past couple of weeks?"

"What do you mean?" She felt herself blushing, saw the almost imperceptible motion of the waiter's head as he tuned his ears in.

"Has he been of help?"

"Yes, he's been a brick."

"Good," he said without enthusiasm.

She blushed again and looked at the waiter, who was having problems with the sole.

"Does he still want you back?"

"I, er—" she said, and faltered. She looked at her watch and pressed the date button: 5/4, it read. She stared at it, puzzled. *May 4?* "What's the date today? It's April still, isn't it?"

She stared at her watch again, confused.

"Alex? Alex?" She heard the words echoing around her head, tried to work out where they were coming from; she saw the face across the table, his mouth opening, closing. "Alex? Are you all right?"

The face went out of focus then came back in again. "Yes," she said. "Yes, I'm fine."

"You've gone very white."

"I'm sorry." She looked down at her watch again and frowned. "What's the time?"

"Twenty to two."

Her watch was correct. "Was there a thunderstorm last night?" she said.

Main frowned, then suspiciously eyed the sole that was placed in front of him. "Was this in a fight?" he said to the waiter, his voice suddenly stern and loud.

"A fight, sir?"

"Looks like it's been in a war."

"I'm sorry, sir." The waiter hesitated, then retreated.

"Thunderstorm?"

"Or an electrical storm?"

"There may have been; it was very humid last night."

Alex felt liberated suddenly. "And could that affect electric appliances—clocks, things like that?"

He frowned. "Possibly. Can cause interruptions in the power supply."

She was silent for a moment, thinking. "Could it affect solar-powered things too?"

He nodded slowly. "Possibly. Why?"

"Oh, nothing."

He looked down and glared at the fish malevolently, then drank some more wine and dabbed his mustache with his napkin.

"What's your opinion of mediums, Philip?"

"Mediums?"

"A friend of mine said I ought to go and see one."

He spooned carrots out of a partitioned dish of vegetables and looked uncomfortable. "Have some carrots," he said. "They do them well here."

She took the bowl. "You haven't answered."

"There are some people who find mediums helpful."

"Who? People who can't accept that someone's dead?"

He shrugged. "Are you a Christian?"

"I suppose so."

"Therefore you believe in eternal life."

"I'm not sure what I believe in any longer."

"Excellent piece of evolution, the Dover sole." He speared a bit with his fork and lifted it. "Used to swim upright." He put his fork down and held up his hand vertically. "Didn't start swimming flat until they moved to the bottom of the sea—realized they would be less visible."

"Smart."

"They had a—problem with their eyes. One either side of their head. Fine upright, but swimming flat, one eye always looking at the sea bed, one up at the sky; one day, pop, both eyes appeared on top."

"What's that got to do with mediums?"

"Can't you see? Evolution is about making nature work. We can prove God did not make man. But what about the other way around?"

"That's an old argument."

"No, it's new; brand new."

"That man may have invented God?"

He speared his fish and held it up in front of his mouth, examining it carefully. "No, girl, not invented. Made! Made! If the whole animal world has evolved from two specks of dust and a bolt of electricity, why not a spiritual world too?"

"You're bonkers."

"I'm smarter than this fish."

"How do you know?"

"Because otherwise it would be eating me."

She grinned. "At least you're cheering me up."

"Yes, well, we all need a bit of cheering up from time to time."

She ate a mouthful of fish. "It's good, even if it does look like something that survived the Glencoe massacre."

He put his knife and fork down, and blushed slightly. "I—er—I was wondering—would you let me buy you dinner one evening? You know—not just yet awhile—but perhaps in a bit?"

She shook her head. "I like my relationships with my clients to be strictly professional."

He lifted his napkin up to his mouth and spoke at the same time, so that his words were muffled. "We—er—could have a strictly professional dinner."

She shook her head. "Don't, Philip. I'm not in any state to start trying to cope with a relationship."

"I'm just offering the hand of friendship; nothing more."

"OK, thanks, I understand. Let's just keep it a lunch-time friendship."

"Are you free for lunch tomorrow?"

She laughed. "Tomorrow's Saturday."

"Saturday's a good day for lunch."

"I'm going to Cambridge tomorrow—I have to sort out Fabian's things."

"Maybe next week?"

"Maybe."

Lunch with Philip Main had lifted her, and she was feeling considerably cheered when she got home. She thought again of the three words on the screen. The strain, she thought. It must be.

The house was quiet and peaceful, and smelled strongly of polish. It was growing dark. The clocks had been set forward. Summer Time had started, but it didn't feel much like summer.

She stood in the hall and suddenly felt as if she were in a vacuum. The last ten days had passed in a haze and now there was a return to normality that seemed flattening. She wished she had taken up Philip's offer of dinner, or her husband's. She did not want to be alone this evening, to dwell on her thoughts. She looked up the television programs in the *Standard,* but there was nothing she fancied. She dropped the paper on to a sofa and went down the narrow staircase into her darkroom.

Photography; there was something intensely personal about photography, and it was instant, told the story without having to wade through the manuscript. Perhaps Philip was right. But there was so much to learn about it. She'd missed the last classes; time, there was never enough time. When David had built her the darkroom she had loved locking herself away down here; she had felt peaceful and safe with the silence and the strange smells of the chemicals. But tonight she felt uncomfortable here; the silence was oppressive.

Philip Main's disgusting contact sheet was still on the drying rack. She unpegged it, hoping Mimsa hadn't noticed it, and was about to tear it up when something caught her eye, a mark, very small, on one of the frames. She picked up her magnifying glass, switched on the light box and looked at the print.

Fabian's face stared back, clearly, from the bottom right-hand corner. And then she noticed it was on every frame, in the same position.

She dropped the magnifying glass; it hit the white Perspex of the light box, cracking it badly, and she stood, shuddering, her skin prickling.

Fabian's face had appeared on the print since she had developed it.

The walls seemed to be closing in. She spun around; the door had moved, she was certain. She grabbed the handle, pulled it open. There was nothing there. "Hello," she

said. "Hello?" She stared through the door, but everything
was quiet.

There was a shrill rasping which seemed to shake the
whole foundation of the house. She let out a small yelp of
fear and clutched the door frame. The rasping ended in a
series of metallic pings. Doorbell! She felt the relief surge
through her. *Don't go away, oh please, don't go away!* She
ran out of the room and up the stairs, desperate to catch
whoever it was before they went away, desperate for some
company, some human contact, any.

She opened the door and stood, gasping for breath, as
she stared at a young man with an earnest, scrubbed face
and short curly hair. He was wearing a shabby gray suit,
too old for him, probably a castoff from someone, she
thought, and a polo neck sweater. She looked down at his
shoes, scuffed, shapeless black shoes that badly needed a
polish. Perhaps they were castoffs too?

He spoke slowly in a gentle voice, carefully articu-
lated. "Mrs. Hightower?"

Alex nodded. He had a familiar look about him, like
an old newspaper she had already read. He didn't look like
a salesman, and she wondered for a moment if he was
another medium sent by Sandy; she did not mind, at this
moment anyone was welcome.

"I'm John Allsop, the curate—I cover your area—er
—the vicar told me of your bereavement, so I thought I
would pop in and introduce myself—if it's convenient."
His right eye twitched sharply, twice.

"Please—yes, of course." She closed the door behind
him. "I'm afraid we didn't use the vicar for the funeral
service—it was done by an old schoolfriend of my husband's—John Lambourne—he's down near Hastings. I
hope the vicar didn't feel his nose put out?"

"No, not at all; this is quite usual."

They went into the drawing room. "I'm afraid we've
been a little remiss about church."

"I wouldn't worry," he said kindly. "But you'd be

very welcome if you'd like to come and worship at any of
our churches."

"Thank you."

"And how are you coping? You look as if you are still
in a great deal of shock."

"You don't expect to go to the funeral of your child,"
she said.

"No," he said. "No; to have a child taken is a terrible
thing. Do you have any other—er—children?"

She shook her head.

"That makes it even worse, if that is possible." He
twitched again. "I suffered a bereavement myself recently
—my wife. I found it very helpful to look at photographs."

She stared at him wide-eyed, and thought of the face
peering out from the photographs of the genitals. How?
How? How had it got there? Was it some kind of macabre
joke? "I'm sorry," she said.

He smiled sadly and nodded. "Thank you."

"Was it—?" She fumbled for words.

"Cancer," he said.

Alex nodded, unsure what to say. "Terrible." Fabian's
face stared at her again. "Terrible." She stood up abruptly,
then wondered why she was standing up. "I'll—er—can I
get you some coffee?"

"Oh, no, really, thank you."

"Do you like coffee, or would you prefer tea—or
whiskey or something?"

"Nothing, really."

But she was already on her way to the kitchen, desperate for a moment on her own to pull herself together.
She made the coffee, opened a pack of chocolate biscuits
and was about to take them back out when she noticed a
business card on the kitchen table. "Iris Tremayne," it
read, with an address in Earls Court. She dropped it in the
bin, then pulled it out and put it on the counter. She
picked up the tray and went back into the drawing room.
"Please help yourself to milk and sugar."

"Thank you."

She was conscious of him looking at her oddly; how bad do I look, she wondered. How shocked?

"Yes," he twitched again. "Photographs; bringing back the memories. It can be very therapeutic. The pain does go, in time, believe me." He smiled and bit into a biscuit nervously, as if worried it might bite him back.

She saw him staring at the bowl of wilting red roses.

"Fabian gave them to me for my birthday—he always gave me red roses; he loved them."

"Do you—er—garden?"

"I'm hopeless, I'm afraid. My husband's the gardener."

"Ah. You're separated, I understand?"

"Yes. My husband used to be in advertising—but wine was always his big love; he decided to pack it all in and start a vineyard. Unfortunately, country life did not agree with me."

"Very difficult, the country; sometimes it can be too peaceful."

"Yes."

"You're a literary agent, I believe."

She nodded.

"I'm writing a book myself. Just a little one."

Alex felt a sense of disappointment; was this the reason why he had come around? "Do you have a publisher?"

"Oh, I'm a long way from finishing it—I don't know that it would be good enough."

"If you'd like me to look at it—"

"Oh no, I wouldn't want to put you to any trouble. Perhaps, if I finish it, thank you."

"Have some more coffee."

"I'll have another biscuit if I may." He leaned forward and took one from the plate. "You might find it comforting, you know, to talk to some of your son's friends. We often know so little about those that are close to us when they are alive, and yet we can learn things after they have departed; things that can be of great comfort."

"Thank you. That's good advice. But he was a bit of a loner really. He had only two close friends that I knew, and one of them was killed in the accident."

He shook his head. "Some things are very difficult to understand, Mrs. Hightower."

She nodded. "Yes."

"But you look as if you are the sort who can cope."

"Yes." She sighed. "I can cope." Then she smiled. "Somehow."

He smiled back and stirred his coffee.

"Do you have any"—she paused and blushed—"any views on spiritualism?"

She saw the frown come across his face, like a cloud.

"I would not advise that, Mrs. Hightower, I would not advise that at all. Have you—?" He hesitated.

"No, absolutely not. But people have been suggesting it to me."

"I have only come across misery caused by that, never any good." He looked uncomfortable suddenly, as if he wanted to go.

"I don't believe in it at all."

"Very sensible. If any friend suggests it to you, they are not truly a friend. Prayer, love, happy memories and time will heal; nothing can be gained by trying to summon up the departed, nothing but disappointment and—" He hesitated.

"And?" she said.

"There are many evil forces, Mrs. Hightower. There is much evil in the world; those that dabble in the occult expose both themselves and others to it."

She nodded. "I'm not about to start dabbling."

"Good." He smiled. "Would you like to say a prayer together?"

"A prayer?" She blinked, and felt herself blushing. "Yes—er—thank you," she said awkwardly.

The curate closed his eyes and they said the Lord's Prayer. He then continued into more prayers and she sat, with her eyes tightly shut; it seemed strange, just the two of them in her drawing room, but when she opened her eyes again, she felt stronger, comforted.

"Would you like me to visit you again?"

"Please, whenever you are passing."

He left, almost as if he was in a hurry to get away, she thought; something had changed in him the moment she had mentioned spiritualism, some concern that she had been unable to allay.

She closed the front door and walked back down the hallway. The light was still on down the stairs to the darkroom, and she wondered whether to go and look again at the photographs. No, she decided, she would look in the morning, in the daylight, when she was rested and her eyes were not playing tricks. She sighed; sometime she would have to tackle Fabian's room, do something with his clothes, his belongings. She wondered suddenly if he had made a will.

She went upstairs into his bedroom and turned on the light. The room seemed very peaceful, almost welcoming. His slippers by the bed, laid out by Mimsa; silly Mimsa, she thought with a smile. Mimsa had taken it badly; violent floods of emotion, the best way to get grief out, she knew, envious for a moment of Mimsa's simplicity, of her Latin temperament. She wished that sometimes she, too, could let her emotion go.

She looked up at the stern portrait on the wall, and Fabian's cold eyes stared down; she shuddered. "Don't look like that, darling," she said. She closed her eyes. "Oh, God, look after my darling Fabian; protect him wherever he is." She opened them again and her eyes were wet. She sat down on the bed and sobbed gently.

Then she stood up, looked at the framed photograph of a Jaguar sports car on the wall and the huge stylized colored posters of old cars, racing. She looked at his books,

rows and rows of science fiction, astronomy. She looked at
the telescope set up at the window, which David had given
him for his sixteenth birthday. She walked over, removed
the lens cap and looked through it. She could remember
Fabian patiently pointing out the stars to her, the Bear, the
Plough, Uranus, Jupiter, he knew them all. She could
never really be sure which was which; she even had difficulty in recognizing the Plough. She stared at the stars
now. They looked huge. She wondered if Fabian was up
there, somewhere, among them.

She opened a drawer and rummaged through his
socks, lurid greens, yellows, pinks; he always wore bright
socks. Something caught her eye at the bottom of the
drawer, and she moved the socks aside. It was a postcard
depicting a long red-brick building with shops and an outdoor café. The Quincy Market, Boston, Mass. There were
more cards underneath, all of different scenes of Boston:
the river, MIT, Harvard University, the harbor, "Scene of
the historic Boston Tea Party," she read. Strange, she
thought, he'd never been to the States, never even talked
about it; why the postcards at the bottom of the drawer,
almost as if he had been hiding them?

She slept with the light on that night, as she had done
when she was a child. It would go in time; as the curate
had said, the wounds would heal. She slept for a while then
woke up, stared at the green glow of her clock, and lay
with a sense of dread, covered in pins and needles listening
to the silence of the night. She looked up at the ceiling,
then across at the wall of Fabian's room.

She saw the words on the VDT. Fabian's face staring
from the photograph.

She closed her eyes tightly, tried to shut them out,
tried to shut out everything.

8

It was drizzling as Alex drove over the River Cam, and into the center of Cambridge, the same as it had been when she had driven Fabian up for the start of his first term. It was strange, she thought, the odd details she could remember. The car crammed full of his luggage. Their conversation. "Had any more thoughts about what you want to do after Cambridge, darling?"

He had stared ahead as if brooding. "No," he had replied flatly, but a little too quickly.

She realized the curate had been right; one knew very little about one's children, however much they hugged you, gave you roses and could sense your own moods. She remembered the day she had told Fabian she and David were separating. "I've known you would for years, Mother," he had said, walking over and kissing her, this strange tall thin son, stronger now than when he had been a child with his weak chest and his fearful rages and his strange dark brooding moods and the hours he would spend in his room with the door locked.

She walked around the quadrangle, listening to the echo of her footsteps, up the stone staircase, along the corridor and found room 35. She was nervous, she realized suddenly, nervous about knocking on the door.

It opened almost instantly, and she jumped.

"Hello, Mrs. Hightower," said Otto.

Why did he always have to sound as if he was mocking, she wondered. She stared up at his brooding, menacing face, made all the more satanic by the cuts and bruising and his strange eyes, smiling, like a pair of conspirators, two hideous cold mocking objects. Had this really been her son's best friend?

"Hello, Otto, how are you?" she said gently.

"Oh, I'm fine, Mrs. Hightower. Would you like some coffee?" She noticed the lilt of German that just took the knife edge off his Eton accent; she could not work out whether he was trying to accentuate or obscure it.

"Thank you."

He poured some coffee beans into an electric grinder, laid out the pot, the cups, the milk, as if performing a ritual.

"This is very nice, Otto. I thought most students only knew how to make instant." She looked around the room.

"Most students probably do."

There were few clues about his personality in the battered undergraduate furniture, the bare walls, the rows of books, mostly scientific. There were piles of papers and clothes strewn untidily around. A couple of empty bottles of champagne lay by the wastepaper basket. "How are you feeling now, Otto?"

"Feeling?"

She nodded. "Emotionally."

He shrugged, put a cigarette in his mouth and lit it. "Would you like one?"

She shook her head. "I hope you don't feel guilty."

"Guilty?"

"Yes. That you—you know—survived."

"I don't feel guilty."

The coffee pot hissed and spat.

"Maybe I will have one," she said. He handed her the pack. "I don't think it's fair that three young boys were killed by a drunk." She leaned forward and took the light Otto held out. "A sad drunk."

"Perhaps it was meant, Mrs. Hightower."

"Meant?" She drew on the cigarette. "Meant that they should be taken or that you should have survived?"

He raised his eyebrows.

"Tell me," she said, and paused, feeling silly. "At the funeral, when I thanked you for coming, you said that Fabian had asked you to come. What did you mean?"

Otto leaned against the window sill and looked down at the quadrangle.

She stared at him, realizing what he must be going through, and said nothing; she sipped her coffee and tapped the ash off her cigarette. "Was Fabian happy here at Cambridge, Otto?"

"Happy? I don't know how you tell if anyone is happy." He turned and gave a strange, leering smile.

"I got the feeling he enjoyed it here; he liked you and Charles very much."

Otto shrugged.

"I think he was very fond of Carrie too. He brought her home a couple of times; I didn't really think she was right for him. All the same, I was sorry when he ditched her. In a funny way, she was quite good for him."

"Ditched her?" Otto marched across the room and stabbed his cigarette out in the ashtray. "He didn't ditch Carrie, she ditched him. She went off to find herself in America."

Alex smiled wryly. "Children never tell their parents much, do they?"

"That depends on the parents," said Otto.

The tone of his voice made Alex feel uncomfortable. "I thought Fabian and I had a close relationship." She shrugged and stared out through the grimy window at the gray sky; the springs in the armchair were tilting her slightly over to one side, and as she moved there was a loud twang beneath her. "He told me that he'd given her up—I suppose he was embarrassed—felt it might be bad for his ego to admit he'd been ditched; one thing he never had any problem with was girls."

"Why do you say that, Mrs. Hightower?"

"What do you mean?"

"He was always having problems with girls."

"What sort of problems?"

"I'd rather not say." He smiled, a curious private smile to himself. She looked at his eyes, puzzled, but they gave nothing away. "I'll take you to his room."

"It's next door, isn't it?"

Otto nodded.

"I'll go on my own first, if you don't mind. If there's anything of his that you'd like—books, whatever—please take them."

"Thank you."

She felt nothing as she walked into Fabian's room; it could have been the room of a total stranger. It was chilly and damp, and smelled of old furniture. She stared at the thin carpet with the floorboards showing through in patches, the single bar electric heater and the grill for toasting sandwiches which she had given him. She looked at the rows of decanters on the mantelpiece. One was half full; she removed the top and sniffed. There was a musty sweetness that reminded her of licorice; port, she thought. Wine racks were piled against the wall, with dusty necks of bottles poking out here and there. Near the floor were several bottles grouped together, their necks wrapped smartly in gold foil, with elegant orange bands around them. She leaned down to read the writing, Veuve Clicquot Ponsardin.

There were some papers on the desk, held down by a ballpoint pen, and she looked at them. "Were Goneril and Regan evil? Or just practical businesswomen? Was Shakespeare trying to tell us all something, centuries before his time? Had the Business Woman of the Year Award existed in Elizabethan times, could they have won it?" Alex smiled. She remembered Fabian discussing this with her only a few weeks ago; she could picture him clearly, walking around the kitchen, hand in his jeans pocket, firing questions at her.

She looked around; it seemed almost as if he had just popped out for a few minutes. She pulled up a chair, stood on it, and lifted his trunk from the top of the wardrobe. The clips opened with dull metallic thuds and she raised the lid, staring at the torn yellowing lining inside, at the broken plastic coat hanger and the single black sock that lay in there, and remembered the first day she had ever packed this, fourteen years before when he first went off to prep school. She could see the clothes lying neatly pressed and folded, the regulation vests and Airtex shirts and the gray prep-school pullovers with the name tags neatly stitched in, and she felt herself crying and did not want to cry in case Otto came in and saw her.

She opened the top drawer in his desk and saw his diary. She flipped through a couple of pages from March, but could see nothing of interest: dates and times of lectures; the start of the holiday marked with a thick line and the word SKIING written after. She turned back a few pages, to January 15. "8 P.M. Dinner. Carrie." The previous day read: "7:30. Cinema. Carrie." There were no more entries mentioning Carrie after the fifteenth. A couple of days were blank, but with large asterisks marked on them. She turned forward to April 7 and smiled through her wet eyes at the black circle around the date, neat handwriting underneath: MOTHER'S B'DAY.

She turned the pages forward and noticed a few other asterisks; they seemed to be about two weeks apart. She noticed an asterisk against May 4 and the date rang a bell. She felt suddenly as if an unseen hand had picked her up and dunked her in cold water; she felt the cold seep through her, as if she were litmus paper. May 4; that was the date her watch had shown in the middle of her lunch with Philip Main.

"How are you getting on?"

She turned around. Otto was standing in the doorway, smiling; that hideous knowing smile, the grotesque slashed and bruised mask that hid, she knew, so many secrets about her son. "OK," she said. "Fine. There's some port in that decanter—you may as well have it."

"Port doesn't last," said Otto disdainfully. "That won't be any good now."

"Oh," she said flatly. "There's quite a lot of wine— you're welcome to that." She wanted Otto to take something, desperately wanted him to take something, but she did not fully understand why, whether it was to have him in her debt, or simply to atone.

He nodded uninterestedly. "I don't think Fabian had that good taste in wine."

"His father was—" she began indignantly, then stopped, realizing she was rising to the bait. "What did you mean just now, Otto, that Fabian was always having problems with girls?"

Otto walked over to the bookshelves and plucked a book out; he flipped through the pages. "I don't think you knew very much about your son, Mrs. Hightower," he said absently.

"Do your parents know much about you, Otto?"

"My mother has been in a home since I was four. My father"—he shrugged—"yes, I see him often."

"What sort of a home?"

"A home."

"A mental home?" she said, gently.

He looked away from her. "What are you going to do with everything?"

"I don't know. Take it back and—" She realized she did not know. She closed the diary and looked at the rest of the papers. Puzzled, she noticed a pile of postcards and a letter addressed to Fabian at Cambridge in a girl's handwriting, all held together by a rubber band. She pushed them into the diary and put it into the bottom of the trunk. She could sense Otto watching her, but each time she turned around he was still leafing backward and forward through the pages. She folded a pair of trousers and laid them in the trunk, feeling embarrassed, as if she were looting.

"I'll take this book, if I may."

"Of course. Take anything you want—it's no use—I mean—I'm just going to give this all away, so take anything."

Otto shrugged. "Just this."

"What is it?"

He held up the cover. It was a slim paperback, F. R. Leavis on T. S. Eliot.

She smiled. "I thought you were studying chemistry."

"I study lots of things."

He walked out of the room without saying anything further.

As she drove back toward London, with the trunk wedged in the passenger seat, the drizzle turned to pelting rain. She watched the wipers clouting away the water, like angry hands, she thought.

The rain turned to hail; the stones rattled on the car's bodywork, drumming on the soft hood above her, and then turned back to rain again. She thought about Otto's strange behavior. He had always struck her as being weird; now he was even more so. Anything was understandable, she supposed, after what he had been through, but there was a malevolence about him which seemed to have intensified, as if it was a joke that he had survived, some sort of bizarre personal joke. And his strange comments about Fabian; maybe it was true, maybe Carrie had ditched him, but his remark about Fabian always having problems with girls mystified her; what had he meant? Was he gay? Had he and Otto been lovers? She thought about Carrie again. A pretty little thing, with her spiky punk blond hair and her chirpy South London accent and the awe in which she had walked around the house. "Like bloomin' Bucknam Palace," she had said. Alex smiled. Hardly.

"Actually, I like scrubbers, Mother," Fabian had said. God, he could be a ghastly snob at times, and then do something totally out of character, like bringing this girl home for Christmas and fawning all over her, as if it were a game. Carrie had been no fool, that was for sure. Alex tried to remember what Carrie had been doing at Cambridge; reporting for some strange left wing magazine, something to do with ecology. She remembered driving down through Streatham with Fabian and his pointing out a dismal Council high-rise complex, telling her proudly that was where Carrie's mother lived.

Suddenly there was a sharp scratching noise on the windscreen in front of her and she flinched; a car passed her in the fast lane, chucking up a heavy spray which blinded her for a moment; there was another sharp scrunch and then another.

Then the spray cleared, and she stared, transfixed with horror, at the single red rose entangled in the wiper arm, sweeping backward and forward across the windscreen.

9

She stopped on the hard shoulder, got out of the car and stood in the lashing wind and driving rain. A truck thundered past, inches from her, the blast of its slipstream catching her, throwing her against the side of the Mercedes. She walked forward, put her hand out, and the wipers swept again, the rose scratching, shrieking against the howl of the wind and the whine of the traffic. She grabbed the wiper arm and lifted out the rose. It pricked her finger badly, and she swore; she released the arm and the wipers swept again, angrily. Another truck passed, close, sucking her in its slipstream, then throwing spray like a breaking wave over her. She jumped back into the car, slammed the door against the elements, and switched on the interior light.

The rose was red, blood red, like the stain trickling down from her finger, which she put to her mouth and sucked. She stared out through her window at the rain, at the demonic lights which hurtled past, at the roars and whines which faded away into the black.

Then she looked down at the rose. Who had flung it from their car, or left it loose on the back of a truck, or . . . ? But no, that was impossible, a coincidence, that was all, she told herself half heartedly. She sat, shaking, wanting to throw it back out there where it had come from, but she could not. Instead she laid it down in front of the gear stick and drove off slowly, frightened.

She carried the rose into the house and stood in the gloomy hallway, leaving the front door open behind her, not wanting to close it yet. She did not know why, but she did not want to cut off contact with the outside world.

She sucked her finger again, which was still painful, and felt the wet damp stem; some of the petals had fallen off. She went through into the drawing room and placed it in the bowl among the roses Fabian had given her for her birthday. It stood out, fresh and vibrant among the others, which were now dying or dead; but she couldn't throw them out, not yet.

There was a loud bang as the wind blew the front door against the·wall; there was another bang and then it slammed shut, as if an unseen hand had hurled it in a rage.

The trunk would have to stay in the car until Monday when she could get Mimsa to help her lift it out, she thought, walking through into the kitchen to turn the heating on, and was surprised to see that it was on, had been on all day, according to the time switch. She suddenly noticed that she could see the vapor of her breath and breathed out again, puzzled, then rubbed her hands together against the cold.

Something moved upstairs, a creak of a spring or a floorboard. She stood and listened. The cold knifed through her, made her tingle; she curled her toes, silently, listening. There was another clunk, and then the sound of water in pipes; the boiler made two loud clanks and switched itself off. She breathed out; stupid, she knew, the house always made strange noises when the heating was on.

She filled the kettle, then walked into the drawing room, glanced nervously at the rose again and switched on the television. There was a roar of applause from a studio audience and the camera panned along a row of beaming antiseptic faces: second-rate showbiz celebrities playing a panel game, trying a little too hard to be jolly; there was a cut to a slick quiz-master holding his microphone up close to a brunette who rolled her tongue around the inside of her mouth. Alex continued to watch for a few moments, cringing. The series had been devised by one of her clients; the critics had called it tasteless, banal and degrading, and they were right. But it had paid the rent for the past four years.

It was too cold to relax. She jumped to her feet, walked across to the roses, sniffed the new one and gave it a light caress with her finger.

She thought of Fabian's trunk lying out there on the front seat of the Mercedes, wondering why she had bothered to bring the clothes back, and worried for a moment that someone might steal it. Then she shrugged; perhaps that would be the best thing.

If David had been around, he could have got the trunk; she wished she had been able to swallow her pride and ask him to. She rubbed her hands together again and shivered and felt sad, wanted to be with Fabian, wanted to hold him, hug him, wanted him to walk in the door and unpack the trunk himself.

She went up to his bedroom; the temperature seemed even lower in here; had Mimsa turned off the radiator? She put her hand on it, then lifted it away smartly, feeling the heat burning her skin. She looked at the brass telescope, the posters on the wall, and then up at the painting, almost expecting a reaction, a slight movement, but there was nothing, just the cold arrogant stare. She knelt down under it and buried her head in her hands. "I love you, darling; I hope you're all right wherever you are; I hope you're happy; happier than you were here. I miss you; I wonder if you miss me; take care, darling, wherever you are. Please God, take care of Fabian." She stayed kneeling, then slowly rose to her feet, and felt more peaceful.

She slipped out, gently shutting the door behind her, stood in the corridor and closed her eyes tightly. "Good

night, darling," she said, and opened her eyes again; they
were brimming with tears. She stopped at the top of the
stairs, sat down and sobbed.

She thought of Otto's lacerated face; thought of him
being catapulted from the car; what had happened, she
wondered, at that moment of impact? How had Fabian
reacted? What had he thought? Who was the driver of the
other car? How could he have done this? The questions
seemed to appear in her mind in bright green letters
printed on a black void. How did Otto feel about surviv-
ing? Why was he so damned weird? He'd given her the
creeps; what did he know? Some secret about Fabian? Was
the whole thing a hoax, some sick joke; were he and Fabian
about to come waltzing in through the door, laughing,
brushing past her and going straight to his room and locking the door, and do what? Watch the stars? Make love?

She heard a roar of laughter from downstairs, and
then applause and a voice saying something she could not
make out; she felt peaceful, sad and a sudden overwhelm-
ing desire to be kind. She thought of David alone in the
farmhouse with the dog and the sheep, tired, lonely, baffled, and she went into her bedroom and dialed his number.

"David?" she said when he answered.

"How are you?" He sounded pleased; she knew,
sadly, that he always sounded pleased when she rang, and
she wished sometimes that he would sound angry, or disturbed from something, or distracted, anything to stop her
feeling guilty about what she had done to him.

"I just thought I'd say hi."

"What have you been up to?"

"I went to Cambridge today—to clear out Fabian's
room."

"Thanks for doing that; must have been a bit of an
ordeal."

"I was OK; except I have a bit of a problem."

"What's that?"

"I can't get his trunk out of my car."

She heard him laugh.

"Want me to come up and help you?"

"Don't be silly."

"I don't mind—I'll come now—or—" His voice became quieter, testing. "Do you have a date?"

"No, I haven't got a date."

"Well, I'll come now; take you to dinner."

"I don't want to drag you all the way up."

"I'll be there in an hour—hour and a half. Better than talking to the sheep."

Alex hung up feeling angry with herself, angry at her weakness; giving David hope, allowing the wound to continue festering. She was startled by the vapor of her breath, and stared at it, thinking for a moment it must be cigarette smoke that she had exhaled. But she wasn't smoking. She watched the cloud, thick and heavy, so heavy she could almost see ice crystals form as it drifted up in front of her; she was cold again suddenly, almost unbearably cold. She felt as if something had come into the room, something unpleasant, malevolent; something very angry.

She got up, went out into the corridor and into the kitchen, but it stayed with her. Her hands were shaking with the cold, shaking so hard she dropped the tea bag on the floor; she heard the clunk upstairs again, a different clunk this time, not like the boiler. She walked out of the kitchen in long positive strides, down the corridor and out of the front door, into the orange glow of the streetlighting.

The rain had stopped and the wind was still strong, but felt warm and enveloped her like an eiderdown. She walked down the street, slowly, hugging it around her shoulders.

She heard the toot of a horn and the rattle of an engine and was engulfed by the stench of pigs, a strange, unfamiliar smell in the middle of Chelsea. She looked around and saw David's mud-caked Land Rover. He was leaning over, sliding open the window. "Alex!"

She waved, surprised. "You were quick! I didn't think you'd be here till well after eight."

"It's half past eight."

"Half past eight?" She frowned, and looked at her watch. No, it wasn't possible. Surely it had only been a few minutes? She shivered. What was happening?

"What are you doing out without a coat?"

"Just came out to get some air."

"Jump in."

"There's a space just there—you'd better take it, you won't get any closer."

He nodded. "Saturday night, I forgot."

She watched him reverse into the space, then jump out. "Aren't you going to lock it?"

"I'm out of the habit of locking cars." He gave her a kiss, and they walked down the road to the house.

How long had she spent walking around outside? An hour and a half could not have gone by. Surely not?

"You look frozen," he said.

"I—er—was a bit hot in the house—had the heating up too much. Let's get the trunk—I'm parked just there."

She staggered backward into the house, sagging under the weight, and heard a crunch as the trunk swung into the wall. "Careful," she said testily.

"Sorry."

They laid the trunk down and David closed the front door; she saw a flat piece of dried mud on the carpet. "For Chrissake, David, you're bringing bloody mud in!" she shouted, livid suddenly.

He blushed apologetically, as if in the house of a complete stranger, bent down and untied his brogues. "Sorry," he muttered sheepishly. "Bit muddy down there at the moment."

She instantly regretted her outburst, and guiltily watched him stooping over, removing his shoes. She stared

at his faded roll-neck sweater, battered tweed jacket with
its haphazard patches and his shapeless brown corduroy
trousers. His beard was tinged with white strands and his
face had a ruddy weatherbeaten complexion. It was hard
to imagine, she thought, watching him standing there in
his gray woolen socks, with his big toes poking through,
that he had once been so fastidious about his appearance;
that he had once worn nothing but sharp designer suits,
silk shirts, Gucci loafers; that he used to gad about in a
Ferrari, that he had loved to strut into Tramp in the early
hours of the morning, greeting Johnny Gold and every
waiter by name.

"You're right," he said, "it is hot in here. Incredibly
hot. How are you?" He leaned forward to kiss her, staggered and nearly fell. "Ooops."

She felt the bristles of his mustache, smelled the alco-
hol, felt his tongue poke through and push in between her
lips. She recoiled. "David," she said reproachfully.

"Just giving my wife a kiss."

"Do you have to get drunk before you can come and
see me?"

He shifted his weight uncomfortably.

"If you got breathalyzed, you'd be really stuck. Want
some coffee?"

"I'd prefer some whiskey."

"I think you've had enough."

God, why had she asked him up, she thought, riddled
with guilt; she just wanted him to go away; she did not
need him, did not need anyone. It had all been a mistake,
tricks of her imagination; or was it? Somehow, she had to
be sure. At least it was comforting, having another human
here; at least she felt safe.

She made him a coffee and took it through to the
drawing room. Angrily, she snatched the glass of whiskey
out of his hand. "Drink this; I want you sober; I need to
talk to you."

"I can stay the night here," he said.

"No, you can't."

"It is my house."

"David; we have an agreement."

He stared at the coffee and wrinkled his nose. God, he really looked like one of those ruddy bucolic picture-book farmers, she thought. How could anyone change so much, so quickly? Just a couple of years; or had he been changing for much longer without her noticing? He was an alien here, hopelessly uncomfortable in the surroundings; she had to concentrate hard to remember that it was he who had decorated this house, his taste, his furniture, his colors. And yet, she felt strangely safe with him here; it was like being in the presence of a great cuddly bear. She sat down on the arm of the chair beside him, trying to sort out the confusion of her thoughts, the violent swings of her emotions, and listened to the noisy slurp as he tested the coffee. She twisted the whiskey glass guiltily around in her hands, then put it down gently beside him.

"This may sound strange, David, but I think Fabian's still around."

He looked up at her, frowning. "Still around?"

"Yes."

"You mean you don't think he's dead?"

Alex took out a cigarette and offered him the pack. He shook his head and pulled a tin of tobacco out of his pocket. "I went to the morgue. I spent six bloody days in France with the body of my son—our son."

"But you didn't see him?"

"No, thank God, I didn't have to; anyway, they wouldn't let me—they said he was too badly—"

Alex shuddered. "I know he's dead, David. But I can —I don't know—sort of feel his presence still around."

"You're always going to remember him—we both will, that's natural."

"Don't you think that dream you had when you saw him, the morning he was killed—that we both had—don't you think that was strange?"

He pried open the lid of the tin and pulled out a cigarette paper; she looked at his grubby hands, the yellow-stained fingers, his filthy nails.

"Coincidence. Maybe telepathy; my mother had a similar experience during the war, the day my father was killed; she swore she saw him sitting under a hedge at the end of their lane. She went to mediums, had séances in the house and claimed she spoke to him regularly."

"What did he say?"

"Nothing; used to tell her it was very blue out there. That's the problem, the dead never seem to have anything very interesting to say." He licked the gum on the paper and closed up his cigarette.

The door suddenly moved, several inches; Alex jumped, her heart racing, and it moved again; she felt a cold chill down her neck and spun around; the curtain was billowing out. "Did you open the window?"

"Yes," he said.

She felt the relief seep through her, like warmth from a bath.

"You're very edgy," he said. "You should have a holiday—go away somewhere."

"I can't spare the time at the moment; I've got two very important deals I have to close."

"Come down to Château Hightower—you can have your own room, come and go as you like. It's peaceful—you can do your deals over the phone."

"I'll be all right."

"If you want to come down at any time just turn up, you'll be very welcome."

"Thanks." She smiled. "Maybe." She hesitated, leaned over, and stroked the side of the whiskey glass. "I want to show you something."

She led him down into her darkroom and picked the contact sheet off the table, then stared at it in disbelief; it had completely fogged into a haze of white and gray tones. She shook her head, picked up the negatives and dropped them on to the cracked light box. There was nothing there; nothing on them. Nothing at all. It was as if they had never been exposed.

"You didn't fix them properly," he said.

"Don't be ridiculous. Of course I did."

"You must have had the solution too long—got too weak—these have all carried on developing. What were they of?"

"That's the whole point; they were pictures a client sent me—a roll of film—he's a bit eccentric—they were pictures of some animal's genitals."

She saw David's probing stare and blushed.

"He knew of my interest in photography. Anyhow, I developed them, made a contact sheet and they were fine; I put it on the drying rack, and when I came down to check it, I could see Fabian's face on every frame—it had just appeared there."

David looked at her, and shrugged. "Double exposure."

She shook her head. "No. No way."

"Did he know Fabian, this client of yours?"

"No; he had no reason to take pictures of Fabian. Anyhow, it wasn't on the negative."

"You mean you hadn't noticed it on the negative."

"No. It wasn't on the negative."

"You sure you didn't imagine it?"

She shook her head.

"Alex, you know you are very tense at the moment—"

"It's nothing to do with that," she snapped. "Jesus, what do you want to do? Commit me to a loony bin?"

"Perhaps you should see the doctor."

"David, I am perfectly OK; I'm coping with everything; it's just that there is something very strange going on. I feel that Fabian is still around, that's why his face appeared."

"And Fabian fogged the film?"

She shrugged. "Maybe."

"What else?"

"Silly things." She shook her head. "Probably nothing. I just wonder—maybe I should go and see a medium. If I did, would you come?"

He shook his head. "Forget it, darling; you'll make it worse for yourself. If you went to a medium and you got in touch with Fabian—what would you say to him?"

She stared at her husband, and then had to look away, red in the face; *I know what I'd say*, she thought.

"And what would you expect him to say to you?"

She shrugged. "I've always been as cynical as you about that sort of thing, David, it's just—" She paused. "Maybe you're right, maybe I should have a break. Help me get the trunk upstairs."

"And afterward I'll buy you dinner; we'll go out somewhere nice, OK?"

She looked at him and nodded.

"Christ it's cold in here," he said as they carried the trunk into Fabian's room. "Where do you want it?"

"On the floor."

"Let's put it on the bed," he said. "Be easier for you. You ought to have the heating on in here; otherwise you'll get dampness."

"It is on. I think the floor would be—" But David had propelled them over to the bed, and they laid the trunk down on to it, with a loud clank from the springs.

Alex watched David look around the room, lost, like a visitor trying to find his bearings in a museum. "There's his telescope; God, I remember giving him that."

"He loved it."

David stared up at the portrait, and Alex noticed the look of discomfort on his face. He looked away. "Still got that Brooklands poster—worth a few bob now."

Alex looked at the old racing car, hurtling around the banking. David walked over to it. "I remember hanging this for him—he can't have been more than seven or eight. I made a real botch-up of it—couldn't get it to the right height—had to take the bloody nail out half a dozen times." He lifted the picture off the wall. "Look, there they all are!" He pointed to the chipped plaster and the haphazard holes.

"It's funny what one remembers," said Alex, watching him carefully rehanging it. For whom?

She walked out into the corridor, suddenly wanting to be away from the room, wanting David away from it as well; his presence there was annoying her, poking about, moving things. Let him rest, she wanted to say, let him rest, you fool!

He came out of the room with his head bowed and the color gone from his cheeks, and she immediately felt angry with herself now for her feelings, angry at being so blind to his own grief. The child had meant so much to both of them, after the endless visits to the specialists, the ectopic pregnancy that had to be terminated and then finally, the last hope; and her secret.

They walked slowly down the stairs and stopped on the landing. She felt David's arm around her, squeezing her, and she leaned into him. It was suddenly cold once more and she wanted to go down and close the window. Grief crept up around her, the cold empty room, the trunk on the bed that Fabian would never again unpack. She felt the warmth of her husband, felt his strong powerful frame, the squeeze of his large hand. She nestled into the soft brush of his face and kissed his cheek. She felt his face stir and his moist lips on her own cheek and she found herself being maneuvered slowly, step by step, in through her bedroom door; she felt his kisses becoming passionate, moving down her neck.

"No, David."

He kissed her chin, then pushed his lips on to hers. She broke her face away. "No, David."

"Yes," he said. "Yes, we must."

It was Fabian's voice; she opened her eyes and saw Fabian's face. "No," she said, pushing him away. "No, get out!" He came back toward her. "Get out!" she screamed. "Get out!"

Fabian stared at her, frozen for an instant in shock, then became David again, and then Fabian, until she could not tell who it was.

"Get out, get out!"

"Alex, darling, calm down!"

She kicked him hard, straight up between the legs, saw the wince of pain, the shock in his face, then pummeled him in the chest. She felt hands grasping her. "Calm down," she heard. "Alex, calm down!"

"I'm calm!" she yelled back. "For Chrissake, I'm completely calm. Just get out!"

"I'm sorry, darling, I didn't mean to—"

She stared at him, wide-eyed, filled with an inexplicable sudden hatred for him. "Go," she shouted in a voice she scarcely recognized as hers. "Go, go, I can't stand you being here." She saw the shock in his face, saw his hands crossed between his legs. "Please, David," she said. "Please go."

"What about dinner?" he said, bewildered.

"I want to be on my own. I can't explain it; I just need to be on my own. I'm sorry, it was a mistake asking you to come." She stared at him, fearful that at any moment he would turn back again into Fabian. "I'm just not ready at the moment, not ready for anything; I've got to come to terms with this myself."

She followed him down the stairs. "Will you be all right—to drive home?"

David looked at her and shrugged. "I drove up here."

"I'm sorry," she said. "I'm sorry."

"Do you want me to call you when I get home?"

"Call?" she said weakly. "Sure, if you like."

She closed the door, went into the drawing room and sank down in a chair. Outside, a short way off, she heard the Land Rover's engine rattle into life and the crunch of the gears.

And then the guilt hit her.

"David!" She ran to the front door. "David. Wait!" She fumbled with the catch, pulled the door open, tripped out, down the steps, on to the pavement. The tail lights were disappearing down the road. She ran after them. "David! Stop, please stop! I didn't mean it. Please stop! Oh please stop!"

She saw the amber flashing indicator getting closer as she sprinted down the road. Then it pulled away from her and vanished around the corner.

"David!"

She ran on after it down the King's Road. *Don't get those lights; please don't get those lights!*

But they turned green and he was gone.

She collapsed, sobbing, against a lamp post. "David. I'm sorry. I'm so terribly sorry."

Slowly, she turned, and walked back to the house. The front door was still open. She closed it behind her, then went through into the drawing room, completely drained, weeping. She lay down on the sofa and lapsed into a doze.

She wasn't sure what woke her, whether it was the chill air in the room again, or the smell of cooking, the tantalizing smell of frying food.

In spite of the cold she felt better, more peaceful. Had David really come, she wondered, or had it all been part of a terrible dream? She sniffed the rich heady smell and thought of Fabian's passion for fried eggs; sunny-side up, always. There were times as a child when he had his moods; he would refuse to eat anything except fried eggs for days.

She looked at her watch. Ten o'clock; the smell was growing stronger and she realized she was feeling hungry; she'd eaten nothing since the apple and a piece of toast for breakfast. She wondered which of her neighbors it was, and walked to the window. To her surprise, it was shut. She stood still, trying to figure out how the smell could be so strong, and then she heard a hissing and crackling, close, so close it sounded like her own kitchen.

She walked out into the hallway and saw the kitchen light on.

The hissing and the crackling were coming from there.

She sprinted the twenty feet and stood, staring at the empty burner. The smell of fried eggs was overpowering. She opened the window and leaned out, but there was nothing: the familiar night odors of the neighborhood, of garbage cans, wet grass, diesel fumes and a faint hint of curry. She closed the window.

The smell was in here.

She saw the vapor of her breath again, smelled the smell even more intensely, felt terror surging through her. She walked out of the kitchen, closed the door, went through into the drawing room and picked up the telephone directory.

Mankletow. Manly. Main. Her finger was shaking uncontrollably. There were seventeen P. Mains listed. She knew the road he lived on, Chalcot Road, but there was none there. She dialed Directory Enquiries, conscious of her strained, high-pitched voice. The operator was kindly, as helpful as she could be. "Sorry, dear," she said, "he's unlisted."

"Could you phone him and ask him to call me?"

"Can't do that, I'm sorry. He's down as 'no connection.' I don't even have his number myself."

Alex walked back into the hallway, stared fearfully at the kitchen door, felt the ice-cold air. She pulled her coat down from the rack, grabbed her keys off the table, went outside and locked the front door behind her.

10

A drunken gaggle of businessmen wandered past Alex; in town for a conference, she judged, by the name tags some of them had forgotten to remove from their lapels.

"Here's a bit of crumpet, Jimmy," said a Scottish accent.

She let herself into the office, and as she locked the door behind her, there was a roar of laughter in the street, probably at her expense, she thought.

It was quiet inside, unnaturally quiet. The room was dark, and the random streaks of harsh white light from the massage parlor across the road flickered on the walls and furniture, giving a strange chiaroscuro effect.

She stared at the intense blackness of the staircase, pressed the light switch, and instantly it was banished and she was in her own familiar surroundings, with the soft grays of the walls and carpets, the crimson lamps and bannister rail and the framed dust jackets lining the walls.

She walked past the receptionist's dark silent switchboard and began to climb the stairs. She saw the shadow on the floor above, and for a moment was reluctant to climb farther; it seemed the shadow was moving. She hesitated, but knew she had to get to the landing, to the next switch. She watched the shadow; when she moved, it moved; when she stopped, it stopped.

Stupid, she thought, suddenly realizing it was her own shadow.

She walked up into the dark, found the switch, pressed it with a quick nervous stab of her finger and jumped as the light came on, then walked up the next flight and on to the landing. Julie's office door was open and the room was pitch dark. She stared at it nervously, reached in and switched on the light, and again felt relieved by the normality. She stared, irritated for a moment, at the black Olivetti sitting there without its cover. Julie was always leaving it off. Why did she do that? The gray plastic cover was screwed up behind the filing tray. She straightened it out, put it on carefully, then the manuscript on the desk caught her eye. *Lives Foreseen—My Power and Others',* with a bookmark halfway through it. She had told Julie to send it back, she thought, annoyed, picking it up and carrying it through into her office. She'd speak to her about it on Monday.

Down in the street below, the drunks were bunched up around the doorway of the massage parlor, peering at the blanked-off windows. She let go of the blinds, walked away from the window, shivering from the cold, switched on the heater, then pulled out her address file. She dialed Philip's number and waited, knowing that he always took a long time to answer. Relieved, she heard the click of the receiver being picked up, and was about to speak when she realized that the phone was still ringing.

Someone in her own building had picked up an extension.

She stood, frozen for a moment, paralyzed with fear.

Who, she thought, who? The cleaner? No, impossible. One of her partners? No. She listened for a sound, for breathing, a cough; the phone rang on. She could feel the presence, feel the person waiting, listening. Who? Who? Who? She was shaking now, heard her own heart thumping, louder than the ringing. She felt a pain below her ear; she was banging her cheekbone with the receiver. It rang on, unanswered. Fearfully, she turned around, looked through her open doorway at the passage. The ringing echoed around her office. Something moved at the end of the passage, or had she imagined it? Lock the door, she said to herself. Lock the door! The key was on the outside.

Carefully, gently, she laid the receiver down on her blotter, and tiptoed over to the door. The ringing continued. She tried to pull the key out silently, but she was shaking too much; it scraped, clanked then fell to the floor, bounced and clattered against the molding, with a noise like two trains colliding. "No," she said aloud, "no, no." She dived on to her knees and scrabbled her hands across the carpet after it. She closed her fingers around it, turned and stared fearfully again down the passage at the stairwell, heard the ringing continue, then flung herself back into the office, slammed the door and leaned against it. She tried to get the key in, fumbled, dropped it again. "No," she said. She picked it up, pushed it in and tried to turn it. It would not move.

She turned it so hard she could feel it bending. "Please lock, please lock." She pushed it in farther, and suddenly it turned easily, without pressure, and the lock clicked home almost silently.

Alex rested her head against the door, relief swimming through her, her heart beating so hard it was like a fist punching her chest. She was sweating, gulping for air.

"Hello? Hello?" The voice sounded tinny, as if a radio had been left on. "Hello? Hello?"

She fell on to the receiver, as if it was the first piece of food she had seen for a week. "Hello?"

She heard the familiar hiss of air and tobacco smoke.

"Alex?" said Philip Main's voice, whispering, almost incredulous.

Suddenly, she was conscious again of the presence and did not want to speak, did not want to give herself away. "Yes," she found herself whispering back, softly, almost hissing.

"Hello?"

"Help me," she hissed louder, suddenly beginning to feel vulnerable again; the door was strong, but it would not hold someone determined.

"Is that you, Alex?"

"Yes." The sound came out, a strange, high-pitched squawk from deep inside her that she scarcely recognized.

"Are you all right?" He sounded gentle, concerned.

She didn't want to say it, did not want the other person listening to know she was afraid. Normal. Sound normal. For God's sake, sound normal. "I want to see a medium. I wondered if you knew anyone?" She was conscious that her voice had changed again, into a flat monotone automaton; it sounded like the voice of a complete stranger.

"Are you sure about this?"

Christ, don't start querying things; for God's sake don't. Not now.

"Alex?"

"Yes, I am sure," said the automaton.

"You sound a little strange."

"I'm fine," said the automaton.

"I don't know about mediums. You ought to think about it very carefully."

"Please, Philip. I have to."

"I don't know. I think we should talk about it."

"Please, Philip, do you know any?"

She listened, agitated, to the silence.

"Not personally, no; good Lord, no." He paused. "You told me that a friend of yours had suggested this—doesn't she know any?"

"She sent one round. She was horrible."

Silence again.

"You must know someone, Philip."

"You could try the Yellow Pages."

"Please, Philip, be serious."

There was another silence; Alex listened hard, trying to hear something, anything. She looked around at the door, stared at the handle. It was moving, turning.

She screamed; a dreadful piercing scream, then stopped as abruptly as she had started; it wasn't moving at all; it was the blinds that were moving in the air of the heater, sending shadows across the handle.

"Alex? What's the matter?"

"There's someone here, in the office; listening to this phone call. Please call the police; I think I'm about to be attacked."

She put down the phone, saw the light on the panel go out. Light. She breathed gulps of air. Light; there was only one light, wasn't there? If there had been someone else listening, then another light would have come on on the panel; wouldn't it? She stared around at the door, then at the window, at the restless blinds, then something caught her eye on her desk: the calendar. She stared at it and was filled instantly with a sensation that felt like ice cold water flushing through her, filling every blood vessel in her body.

The date on the calendar read: "Thu. May 4."

"Oh, God," she said. "Don't let me be mad; please don't let me be mad." She stared again at the letters, the digits, checked the date on her Rolex. April 22. She looked around the room, expecting to see something, a phantom, a specter—a—she hesitated, thinking about the smell of eggs, the rose in the windscreen. Fearfully she looked to her right, at the VDT screen that was under its cover. She wanted to lift the cover, stare at the blank screen. Then suddenly, she felt angry. She wanted to get up, throw open the door and shout out, "Here I am. Take me. Do what you want." Instead she found herself pulling out the Yellow Pages.

She heaved a section of pages over. Mediums. Mediums. Nothing under Mediums. What else? Psychics? She turned more pages. Again nothing. Then she tried Clair-

voyants. Something, there was something. "See Palmists
and Clairvoyants."

The list was short. There was an Indian-sounding
name, repeated twice, and only one other. She hesitated;
the names didn't feel right. She stared at Stanley Hill's
manuscript, *Lives Foreseen—My Powers and Others'*. Reluctantly she opened it and flipped through the pages. The
manuscript seemed comfortable suddenly. She was on familiar territory.

Then she realized the words were blurred; she
couldn't read them. She saw her hands shaking wildly, and
put the manuscript down on the desk.

A name caught her eye. Morgan Ford. She saw it
again, a couple of pages later, and then again, her eyes
drawn to it as if by a magnet. "Modest trance medium
Morgan Ford would strenuously deny that he frequently
arranges sittings for royalty in his Cornwall Gardens flat."

"Modest." She liked that word. She pulled out the
directory from the shelf behind her, and leafed through the
pages.

She picked up the receiver and listened to the harsh
crackle, then the rasping hum; she waited for the click of
the extension again, watching the panel for the telltale
light, but nothing happened; the line was private now. She
punched the number and waited.

The tone of the man's voice surprised her. For some
reason she had expected it to be kindly, warm, welcoming;
instead it was cold, irritated, the Welsh accent further
alienating him. She had expected him to say, "Yes, Alex,
I've been expecting you. I knew you would call, the spirits
told me." Instead he said, "Morgan Ford, who is speaking?"

Name. Don't give him your name. Think of a false
name. "I hope you don't mind my calling you at this
hour," she said nervously, unsure how to react, and listening, all the time listening, for the sound of the receiver
being picked up below her. "It's just—so terribly urgent."

"Who are you, please?"

"I need help. I need to see a medium. I'm sorry, are you a medium?"

"Yes," he said, as if she was mad.

"Is it possible to come and see you?"

"You'd like a sitting?"

"Yes."

"I have a cancellation on Monday, 10:30 A.M. if that's any good?"

"I don't suppose there's any chance tomorrow?"

"Tomorrow?" He sounded indignant. "Absolutely not, I'm afraid. Monday—or—otherwise it won't be until May, I'm afraid. Let me see. May 4, I could do it."

May 4. She stared at the calendar again. *What was it? What the hell was it?*

"No, Monday, please." She was conscious of the sound of a car approaching fast and pulling up outside. She heard a door slam, the bark of a dog.

"May I have your name, please?"

"It's—" She hesitated. *What name? What name?* "Shoona Johnson," she said wildly. She thought she could detect cynicism in his voice as he repeated it, as though he could tell somehow that she was lying, and she felt embarrassed.

"And may I have a phone number?"

"I'm, er—staying—" Don't give a number where he could check up and find your name, give him no clues. She stared around for inspiration, read the wording "South East Business Systems" on the base of her VDT, and gave him the number printed beneath it. "See you Monday," she said.

"Goodbye."

She did not like the way he had sounded, as if she had been a nuisance to him, as if he had not cared whether she'd rung him or not. It was now a quarter past ten on a Saturday night, she reminded herself; she wouldn't have been too impressed if someone had rung her at this hour, asking if she'd look at a manuscript. She heard a harsh rattle. Oh, Christ, someone was trying to get in the door.

She spun around, but there was nothing. She heard the sound again, distant, below her, and the bark of a dog again. She ran to the window and looked down. She saw a car with its wheels on the curb, then Philip Main looking up, anxious.

Already? How could he be here already? She fumbled with the window lock, pushed it open and stared down. *No, he couldn't be here yet, too soon. Much too soon.*

"Alex, are you OK?"

Chunks of time were disappearing. *What was happening? What the hell was happening?*

"Alex? Shall I break the door down?"

"No," she said weakly. "I'll give you the keys." She threw them down, saw him jump out of the way, heard the faint clank as they hit the pavement.

Sighing with relief, she walked across her office. There was a growl outside her door. She opened it and saw a small black bull terrier standing belligerently, baring its teeth, with a stream of slobber dribbling from its black gums. It gave a low rumbling growl.

Footsteps raced up the stairs and Main appeared on the landing, puffing, disheveled. "Black!" he shouted. "Leave!"

The dog glared at Alex, hungry for action.

"Black!"

Reluctantly, it backed off.

Main put his hands out and rested them on her shoulders. "Are you all right?"

"Yes, I'm OK."

"I decided to come myself. What's the matter? What's happened?"

Alex stared at him, then burst into tears. "I don't know, Philip. I don't know what's happening."

"Oh, Lord." He fumbled in his pockets and pulled out a handkerchief. "You are in a bad state."

"It was the phone; I heard someone on the phone."

"In here?"

She nodded and took the handkerchief.

"Sorry, it's a bit grubby."

She squeezed it tightly, then dabbed her eyes with it. He led her over to the sofa and they sat down. He fumbled in his pocket and pulled out his cigarettes. She watched the dog look around, uninterestedly, then trot out of the room.

"Someone lifted up the receiver when I was calling you."

"There's no one here now, I looked as I came up; the windows are all locked, as far as I could see. Are you sure?"

She nodded.

"It wasn't a crossed line, outside somewhere?"

She stared at him. "It felt so close."

"What did?"

"The person, whoever it was."

Main offered her a cigarette. "What are you doing here, at this hour, on a Saturday night?"

"I—I needed your number—I didn't have it at home. I'm sorry—did I disturb you?"

"No more than the chap from Porlock disturbed Coleridge; you may have deprived mankind of the greatest poem of all time—I was about to write it—" He smiled.

"I'm sorry; I don't know what is happening."

"I'll drive you home."

"No." She shook her head. "I don't want to go home."

"You're not staying here, I won't let you. I think you need some rest." He held out his lighter. "You can come and stay at my place." He caught her eye and stared straight back. "In the spare room. OK?"

She smiled and nodded, then winced at the strength of the cigarette. She stood up and took Stanley Hill's manuscript back into her secretary's office, replacing it where she had found it. "I didn't know scientists wrote poetry," she said, walking back into her office. "Are you ever going to let me see any?"

"We'll see." He smiled mysteriously.

She felt better after the first whiskey, curled up on the floor on the thick rugs in front of the log fire. The walls of the room were lined with books, shelves of battered, loved books that went up to the high stuccoed ceiling. There was wood and leather everywhere; fine wood paneling, solid wooden furniture, antique but simple, well restored, and leather chairs, big, thick leather chairs and a massive leather sofa.

"I don't understand. Why are you so against it?"

"Mumbo jumbo, it's a load of nonsense; we die and we're gone." He clapped his hands together, suddenly, violently; it made her jump, and the dog rushed over to him, barking excitedly.

"How can you say that?"

"I know it; it's proven. Down, boy, down! Good Lord, you're an intelligent woman, you can't still believe in God! Darwin's proven; the game's up for the Holy Joes." He exhaled a lungful of smoke and the sharp gaunt features of his face became hazy and soft for a moment as the smoke wafted up around him; he looked demonic, she thought, satanic, and for an instant she felt a tiny shudder of doubt about him.

"If we were part spirit, part man, we'd have free will, girl. We don't, we're all prisoners of our genes; it's all laid out, the DNA, the computer program in your genes, from your mother and your father; the color of your eyes, the size of your fanny."

She grinned, relaxing again.

"Even the way you're going to think."

"We have free will, Philip."

"Rubbish. You and I have no more free will than a dog, than Black."

"I thought dogs had free will."

Main pointed a finger at his dog. "Black kills cats; if he sees a cat when he's not on the lead, he'll kill it; it's in his genes, he can't help it, and he can't be stopped."

"What do you mean?"

"You saw how obedient he was in your office. I told him to stop and he did. He'll obey me on everything, except a cat; if he sees a cat, that's it; he'll tear its throat out."

"That's bad training."

"No, there's nothing I could do about it; there's nothing any trainer in the world could do about it; it's in his genes and it can never be removed."

"You said that spirits could have genes too."

"We've evolved God in our minds; it's our survival mechanism, dates back thousands of years, when man first tried to explain why he was here. You've met spiritualists, mediums; they're all loopy or else they're very smooth. The loopy ones think they're genuine, the smooth ones are hoods; they're good at telepathy, they pluck Uncle Harry out of your memory banks, tell you things you already knew, throw in a few others for good measure, you go 'Gosh, Wow, Triff!' Then you think a bit, and you say, 'How is Uncle Harry?' And he says, 'Fine,' and you go away, and you start thinking about it, and the doubt sets in. Look, you think, I buried Uncle Harry last week. He's in his grave, or his ashes are in this urn, and now we're talking to each other again. And you want to talk more and more and you'll find you can't, because Uncle Harry can't think of anything else to say."

He drew deeply on his cigarette, and smiled. "He was a boring old fart when he was alive and you suddenly expect him to become interesting because he's dead." He stopped, seeing the tears in her eyes. "I'm sorry, girl, but you'll only do yourself harm up there." He tapped his head. "Your son was a nice lad; but you've just got to accept that he's dead."

She stared at him for a long time. "I can accept it, Philip. But I'm not sure he can."

11

The bright London Sunday morning unfurled through the grimy windscreen of Philip Main's Volvo; it was like trying to watch television through a frosted glass window, Alex thought. London looked different on Sundays, the sense of urgency had gone from it. There was time on Sundays, time to walk, time to think; London was a good place on Sundays.

She felt rested, having slept well for the first time, she realized, since the news about Fabian.

She looked down at the car's ashtray, jammed open and thick with butts, at the piles of papers, magazines, documents, cassettes lying in the floorwell around her feet. "Thank you," she said, "for last night. It did me a lot of good."

"We managed," he said gently.

"Managed what?"

"Managed."

"You talk in riddles sometimes."

"Managed to restrain ourselves."

She smiled and looked at him, cigarette protruding from his mustache, head hunched slightly forward, as if he was too tall for the car. "You have quite an ego, don't you?"

"No—just sometimes—" He trailed off.

"Sometimes what?"

"Sometimes—" The words trailed away and evaporated. He leaned forward, pushed a cassette into the player, and a second later Elkie Brooks sang, loud and clear, all around her. He grunted, leaned forward again and turned the volume down. "So, the vicar told you to try to find out more about Fabian?"

"The curate. Yes."

"And what have you found out so far?"

"That he didn't ditch his girlfriend, Carrie—she ditched him."

"What does that tell you? That he was proud?"

Alex laughed. "I feel so stupid, you know, about last night."

"The mind plays tricks when you get tired."

"Have you ever heard of a medium called Morgan Ford?"

He shook his head and inhaled deeply on his cigarette.

"How can you tell a genuine one from a fake?"

"There are no genuine ones."

Alex stared at him. "You scientists can be so damned smug, you're infuriating."

He pressed the horn irritably at a small rented car, all four of its occupants gawking at Liberty's façade. "No, we just state truths people don't like to hear."

"That's equally smug."

She was mildly surprised to see her Mercedes standing where she had left it, not towed away, ticketed or vandalized. She leaned over and gave him a kiss on the cheek.

"You're going to be all right now?"

"Yes."

"I think I'll take you out to dinner tonight, just to make sure."

She shook her head. "I don't really like going back to an empty house in the evening. Come around to me and I'll make some supper."

"About eight?"

Alex drove off feeling cheerful, relaxed; but the pain would come back, she knew. It was all piled up in her head, waiting to avalanche; it would be worst in the late afternoon when the sunlight began to fade; the depression would come, the way it always had, late afternoon on Sundays, all her life, since she was a small child.

She drove south over Vauxhall Bridge and down toward Streatham, not relishing the task she faced of trying to find Carrie and breaking the news to her. She didn't even have an address. All she could remember was that they had been passing an antique shop with a row of chairs out on the pavement, when Fabian had said, "That's where Carrie lives, Mother," and she had looked over to the right and seen the tower blocks. It was at the start of a hill, very similar to the hill she was on now; she saw an antique shop, closed, boarded up, and two gray towers in the distance to the right. She turned and headed toward them, down a narrow street lined with beat-up cars and grimy vans: a tight hemmed-in street. Two black kids were playing a game on the pavement; they stopped and looked at her and she felt herself blushing, felt somehow that she had no right to be here, that she was out of her allotted territory.

The road wound around and up through a seemingly endless row of two-story council dwellings, stark metal staircases leading to the upper floors. Towels, sheets and underwear hung from the balconies and windows; it felt like a ghetto.

The two tower blocks now loomed straight up in front of her, crumbling, precast concrete; they stretched into the sky like a pair of giant dismal tombstones.

Alex got out of the Mercedes, locked it carefully and walked into the lobby of the nearest building. Most of the glass from one door panel was lying on the floor and the other door was wedged permanently open. The word FUCK had been spray-painted across a wall in large crimson letters, and there was an unpleasant smell she could not identify.

She looked down the name panel. It was there: E. Needham. She felt a confusion of emotions suddenly. It would have been easier if there had been no name; the decision would have been made, and she could let it rest.

She pushed the button and the huge elevator door slid open; it was more like a freight elevator than a passenger elevator. SUCK YOUR BALLS. The graffiti artist had been at work in here too. She pushed the button for the third floor and the door shut slowly, jerkily. She wondered if it would have been more sensible to have walked. There was an almost imperceptible jolt and the doors in front of her began to slide downward slowly, almost agonizingly slowly. The lift smelled foul, like a public lavatory, and suddenly she noticed, to her horror, a puddle of urine on the floor beside her. She moved away. There was a clunk and a shudder and the elevator passed a marker for the first floor.

Finally, it jerked to a halt and she stepped out into a grimy stone-floored corridor. There was a faded ban-the-bomb roundel sprayed on the wall, and farther along someone had carved PIGS into the wall with a chisel. She stopped outside number 33, a blue door with a spyhole, and looked for the bell. She pushed it, heard a rasp like an angry insect, and waited. A moment later a woman's voice called out. "Yeah?"

Alex stared at the door. "Mrs. Needham?" She waited, but nothing happened. Somewhere down the corridor she could hear a baby crying, and above her the faint blare of pop music. She rang the bell again.

There was another long pause. "Yeah, who is it?"

Alex stared at the door. "Mrs. Needham?"

"Who is it?" The voice was closer now and she heard the shuffle of footsteps, saw the glint of movement in the spyhole. "What yer want?" said the voice, hostile.

"I want to speak to Mrs. Needham, please."

"You from the Council?"

"No. My name's Alex Hightower. My son used to go out with your daughter."

There was a long silence. Alex heard a hacking cough, then silence again. "Hello?" she said nervously.

"So what yer want? I've paid me TV license."

Alex frowned, baffled. "I just want to have a word with you about your daughter, Carrie. Do you have a daughter, Carrie?"

A pause. "Yeah." Another pause. "What she done?"

"Nothing, Mrs. Needham. I have some news to give her. Please open the door."

There was another hacking cough and she heard the sound of bolts sliding; the door opened a few inches. She saw a much younger woman than she had expected, someone her own age, but with a pinched, hardened face, aged by neglect, sourness and a sallow complexion that was desperately in need of some fresh air. She must once have been very pretty, and she could be attractive now if she made the effort. She stood there, her hair a nest of curlers, cigarette hanging from her lips, in a dirty blue dressing gown, looking her up and down. "You're not from the Council?"

"No."

"Yeah, well, they got some funny ideas." Alex saw the eyes stare at her shiftily, then dart nervously around. The woman jerked her head and stepped back; Alex took this to be an invitation and stepped into a short hallway which stank of sour milk and cigarette smoke. Through a door to the right she could see the kitchen, the table stacked with a pile of empty beer bottles. The woman led her into an L-shaped bed-sitting-room. "Carrie, you said?"

Alex nodded and stared around at the unmade bed, the bare walls, the clothes, trash, magazines and unwashed dishes strewn around at random, at the filthy windows and the magnificent views out over London beyond.

"My son, Fabian, used to go out with your daughter

—until quite recently; I think they split up just after Christmas."

The woman stared blankly, drew heavily on her cigarette, even though it was down to the filter, screwed up her nose, took another drag and stubbed it out. "Ain't seen her; she don't come here much." She turned her face away from Alex and coughed again, a long, hacking cough. She turned back. "Sit down, throw those papers on the floor. I'm afraid it's not much here; they don't give you much here; they don't give you much now, the Council, if you're on your own."

Alex removed a pile of newspapers and a half-completed football pools coupon from the sofa, and sat down.

"Gone her own way, if you know what I mean."

Alex sensed the woman eyeing her up and down. "All children are difficult, one way or another."

"I don't know about no Fibbin—wozzisname, Fibbin?"

"Fabian."

"Don't know about 'im. She din't say nothing about him."

"He was killed in a car crash two and a half weeks ago. I know he was very fond of Carrie; I thought she ought to know."

"Oh yes?" the woman said, matter-of-fact, and Alex wondered if perhaps the woman had misheard her.

"I thought Carrie might have come to the funeral, you see." Alex bit her lip; she wanted to get out of here, away from the stench, this wretched woman, the filthy flat.

"I'll tell her when I see her, dear—dunno when that'll be. I'm sorry, haven't offered you nothing—don't get many visitors, see, except from the Council."

"I'm fine, thanks."

"Cup of tea or something."

"No, thank you, really."

"She's in America." She nodded at the mantelpiece and Alex saw a postcard with a picture of a skyscraper.

"How long has she been there?"

The woman shrugged. "Dunno how long she been anywhere; just get postcards, nothing else; get 'em regular, I suppose." She shrugged. "Know some mums don't even get that."

Alex smiled. "I thought Carrie was very nice; pretty girl."

The woman shrugged. "I wouldn't know, wouldn't know what she looks like these days; had some photographs of her once, dunno what I done with 'em."

There was a rasp from the doorbell and an urgent pounding on the front door.

"Who is it?" she shouted sharply.

It rang again twice and there was more urgent knocking.

"All right, all right!" She stood up, coughing, and shuffled out.

Alex went over to the mantelpiece and looked at the postcard. In small white print at the bottom were the words: "John Hancock Tower." There were several more cards stacked up beside it. Massachusetts Institute of Technology, Cambridge, Mass. Newport, Rhode Island. Vermont, New Hampshire. She heard the click of the door opening, heard laughter and footsteps, looked around nervously and slipped the card from the Massachusetts Institute of Technology into her handbag.

"Bugger off! You fuckers!" she heard Mrs. Needham yell; there was a crash as the door slammed shut, and Mrs. Needham shuffled back into her room, holding a beer bottle, her face flushed with rage. "Buggers, the kids round here. Buggers." She prised the top off the bottle, took a swig and offered it to Alex.

She shook her head. "No, thank you."

The woman wiped her mouth with the back of her hand. "Get 'em all the time. The Council say they can't do nothing." She took another swig from her bottle. "How did you say your son was?"

Alex looked at her, horrified, as she realized that the woman was drunk and had been all along.

"He's dead, Mrs. Needham," she said as calmly as she could, feeling pity and anger fighting their way up her throat. "Dead."

"Yeah, well, get's us all," said Mrs. Needham.

12

Alex drove down the King's Road, glad to be out of Mrs. Needham's flat and away from the claustrophobic desolation of the neighborhood.

She felt anger rising in her, anger at the woman for living like that, for not caring that Fabian was dead; anger at her being so pathetic, anger that anywhere as ghastly as that place could even exist. Then she thought of the view, that stunning view from the window, and it seemed absurd that the only thing of beauty about the whole place should be the view of somewhere else.

The house was peaceful; she picked the Sunday papers off the doormat and took them through to the kitchen. She heard the whirr of the kitchen clock, the soft breathing of the boiler. Everything felt normal, smelled normal, sounded normal. The house hummed, sighed, creaked, like the old friend it had always been. She felt comfortable, safe. Home.

The phone rang; it was David. "Alex, are you OK?"

His voice sounded clumsy, intruding on her peace, and she felt instantly annoyed with him. Then she remembered how she had treated him and felt sorry. "Hello, David," she said, making an effort to sound pleased to hear him. "I'm fine—look—I'm sorry about last night—I don't know what happened—"

"It must have been the strain, darling. We've both been under terrible strain; the shock of the whole thing."

Swear at me, for Christ's sake, be firm with me, don't be so bloody nice to me all the time; call me a bitch, shout at me; make me afraid of you, she thought, but could not say it. "Yes, you're right," she said flatly. "I ran after you last night, shouting at you, waving—everyone must have thought I was bonkers."

He laughed. "Why?"

"I wanted to apologize."

"I rang you when I got back; there was no answer; I was worried sick."

"I went to the office."

"The office?"

"I thought I'd try and do some work; I ended up sleeping there."

"I think it's good to work hard at the moment, take your mind off—you know—but don't overdo it—you must try and rest."

She watched her reflection in the toaster, saw her eyes and looked away, unable to face them. It was a lousy feeling, lying when you knew you were being believed, she thought; it was like cheating against yourself. "I went to see Carrie's mother today."

"Carrie? Did she know?"

"No. Nothing. She hardly ever sees Carrie, apparently. She's in the States somewhere at the moment."

"She was a sweet little thing." His voice trailed off. "How about some dinner one night this week?"

"That would be nice."

"How's your schedule?"

"I've left my Filofax in the office. Let's talk tomorrow."

She sighed as she hung up, thinking for a moment of the times they had been together, when they had been happy; or had it all been a pretense then? All just a larger lie? She made a sandwich, then went through into the drawing room, lit the fire, put on a cassette of *Don Giovanni* and curled up on the sofa.

It was late afternoon when she woke up with a start out of a heavy dream. She felt confused and hot; she had been driving somewhere with Fabian; he had made a joke about something and they had been laughing. He had seemed so real in the dream, so incredibly real, it took her several seconds to remember . . . that they would never drive anywhere, never laugh together again. She felt sad and cheated, cheated by the dream and cheated by life, and she stood up with a heavy heart, walked to the window and drew the curtains against the darkening light.

She wished her mother was still alive, that there was someone older and wiser in whom she could confide; someone who had been through it all before. There were things about being an adult she had never got used to; sometimes it seemed she had become a parent without ever having ceased to be a child.

She opened her handbag and took out the postcard she had taken from Carrie's mother: it was a wide riverside panorama, showing an avenue of grand university buildings. She turned it over. "Massachusetts Institute of Technology, Boston, Mass." was printed on the bottom. Boston, she thought; Boston, Boston, Boston. She looked at the handwriting, large neat upright letters:

> "Hi Mum, This is a really friendly place, lots of
> things happening, met some great people. Will
> write again soon. Love C."

There was one halfhearted *X* after the initial. She carried the card upstairs and went into Fabian's room.

His trunk sat on the bed, like a coffin, she thought, shuddering. "F.M.R. Hightower" was stenciled in faded white letters amid the scratches and dents on the lid. She opened the first catch, which sprang back sharply and caught her finger a painful blow, and opened the second more cautiously. She raised the lid, rummaged through the clothing, and pulled out Fabian's diary. She opened it up and pulled out the blank postcards she had found in his desk at Cambridge, and compared them with the one she had in her hand from Carrie; although the pictures were different, the printed layout on all of them was exactly the same. She frowned, puzzled, looked around the room, caught Fabian's eye staring down from the portrait and looked away guiltily, embarrassed about what she was doing.

There was a zipped pocket at the back of the diary, which she opened; inside was some pink notepaper, with handwriting that looked like Carrie's, and it was dated January 5. The address in Cambridge was also handwritten:

Dear Fabian,
    Please stop these persistent phone calls
which are annoying and distressing for everyone. I have told you I do not want to see you
again, and there is nothing that is going to
change my mind. There is no one else, as you
seem to insist. It's just that you've changed—or
maybe I never knew the real you. I can't cope
with your weird habits anymore. So please
leave me alone.
                                    With love. C.

The same curly *C* and the same style of handwriting as on the postcard, but something struck Alex as being different about it, and she could not figure out what. She read the letter again. Weird habits. Weird habits, she thought, puzzled, conscious that she was beginning to feel cold again in the room, cold and uncomfortable. The door-bell rang. She looked at her watch: it was six-fifteen. She slipped everything back inside the diary, laid it on top of the trunk and went downstairs.

She opened the front door and felt immediately unsettled by the large woman with the peroxided hair who stood there.

"Hello, Mrs. Hightower."

Alex stared at her neat black pillbox hat, her leather gloves and her immaculately pressed white blouse.

"Iris Tremayne; I popped around last week."

Alex watched her tiny rosebud lips parting as she spoke, like a secret door in the soft folds of her face. There was a determination in the woman's eyes, a determination that this time she would not be sent away. "Come in," she said, unable for a moment to think of anything else to say.

"You need me, dear, I can tell," the woman said, stepping possessively into the house.

Alex still had the words of the letter going around in her mind. Weird; weird; the glare of the portrait, the sudden chill in the room. Surely it was Morgan Ford she was seeing, and that was tomorrow. "I think there's a mistake—" she began.

Iris Tremayne stared imperiously around the hallway, then followed Alex into the drawing room. "You're being troubled, dear, aren't you?" There was a gentleness that just stopped her voice short of being bossy.

"I've been a bit jumpy, that's all."

"I should think you would be, with what's been happening."

Alex stared at her warily. "What do you mean—with what's been happening?"

"You're being troubled, dear, aren't you? I could sense it when I came around before, you were going to be troubled; tell me, I'm right, aren't I, dear?"

Alex glared at her, annoyed suddenly for the intrusion into her privacy. She had the appointment for tomorrow; she did not need to speak to anyone now. She wondered if Morgan Ford and Iris Tremayne were connected, whether he had tracked her down through the Olivetti service number she had given him and sent Iris Tremayne around. Ridiculous. "Would you like a cup of tea?"

"Oh no, dear, thank you."

She looked around her again. "This is a very nice house, dear." A painting on the wall caught her attention and she walked over toward it, then pointed her finger. "Is that a Stubbs?"

"No."

"He's the only painter of horses that I know."

"It's one of my husband's."

"He's a painter, is he?"

Alex looked at her coldly. "No, the horse; he used to own it. One of his hobbies."

"Not a betting person myself; suppose I should be . . . with my sensitivity . . . but it never seems to work for us sensitives, dear. I never knew anyone who could predict winners for themselves. Restful, aren't they, pictures of horses."

"I've never really thought about it." Alex stared at her impatiently. "What did you mean just now, when you said I was being troubled?"

"His spirit is restless, isn't it, dear? He wants some help." She lowered herself carefully into an armchair, like a crate being lowered into a hold, thought Alex. The woman closed her eyes tightly, inclined her body forward and, keeping her gloves on, held her right wrist in her left hand. She opened her eyes and looked up and Alex detected, for the first time, a flicker of doubt in the woman's positive manner.

"Don't worry, dear." The lips parted, stretched into a nervous smile then shrank back, as if they had a life of their own. "There's no charge, no charge at all. Of course, you can give a donation to charity if you wish, but that's optional, quite optional." She raised her large false eyelashes up to the ceiling, frowned, as if detecting a flaw in the paintwork, then smiled again uncertainly. "Coping, are you, dear?"

"Yes," said Alex coldly. "I'm coping."

"He's around, isn't he, dear?"

"What do you mean?"

Iris Tremayne shook her head and breathed in sharply; her shoulders suddenly contracted, then relaxed again. She closed her eyes and sat very still. Alex watched her curiously, and felt a sudden deep sense of dread.

The woman began to twitch, almost imperceptibly. Then suddenly she stopped and stood up straight, opening her eyes. "I'm sorry, dear," she said, "I've made a terrible mistake. I shouldn't have come." Her voice had changed, it was icy cold now; the calm had gone from her face and she looked almost as if she was frightened. "No, I shouldn't have come at all. A terrible mistake."

"What do you mean?"

She shook her head. "I'd better go now, dear," she said abruptly, picking up her handbag.

Alex felt afraid suddenly. "What do you mean?"

"It'll be much better if I go, dear; it's not what I thought at all."

Alex stared at the round whiteness of her eyeballs, the dark pupils scanning the room, darting about, the furrows of the frown lines in her fleshy forehead. "Can't you at least tell me what you mean?"

Iris Tremayne sat down for a moment, rummaged in her handbag and took out her powder compact. She opened it with a loud click and stared at the mirror. "I look a sight," she said, dabbing her nose with some powder.

Alex felt her anger rising. "Please tell me what this is all about."

The woman looked at her, then snapped shut the compact. She hesitated, then shook her head. "You must believe me, dear, it's better if I go, best not to talk about it, forget it, dear, forget I came. You were right, you were quite right last time." She stood up again and edged toward the door. She stopped, tried to give Alex a kindly smile, but she was trembling too much. "I really think I'd better go; leave it all alone, I think that would be best. Don't worry about any payment."

"Look, I want an explanation. Please?"

There was a dull crash from upstairs; Alex wondered for a moment if she had imagined it, but she saw the woman's nervous glance.

"He's troubled, dear."

"I'll just go and see what that was."

"No, dear, I wouldn't; I've disturbed him, you see," she said hesitantly. "He's not pleased about my coming, not pleased at all." The woman shook her head. "Leave it, dear, take my advice—I've never had—never known—not like this, you must leave it alone, leave him alone; ignore him." She suddenly took a step toward Alex and gripped her hand firmly. Alex felt the cold leather of the glove. "You must, dear." She turned and marched out into the hallway. There was a click of the door and she was gone.

Alex stared around the room, her head spinning, and walked to the window; she parted the curtains and stared out. She could see Iris Tremayne walking down the street, in short ducklike steps, each one growing faster, more determined, almost as if she was trying to run but wasn't quite able to.

13

Alex released the curtains and stared around the room. What had Iris Tremayne seen, she wondered. Was she a loony, or—? She lit a cigarette and took a deep drag; it had a foul, unfamiliar taste, like burned rubber. Fabian hated her smoking and she had always tried not to when she was with him; she felt suddenly as if she was cheating on him now, took another drag, almost surreptitiously, and stubbed it out, screwing her nose up at the stench.

She went through to the kitchen, trying to ignore the crash from upstairs. Just another trick of her mind, she told herself, but she could still see Iris Tremayne's face, the fearful glance upward. Probably just the boiler again. She opened the freezer door, and rummaged through the frozen packs, wondering what to cook for Philip, then closed the door again, restlessly. She looked at her watch: seven o'clock. He would be here soon. He could decide and she'd pop it in the microwave.

She looked up at the ceiling and listened. Everything was quiet. What the hell had she meant, the damned woman? She walked down the passageway, climbed the stairs, stood on the landing and listened again. She felt nervous suddenly, uncomfortable, wished for a moment she was not alone. In the distance she heard the siren of an ambulance. She opened her bedroom door and turned on the light; everything was normal. She checked the bathroom; nothing wrong there either. She went down the corridor, stood outside Fabian's room and listened again. She pushed open his door, turned on the light and felt the blood drain out of her.

The trunk was lying upside down on the floor, the contents spewed out all around it.

She felt herself reeling and clutched the wall for support; it seemed to slide away from her and she stumbled, grabbing the side of his armchair. She closed her eyes, breathed deeply, opened them again, looked around, bewildered for a moment, then went out of the room, down the corridor and into his bathroom. Had there been someone in here? No, impossible; the windows were all closed, secure. Could it have fallen by itself—had she left it balanced on the edge of the bed? No, that was not possible. So how? How?

She went back into the room, stared at the jumble of belongings on the floor, clothes, books, his diary, his battered straw boater, then up at his portrait. How?

The doorbell rang. She turned off the light, closed the door and went downstairs.

"Sit!" she heard, followed by an angry snarl. "Sit!"

Shaking, she opened the door and saw Philip Main standing there in a battered cord jacket, holding a crumpled paper bag under one arm and Black's leash, with some difficulty, in the other.

"Black, sit!" Main looked at her. "Sorry if I'm a bit early, couldn't remember what time." He turned back to the dog. "Sit!"

"I don't think I said a time."

He thrust the paper bag at her. "Didn't know what we were eating, so I bought red and white."

"Thanks." She took the bag.

Main was physically jerked backward. "Black, sit!"

The dog let out a slow rumbling growl, like a powerful motorbike idling. "Come in."

Main jerked the dog leash hard and Black gave a surprised choking cough. "He's—er—not pleased—hasn't had much of a walk today." The dog dug its toes into the concrete step and slid, reluctantly, a few inches under Main's determined pull. "Black!" The dog looked up, sensing defeat, and reluctantly followed its master into the house, then stopped inside the hallway and sat down.

"Hello, boy," said Alex, patting him, but the dog ignored her completely and stared, suspiciously, at the ground. Main unclipped the leash. "Gets these moods."

"Must be difficult, keeping a dog in London."

"Sometimes." He rolled the leash up and pushed it into his pocket. "We seem to manage."

They went through into the drawing room. "What would you like?"

"You look terrible."

"Thanks a lot." She smiled.

"White; you look white as a sheet."

"Scotch?"

"I don't suppose you've any Paddy?"

"Paddy?"

"Irish whiskey."

She shook her head. "Sorry." She was conscious of his stare and felt uncomfortable. "I'm probably a bit tired."

He sat down and slowly eased his cigarette pack out of his jacket pocket.

She handed him his drink. "Actually, I've had a bit of a bummer of a day. How was yours?"

"All right." He leaned forward and sniffed his whiskey.

"Make any progress? Am I any nearer getting a book?"

"A little bit." He sniffed the whiskey again. "A little bit."

"I wouldn't make much of a living if all my clients were like you; three years and I still don't know what it's about."

"Did all right with the last one, girl."

She smiled; his last one had been published in fifteen countries; it had been translated into twelve languages, and it was incomprehensible in all of them. "Will I be able to understand this one?"

"The whole world will be able to understand it, girl. But they won't want to." He struck a match and held it to the end of his cigarette.

"You're very determined, aren't you?"

"Determined?"

"To prove that God does not exist."

He shook out the match. "Hokum, girl; there's too much hokum in the world."

"Are you sure it's not a vendetta?"

"Vendetta?"

"Against your father. He was a clergyman, wasn't he?"

He shook his head in a cloud of smoke, then stared sadly at the carpet. "Lost his faith; decided he had it all wrong, that he wasn't a vicar at all."

"So what was he?"

"He became a medium."

Alex stared at him. "You never told me that."

"No, well, there are certain things one doesn't tell."

She shrugged. "Why not, it doesn't matter. Did he get you involved in anything?"

"Good Lord, yes; all the time."

She watched him sitting there, his tall frame crumpled awkwardly in the chair, gripping his glass clumsily with both hands, like an old man. She felt comfortable with him, safe with his mysteries and his answers and his knowledge; he always gave her the impression that somewhere, deep inside him, was the truth about life, that only he knew it, and one day, if she pried hard enough and deeply enough, he would reveal it to her. "In what sort of things?"

He went red and stared hard at his glass, as if trying

to read something that was written in the whiskey. "Spirit rescues, he used to call them."

"Spirit rescues?"

"Hmmm!" He shuffled awkwardly about in the chair.

"Tell me about them."

He looked around, embarrassed, as if to check no one else was listening, then gave her an apologetic smile. "Used to take me along, as a sort of earth." He shrugged. "Exorcisms, spirit rescues, that sort of thing."

"I don't understand."

"There was a stretch of road, near Guildford, that people seemed to think was haunted; some chap wandering around in the middle of the road. Several police patrols saw him too. My father went along, took me with him, took me because I wasn't psychic, couldn't be affected by spirits; I was like an earth wire on a plug." He pushed his cigarette into his mouth and drew deeply on it. "It turned out to be a truck driver who had been killed in a crash a few years before; he didn't realize he was dead, was wandering around trying to find his wife and kids. My father told him what had happened, explained he was dead and put him in contact with some spirit guides; they took him off and he was quite happy." Main looked up at Alex sheepishly, then looked down at his whiskey and turned the glass around in his hands.

"Did you see this man?"

"Lord, no. Just heard my father speak to him."

"And what did you think about it?"

He drank some whiskey and looked up at her. "I thought my father was round the bend."

Alex stared at him, and they sat in silence for a long time. "I don't think you did," she said finally.

He shifted again uncomfortably. "It was all a long time ago." He paused. "Gosh yes, a very long time."

"And you've spent the rest of your life trying to prove him wrong?"

Main sat and stared silently at her. "My father ended up in a funny farm."

"I'm sorry," she said.

He shrugged.

"Perhaps he couldn't cope with his powers."

"Hmmm."

She shuddered. "Creepy."

"There's a link between the old brain, mental illness and pyschic powers. Weird lot, mediums."

"I've never heard of a vicar becoming a medium."

"Have you ever heard of a vicar who ended up in a funny farm?"

She looked at him, uncertain whether to smile. "Was there ever a time when you did believe in it?"

"It destroyed my father." He looked down at his drink.

"Don't you think sometimes good comes of it? People with healing powers?"

"The National Health has healing powers; and statistically a better record."

"And when they fail?"

He stared into his whiskey. "Nothing's proven."

"People have been healed when doctors have given up hope."

"They've done that for centuries, girl; long before mediums."

"And before Christ?"

He shifted again. "You need rest, girl, a holiday; get away from it all; you don't need mediums stirring it all up again for you."

"One came round this afternoon."

"That explains it."

"What?"

"Why you looked white as a sheet when I arrived."

"She was odd. She really spooked me." She looked at him, but he said nothing. "I hadn't asked her to come; she said she sensed I was being troubled, that—Fabian—was still around." Alex smiled nervously and pulled out a cigarette. "She sat down in here, closed her eyes and started shaking like a leaf; then she stood up, looking very frightened, and said she had made a mistake, a terrible mistake, that I should leave him alone."

"Very sensible."

"Then there was a crash upstairs."

Main looked at her, his eyes probing. "Some stupid woman trying to con you into something."

"No," said Alex, "that's the point—she wasn't. She just left; wouldn't say anything, wouldn't answer me. Just rushed out, looking terrified."

"Loonies; they're all loonies."

"Even Morgan Ford?"

"Yes, girl. Bound to be."

"Thanks a lot; I should have a great time with him tomorrow then."

"I've already told you."

She shrugged. "I want to go; I can make up my own mind. I especially want to go now, after what's happened —I—"

He was looking at her, his eyes penetrating. "Something else has happened, hasn't it?"

She twiddled with her cigarette. "I brought Fabian's old school trunk down from Cambridge yesterday; it was on his bed, full of stuff, very heavy. The crash I heard—I went upstairs; it had fallen off his bed, on to the floor. There's no way it could have fallen on its own, Philip."

"So how do you think it got there?"

She smiled nervously and felt herself blushing. "This may sound crazy—maybe you should put me in a funny farm too—Fabian always used to have a violent temper; most of the time he was sweet and gentle, but when he didn't get his way, particularly as a child, he used to have the most terrible tantrums. Sometimes he was so strong, I couldn't hold him. Maybe he got angry just now, with that woman." She smiled again and stared at Main hopefully.

He grinned. "There are a hundred reasons why something can fall on to the floor."

She shook her head adamantly. "No. There's no way; that trunk did not fall." She looked at him. "Why are you grinning?"

He shook his head slowly. "Yesterday you were being attacked in your office; today someone's throwing trunks around your bedrooms. Think about it."

"It's different, Philip. Last night I was all wound up, I admit that; but not tonight, tonight I was feeling OK." She paused. "Come and see for yourself."

He shrugged and stood up.

For a dreadful moment Alex thought they were going to walk into the room and see the trunk lying on the bed again, still neatly packed. She pushed open the door and turned on the light; the trunk lay there, everything spilled out on the floor, as she had left it.

"See?"

He looked down at the trunk, studied the clothes and the books strewn around. "It was on the bed?"

"Yes."

Main looked around the room, stared up at the portrait of Fabian and lingered on it thoughtfully. He walked over and fondled the telescope. "Fine instrument."

"You can have it if it's useful."

Main knelt down and stared through it; he focused the eyepiece. "Bad place, London, for astronomy; too much pollution in the air."

"Take it if you like."

He shook his head. "Not my field. Queen Victoria used to loathe microscopes. Said they enabled you to see things so closely, you could not tell what they were. I feel that way about telescopes; they enable you to see things so far away you still cannot tell what they are."

She smiled.

"Give me a microscope any day. It's all there, girl,

under the microscope; all of it." He stood up, stretched, looked down at the trunk. "Want a hand?"

"No. I've got to sort it out anyway; might as well leave it there." She saw Main stare at the portrait, then look away uncomfortably. "Has that effect, doesn't it?"

"The portrait?"

She nodded.

"Looks like one of those van Eyck characters." He looked up, then turned away again sharply.

"Are you hungry?"

"Well," he said, sighing, "I suppose a chap could eat something."

"Perhaps a chap would like to choose it? And the chappess will cook it."

"Bona," he said, turning and staring at the picture again. A perturbed look came across his face and he walked out of the room, a little too hurriedly, thought Alex, surprised at the sudden change that had come over him.

14

Black made a noise like a child gargling, and Alex jumped. The pitch deepened again into a low rumble.

Main picked some lasagne out of his mustache, dabbed his lips with his napkin then turned his head toward the passageway. "Quiet, boy!"

The rumble continued. He picked up his wineglass and drained it. "Bona," he said.

"You've been very quiet."

He leaned back in his chair and pulled his cigarettes out of his jacket. He lifted the bottle and poured some wine into Alex's glass, then refilled his own.

"Nice wine."

"Montepulciano d'Abruzzo."

"Pardon?"

There was another rumble from Black. Philip turned and looked at the passageway again. "Quiet!" he shouted. "Some remarkably good wines, from Italy. Stunning."

"You should get together with David; write a book."

He paused, then looked up at her. "Jesus knew a bit about wine."

"Jesus?"

"He didn't turn the water into ordinary plonk. Someone asked the host why he'd saved the best wine to the end."

She smiled. "Italian?"

"No, good God, no. Probably Lebanese."

Black rumbled again. Philip frowned but said nothing.

"So what do you think about the trunk?"

He did not speak until he had lit his cigarette, as if it was a drug he needed to give him the power of speech. "I think you had it too near the edge of the bed."

She looked down. "No, Philip, I didn't, and you know I didn't."

Main stood up and ambled toward the doorway. "Black!" He walked down the passage and saw the dog standing staring up the stairs. It started its low slow growl once more. "What's the matter, boy?"

The dog ignored him.

"There's nothing up there, boy." Main stared at the dog, puzzled, beginning to feel uncomfortable himself. He turned back, walked a short way down the passage and went into the lavatory under the stairs. He closed the door, turned on the light and lifted the seat. He found himself shivering. It was like an icebox in here. He looked at the sharp black and white pattern on the wallpaper and noticed a sheen on it; he ran his finger along a strip and it felt wet. He looked at the moisture on his finger; the temperature seemed to be dropping as he stood. There was a crack like a pistol beside his right ear; he saw a shadow and flinched reflexively. An entire panel of paper fell away from the wall and on to him. He fielded it off with his arm and it dropped down beside him; he saw another panel in front of him begin to slide slowly down. He opened the door, snapped off the light and backed out, closing the door firmly. He stood in the passageway for a moment, wondering if he had imagined it. He put his hand on the handle again, then turned away and walked back into the kitchen.

Alex was looking at him, anxiously. "Everything all right?"

He said nothing.

"You look worried about something."

"Have you had that dampness in the loo long?"

"Dampness? What dampness?"

"The wallpaper's dripping; it's coming away from the walls." He saw the frown on her face.

"Can't be. The house is bone dry."

"Perhaps you've got a leaking pipe."

"I'll call the plumber in the morning."

"I'll have a look; may be something simple." He took off his jacket and hung it on his chair.

"I'll make some coffee," she said as he walked out of the room.

She heard Main scrabbling about upstairs as she carried the coffee through into the drawing room. Black was sitting by the front door. "Hello, boy!" she said. "Want to go out?" The dog ignored her.

She put the tray down, pulled *Don Giovanni* out of the tape player and pushed in a Mozart compilation tape. She saw the stack of unopened letters on her bureau, walked over and sifted through them. She recognized the handwriting on one or two of them, but could not bring herself to open them; not yet, she thought. Later, one day when she was strong again; for a moment, she wondered if she ever would be strong again. She filled her cup and sat down on the sofa.

Main came into the room, wiping his hands on his corduroy trousers.

"Black or white?"

"Black, please."

"Did you find the problem?"

"No."

"Thanks anyway."

He sat down beside her and began to stir his coffee thoughtfully. "I'll bring some tools round tomorrow. Lift up some floorboards; probably a leak in a joint somewhere."

"I didn't realize you were such a handyman."

"No, well, we all have hidden talents."

"You could write a book on do-it-yourself."

"Going to be busy, with do-it-yourself and the origins of life."

"Not to mention poetry."

Alex sensed him tense up. Suddenly, he looked over his shoulder.

"Everything OK?" She found herself turning around too, and felt a prickle of anxiety. Philip was looking uneasy, frowning. She listened to the music and said nothing. Slowly she felt him relax again; she watched him put down his cup and felt his arm gently touch her shoulders. She leaned back slightly, affectionately, but still she didn't feel comfortable. She shivered.

"Figaro?"

"Yes. An excerpt; various different Mozart—"

She wanted to speak, converse, to hear his voice, put this strange fear that was engulfing her out of her mind. Her Sunday afternoon fear had come late today, she thought. "You're very quiet."

He raised his eyebrows.

"Penny for your thoughts."

"You won't get rich on that; you're meant to be my agent."

She laughed, then was silent again, and listened to the music. A French horn was blowing a gallop; it was Mozart at his most rousing, most cheering. She found her feet tapping to the tune, felt the rhythmic thump of Main's arm on her shoulder. She sighed. "Oh God," she said, "why did this have to happen, why?"

"Hrrr."

"Is that your explanation for the origin of life?"

"What?"

"Hrrr!" she imitated.

She felt him lean forward, heard the clink of the cup,

the faint slurp, the clink of the cup again. "You'll get over it, old girl; it'll take time, a long time. I wish I'd met him."

She suddenly had an impulsive wish to say, "You will!" She felt a sudden strange tingling of excitement, of optimism. She drank some more coffee. "You know, it's funny—my mood swings so much at the moment—I go up and down, often several times in an hour."

He nodded. "That'll keep happening, for a while."

She looked at him. "Are you an expert on everything?"

"No, gosh, my word no. A little knowledge is a dangerous thing."

"So you have a lot?" She felt his arm squeezing her shoulder.

"No, good Lord no." He sat in silence for a moment. "There was a master at school, a pompous little man, who used to tell us with great satisfaction that he had never driven a motor car and did not know how to. But he was, however, fully qualified to drive a steam locomotive."

Alex smiled.

"He'd driven one in the 1926 General Strike: from King's Cross to Edinburgh nonstop. He claimed still to hold the unofficial record for the fastest time."

"Life's full of odd little people doing odd little things." She saw Main's face close to hers, saw the pockmarks in the white bony flesh, the gingery bristles of the mustache; she jerked back, surprised, then felt the soft bristles brushing her nose, brushing around the top of her mouth, saw his blue staring eyes going out of focus, like the view of a dentist's eyes, she thought for a moment.

Then suddenly the face changed and it was Fabian.

"No!" she screamed, pulling sharply back. "No!" Fabian's face dissolved, and she saw the shock on Main's face; it remained there, frozen for a moment, and then turned to an embarrassed sheepish expression.

"Sorry," he said lamely. "I—er—"

She continued to stare at him, shaking, wide-eyed.

She had seen him so clearly, so vividly. There was something touching and at the same time hideously obscene; Christ, what weird tricks her mind was playing. "I'm sorry, Philip," she said. "I'm really not—I don't know—ready." She felt his arm slip away from her shoulders, saw him lean forward, rest his elbows on his thighs.

"No, my fault, my fault entirely," he said. "I just find you—so immensely attractive, I—I—" He sat upright, gave her a benign, lost smile.

"I think maybe I'd better go to bed now," she said.

He looked at his watch. "Yes, good Lord, it's getting late." He stood up slowly and looked around again, and she saw the sudden expression of fear on his face. "You'll be all right?"

She nodded, and grimaced. "I'll have to be, won't I?"

Main wandered out into the hallway. It felt cold out here now; he rubbed his arms and walked into the kitchen. It was freezing. He looked around; were the walls damp in here too, or was it his imagination? He suddenly felt very uncomfortable, an intruder; the house didn't want him, was telling him to go. He removed his jacket deliberately slowly from the chair and pulled it on, then stood still and looked around. He felt the cold seeping through his skin. He walked over and touched a wall, ran his finger down and lifted it away; it was dry. He looked up at the ceiling, feeling so cold he could barely stop himself from shaking, then marched to the door, turned and stared back at the kitchen. "Fuck off," he said loudly, firmly; then he turned and walked through into the hallway.

"Did you say something?" said Alex, carrying the tray out of the drawing room.

"Me? No."

"I was sure I heard you speak."

"Just to Black, that was all."

"Ah."

He pulled the dog's leash out of his pocket and Black

suddenly became animated, jumping up, barking cheer-fully.

"Home, boy!"

"Good night, Philip."

"Thanks for supper."

"Thanks for the wine." She leaned forward and gave him a light kiss on the cheek. "Drive carefully."

"You can come and stay with me if you—er—if you want. You can have your own room, come and go—if you don't feel like—"

She shook her head. "Thanks, but this is my home. I've just got to get used to it again, that's all. Fabian was never here much, you know, anyway." She closed the door, heard the dog bark cheerfully at the night and turned the key. She felt peaceful suddenly. Immensely peaceful and relaxed, as if an evil presence had suddenly been exorcised from the house.

15

She parked in the gloomy terrace off the Gloucester Road and crossed her fingers that she would not get clamped or towed away. The numbers on the buildings were illogical, and she paced the length of the terrace, crossing the road, getting increasingly anxious that she was going to be late and miss the appointment altogether.

Then she saw it. Forty-nine. On the building directly in front of her car, staring her in the face, almost taunting her, she thought, angrily. She walked up the steps and scanned the names on the entryphone panel. Goldsworthy, Maguire, Thomas, Kay, Blackstock, Pocock, Azziz. Several of the names had been written in a scrawling pen; one, Azziz, had a line through it. Among them she found a fading yellow label with neat typing which simply said "Ford."

For an instant she felt relieved; then she began to feel nervous. She looked around uncertainly, wondering whether the neighbors all knew, whether the people walking past on the pavement were nudging each other and pointing at her. She wondered whether mediums made a lot of money. Morgan Ford certainly did not spend any on the outside of the building. The porch tiles were cracked and the plaster was peeling off the columns.

A cold unwelcoming voice crackled through the entryphone: "Yes?"

"It's—" Oh, Christ, what the hell was the name she had given? She couldn't remember; stall, she thought, stall for time. "Johnson!" she said suddenly, feeling the relief. "Mrs. Johnson." She'd given a Christian name too; what was that? She racked her brains again feverishly.

The grimy, dimly lit hallway gave nothing away about the identity of the tenants. There were several piles of mail on a shelf and a battered bicycle leaned against the wall.

Ford's flat was on the third floor and the door opened as she reached it. His appearance surprised her and she wondered what she had been expecting—some aging bearded weirdo left over from the sixties, dressed in a kaftan and sandals and holding a joss stick. Instead she was staring at a short man with neat gray hair and a neat gray suit; in his early fifties, she guessed.

"Shoona Johnson?"

For a moment Alex nearly said, "No, no, Alex Hightower," but just managed to stop. She stared through a doorway behind him, into a tiny office where a pile of letters and newspapers were laid out neatly on a small desk. "Yes." That was it, Shoona. Why the hell had she chosen Shoona, she wondered? She'd never met anyone called Shoona in her life.

He held out a small pink hand dominated by a vulgar rhinestone ring, a hand so small she wondered if it was a deformity. It was like shaking hands with a child.

"Come in. Thank you for being so punctual." There was a warm singsong lilt to his Welsh accent that seemed totally different from how he had sounded over the phone. "I'm afraid I'm a bit disorganized today, my secretary hasn't turned up."

Alex felt a sense of disappointment as she stepped into the plain dim hallway. It all seemed so ordinary; there was no feeling of magic, of occasion, of great ceremony. Business suits, secretaries, an office. She hadn't somehow expected him to be doing this for a living.

The drawing room changed her opinion. A huge burgundy-colored room with a view out across the gardens. It was overfurnished with fine antiques in an almost vulgar display of money. A gas log fire burned with a low hissing sound. Two cats sat on either side of the grate, motionless, like sentinels, a ginger tom and a smoke gray Burmese; the tom jumped forward on to the carpet and circled curiously around her.

And then she saw the bowl of red roses on the table in the center of the room.

She began to tremble, and started to back away. The phone rang.

"Please, take a seat." Ford brushed past her and picked up the receiver. "Hello." She watched him stiffen, saw him speak in the same cold, aloof way he had done the other night. "I have a cancellation on Thursday at half past eleven. I could fit you in then. Very good, and what is your name, please?"

Did he tell everyone that he had a cancellation, she wondered. She sat down in an uncomfortable Victorian armchair and stared at the roses again.

"Just one second, I'll fetch my diary and confirm that." She looked up and caught his eye. "Like roses, do you? They're nice those, aren't they?"

She wondered, as he left the room, whether it had been an innocent remark, or whether she had detected a mischievous wink in his eye. She looked again at the roses; no, maybe it was just coincidence; they went with the cats and the fire and the ornate furniture. A strange room for a middle-aged man, she thought; it seemed more like the room of an elderly titled widow.

She stared at a painting on the wall. Three phantom-like faces with slits for their eyes, huddled together, white on a white background. On a shelf just below them was a menacing Buddhaesque statue. She noticed more paintings as she looked around, all sinister; the room was beginning to frighten her. She stared at the roses, so like the ones Fabian had given her. She went over to the bowl and counted them. The same number. The same color. Was it a message, she wondered. A sign? Ridiculous. As she watched them, they seemed to be glowing. She closed her eyes, shook her head and turned away. She heard Ford's footsteps, a loud snort as he blew his nose. Instantly she sensed the atmosphere change as he entered the room. Everything became calm, peaceful again; she felt at ease. She glanced again at the roses; they were pretty, cheerful, and made her suddenly, inexplicably, feel good.

The tom looked up at her, then jumped on to her lap. She smiled down at it nervously, wondering whether it was about to attack her, and tentatively stroked its neck. It settled down, resting its head on her thigh, and looked up at her unblinkingly. She felt comforted by the contact, rested her hand on its belly, felt the warm skin beneath the fur, its assured relaxed breathing.

"Put him on the floor if he's a nuisance."

"No, he's fine."

"Some people are funny about cats."

"He's a nice chap."

Ford stood in front of her, hands clasped behind his back, and gave her a gentle smile. He looked up at the mantelpiece. "We've started a little late, so I'll give you some extra time."

Again Alex felt unsettled by his businesslike attitude. Surely you couldn't be a medium in units of quarter of an hour, like a lawyer or an accountant?

"Do you have anything I can hold?"

"I'm sorry?"

"Something you wear a lot. Your watch, a bracelet?"

She took off her Rolex and handed it to him.

"Now, is there anything in particular you want, or shall we just start and see how we go?"

She shrugged, wondering what to say.

Without waiting, he sat down in a chair beside her, held her watch outstretched in his hand for a moment then curled his fingers over it. "Upheaval," he said gently. "I sense upheaval. Something's upset the rhythm, something tragic, I feel, recently, very recently, within the last few weeks perhaps?" He looked at her.

"Do you want me to answer you?"

"As you like." He smiled. "There's no need if you don't want to, but it would be helpful, guiding me, if I'm on the right track."

"You're on the right track."

He sat still and frowned, then tilted his head back, keeping his eyes wide open. "Yes," he said. "Yes, I'm feeling something very distinctive, something very close, young, energy, a lot of energy. It's a child—no, not a child, but not an adult, definitely. Someone in their teens perhaps, or early twenties?" He stared questioningly at her. She said nothing. "Male." He frowned, and Alex saw the strange, nervous expression she had seen on Iris Tremayne's face the previous day. He sat very still for a moment and said nothing.

Alex stroked the cat, looked again at the roses, at the three phantoms, at the leaping flames with their hypnotic pattern, then again at Morgan Ford. His whole body seemed clenched like a fist, shaking, grim determination on his face, as if fighting a tremendous battle of will.

"This is extraordinary," he said, continuing to stare straight ahead. "He's trying to tell me his name. But it's too soon, much too soon, it takes several months for the spirits to settle down, they're too frisky in the first few weeks, it's difficult." His voice trailed away. "Clarity, clarity is difficult. Something violent, not here, not in England, somewhere overseas, I sense flames, an explosion. A truck is involved? Yes, a truck, someone's shouting about a truck!"

Alex watched him, his eyes shut now, trembling like a child.

"Something else now, someone's shouting, Harry? No, not Harry, sounds like Harry. I can sense terrible anger, terrible violence, someone is screaming 'Truck! Truck!'

There's an explosion, someone's shouting out 'Harry' again; this Harry seems very important."

Alex watched him, transfixed, as sweat poured from his sheet-white face.

"Now it's clearing a little, there's this young person again, a young man, he's trying to tell me his name. It's not clear, not clear at all, David could it be? No, Adrian? Maybe Adrian." He shook suddenly, violently, as if an electric current had been passed through him. "Something's not right, not right at all; there's a terrible conflict going on, something very disturbed; there's a lot of anger, so much anger. Fabian, could it be Fabian?" He continued without opening his eyes. "Yes, he's telling me something, he's clear now, incredibly clear."

Alex felt the cat breathing softly under her hand. She looked at the roses, at the medium, felt herself trembling strangely, almost as if she wasn't actually sitting in the chair but was suspended a few inches above it.

The medium suddenly shouted out at the top of his voice, and startled her. *"My God he's clear!"* His hands were shaking, as if the watch were a mad wild thing. "There's someone else now, trying to come through; a girl, she's trying to tell me something, but it doesn't make much sense, she's saying her name's Harry. There's so much disturbance, Fabian's making this disturbance; it's a game, he's larking around, that's the trouble, it's too soon, he's too frisky, it's all a game at the moment. Now, she's coming through again, more clearly now, no, there's Fabian again, it's almost as if he's trying to—yes—trying to stop —jealousy, of course, oh it's become all so unclear again." Alex saw Ford relax, lean back, turn to her. "It's as bad as the telephone system up there sometimes."

She stared, puzzled for a moment by the remark, then realized he had cracked a joke.

"Extraordinary, quite extraordinary; I've never known anything like this, never." He leaned toward her. "This is something really quite incredible."

Alex stroked the nape of the cat's neck mechanically and listened to it purring. "In what way?"

"Extraordinary; did it make sense?"

"I'm very confused."

"I'm very confused too." Ford smiled.

"What do you mean?"

"Have you had much experience in this field, Mrs.—er—I'm sorry—I can't remember your name."

"High—Johnson."

"Ah, yes."

"What do you mean, experience?"

"In the spiritual world?"

"No."

"Your son came through very clearly; I am correct, yes? It was your son you wanted to contact? His name is Fabian, or Adrian?"

He knew who she really was; somehow he had found out.

"You've done your research well," she said coldly. "You've been very thorough; but you've made just one mistake."

He raised a single eyebrow.

"My son wasn't killed by a truck, but by another car."

"Mrs. Johnson, I wasn't there; I can only go by what I'm told."

"Or by what you've read."

He pulled out his handkerchief and blew his nose. "Read?"

"The crash was reported in the newspapers, Mr. Ford," she said. "I don't know how many papers, but it was in the *Daily Mail*. They reported that it was a truck. I noticed, as I came in, the *Daily Mail* on your desk." She waited for the explosion of anger, but none came. Instead, he looked hurt, puzzled, and shook his head thoughtfully.

"I'm sorry," he said quietly. "You obviously have a poor opinion of the integrity of mediums."

The sincerity of his voice made her hesitate, and she felt herself beginning to blush. She looked at his neatly groomed hair, his immaculate white shirt and snappy gray tie and the matching handkerchief puffed out of the breast pocket of his suit. She looked at his tiny pink hands with their manicured nails and the huge vulgar ring, and then back at his face. Smooth. He could have been an insurance salesman.

"I don't do research, Mrs. Johnson. I don't read obituary notices, I don't scan the papers for reports on road accidents and try to link them up with my clients; I don't delve back into the old school records of my clients, trying to dig up facts they've long forgotten that I can hit them with." He smiled. "In any event, with the amount of people who come here giving me fictitious names, how could I get anywhere with any consistency?"

Alex looked away guiltily from his searching eyes, and heard his gentle voice continue.

"Nor do I dole out only good news to the bereaved; I relate what I hear. That's my gift, that's all I can do." He raised his eyebrows apologetically. "We have a misconception about the departed. We think that because they have moved on, they have gained integrity." He shook his head. "It takes more than one life and passing to gain integrity—and integrity is just one of many things we have to learn in our journeys through this life and the next. Spirits can tell lies, frequently they do; they can get things wrong too. You see, things don't get improved suddenly by passing into the next plane. If you have a lousy memory in this life, it isn't going to alter suddenly in the next."

She saw his meek, apologetic smile and did not want to hurt him. "My son had a very good memory."

"Accidents happen very fast. They can be very confusing; the whole business of going over is very confusing, that's why I don't like to try to communicate with the very recently departed, not really before at least three months; this was only in the last few weeks, wasn't it?"

She nodded.

"Normally, I am not aware of much of what I am saying during a sitting, and at the end I can scarcely remember it at all; this is quite different; never in all my life have I known anything so vivid. Please don't be cynical, we should continue."

"You got something else wrong too," she said.

He smiled. "What was that?"

"You were talking about someone called Harry—you said that something was odd, that it seemed to be a girl called Harry."

"Yes?"

"Could she have been called Carrie?"

"Carrie?"

Alex nodded.

"Sometimes," he said, "with all the interference—things aren't distinct. Carrie? Yes, Carrie." He closed his eyes for a moment and then opened them again. "Yes, it could have been."

"Tell me, at these sessions, do you talk to the living or the departed?"

He stared at her, unruffled. "I'm what is called a medium, Mrs. Johnson; I'm a link between the earth plane and the departed."

"Then I don't understand how you could have spoken to Carrie."

"Why not?"

"Because she's not dead. She's very much alive, and well, in America."

She saw doubt flit across his face, like the shadow of a bird, saw a strange look appear in his eyes, as if something had profoundly disturbed him. He shook his head. "She was trying to come through, Mrs. Johnson, that's all I can tell you. You're sure that she's still on this plane? That she hasn't been in an accident?"

"Isn't it possible you might have picked her up telepathically?"

"That's how a lot of people try to explain mediums, Mrs. Johnson. That we pick up the information telepathically from our client's brain. You couldn't use that old chestnut today, could you? Because I've stated two things that aren't in your brain: that your son was in collision with a truck; and that Carrie, whoever she is, has passed across to the other side."

She stared at him, trying to think clearly.

"I'm sorry that you're skeptical, Mrs. Johnson. I don't know how I can change that, but I've got to, somehow."

"What do you mean?"

He sat in silence for a long time. Alex listened to the hiss of the gas, the purring of the cat; outside she heard the rattle of a taxi and the slam of its door, and wondered if it was his next client arriving.

Suddenly he leaned toward her, until his face was close to hers, so close she could feel the warmth of his breath.

"Mrs. Johnson," he said. "Fabian wants to come back."

16

She felt confused and disillusioned as she drove away. Main had been right in his advice; it was exactly how he had told her she would feel. The curate had been right too. Nothing could be gained by summoning up the departed, he had said, nothing but, what was it—disappointment and evil? Strong words from the fire-and-brimstone brigade. Pastoral care, he had recommended; that had a nice gentle ring to it.

She thought about the evil; mischief, perhaps, but not evil. Games, perhaps; tricks. She thought about his room, how it had seemed so menacing without the presence of Ford; did evil take place there? Did he hold strange séances where they drew the curtains, turned up the wick and sat in circles with the cats sitting, watching? She shuddered. There seemed to be so much about life, so much that went on in the world that she could never know, that most human beings could never know: secret societies, strange practices, communions with gods, devils, departed ones. Did any of them know the secret? The truth? Was Morgan Ford, in his smooth suit and his grand drawing room, one of the few people on earth privy to the meaning of life? Had he alone been entrusted with the secret? And if so, what had he done with it? What was he doing with it? Sitting in his strange room telling lies to grieving women?

She heard angry hooting behind her and looked up;

the light was green. She glanced in the mirror, saw the
nose of a taxi, raised a hand and drove into Hyde Park.
She pulled over to the left, driving slowly, and put her
indicator on. Where was she going? It was eleven o'clock
on Monday morning and she had important work to do in
the office, but she couldn't face it, not yet; it seemed unimportant compared to her disappointment. What had she
been expecting, she wondered, and shrugged privately to
herself.

It had really seemed, she thought sadly, that Fabian
had been trying to tell her something; that there had been a
meaning to all the strange goings-on, to the weird tricks
her mind had been playing. She had been convinced, she
knew, that Fabian had been telling her to go to a medium.
She smiled, and felt her eyes watering. She had hoped, she
supposed, that she was going to discover some point to his
death, that he would explain it to her; but now all that had
been shattered; it had been a delusion, another of life's
dirty tricks.

Yes, Main was right. He and his kind were closer to
the truth, sitting there in their laboratories with their pi-
pettes and their glass tubes and their Bunsen burners, and
their computers, searching all the time for their equations,
searching for that one big ultimate equation.

Was it there, a palimpsest, lying quietly somewhere
under the DNA code, waiting for that one scientist more
patient, or just luckier than the rest, who would forever
render the entire paraphernalia of religion redundant?

She parked and walked along beside the Serpentine,
feeling the enormity of the world all around her. She
looked at the London skyline beyond the trees, the buildings bunched together, rubbing shoulders like passengers
in a crowded tube. An old man sat staring out across the
water, raising his arms up and down as if making a strange
gesture to the futility of it all. She shivered, wrapped her
arms around herself, afraid suddenly of being old, old and
staring at the water and making futile gestures.

The roses in the room; the rose on the car windscreen. What were the odds of that happening? The odds of there being the same number of roses in the bowl? The same color?

What were the odds for Morgan Ford? Had he known who she really was? How? Was linking her with the car crash he'd read about in the papers a good guess, or had she given him some clue when they'd begun to talk? Had he picked it up telepathically? That was the only other rational explanation—but then how had he made the mistake about the truck? And the mistake about Carrie?

Too many things were contradicting each other. Where was the truth? Was there a personal palimpsest put there by Fabian? Was she looking at the face value of everything, and not beneath? She shook her head, stared at the boathouse, watched a horse canter by on Rotten Row, a smart young girl in one of those new-style crash helmets; change, she thought, change, progress. Everything seemed to be converging to a vanishing point somewhere in the distance. There was a growing sameness about everything; even horse riders now all looked like mounted police. God, she had never been any good at puzzles, riddles; was there a vanishing point for this riddle now? Would the puzzle stay unresolved forever, parallel lines that would never change, or was there a junction, somewhere in the distance out there, where the answer lay?

Otto came into her mind, quietly, unobtrusively at first, as if he had slipped in through an open door and was waiting quietly in the shadows for her to notice him. She watched a young girl with her nanny throwing crumbs to the ducks, and felt Otto lurking, smirking. Why? What was he doing, she thought, irritated. She tried to ignore him, to put him out of her mind, but that only made him clearer still. She could see his room, the empty champagne bottles, the hum of his coffee grinder, the careless, arrogant stirring of the cups, and the contempt in his eyes, with their secrets about her son, and the look which said, "I could have you anytime I wanted, but I wouldn't bother."

What did he know?

She found herself walking back to the car, working out in her mind the best route to the motorway, wondering if he would be there, or would she have to wait out in the corridor? It was no good resisting, there was nothing she could do to stop herself. She could think of nothing, nothing except the dark oak door of his room.

She arrived in Cambridge shortly before two, parked outside Magdalene and ran through the archway. She hurried up the steps and down the corridor which now seemed familiar, then stopped outside his door, breathless, and hesitated, listening, for floorboards creaking, for a clink of a cup, for music, voices, a rustle of paper. There was nothing. She knocked, timidly, knowing it was futile, heard the dull echo of the knock, sensed the flat emptiness of the room beyond.

The door opened, and she jumped back. Otto stood there, one hand in the pocket of his heavy cardigan, and nodded at her, the knowing smirk on his lacerated face, the leer in his eyes. "You're earlier than I expected."

She frowned, thrown by the remark, stared back into his eyes, trying to understand what he meant, then looked away, uncomfortably, and gazed for a moment at the flaking lintel above the door. "I'm sorry, I don't understand— I didn't leave any message."

He turned and walked inside. "I've put coffee on. Would you like some?"

She saw the percolator bubbling, the two cups laid out beside it.

"Thank you."

"I knew you were coming," he said matter-of-factly.

"How?"

He shrugged. "I know a lot of things."

"What sort of things?"

He gave a short contemptuous laugh, and for an instant she would have loved to hit him.

"You didn't know enough to save my son from being killed," she said suddenly, vitriolically, unable to prevent the words from coming out.

He knelt down beside the percolator and lifted it up. "Black, no sugar."

"Thank you."

She waited for his retort, but none came; he stayed kneeling by the coffee pot, and she watched him, feeling strangely sickened.

When he finally turned around, his eyes were livid.

"I'm sorry, Otto," she said, nervous suddenly. "That wasn't very nice of me." She felt the rage burning silently inside him; he seemed much older than a student suddenly, older than she. "Sometimes I say things," she said, "things I don't mean."

He sat down on the floor and leaned against the wall, his anger subsiding, the youth returning.

She smiled tentatively. "How did you know I was coming?"

He sounded distant, as though he were dictating into a microphone. "I get feelings about things sometimes, something that's going to happen, sometimes big things, sometimes little things, sometimes nothing."

"And what happens?"

He took a sip of his coffee. "They come true." He stared, probing. "But I can't do anything about them; it's all useless, this information."

"Why?" she said uncomfortably.

"It's as though it has already happened; so I can do nothing."

"You got the coffee ready for me."

He shrugged. "Got the coffee ready, sure; but that's really no big deal."

"Did you know about the accident? That it was going to happen?"

"No. Nothing." He paused. "Even if I had—" He shrugged.

"Do you know why I've come?"

He said nothing.

She looked into his eyes, tried to read them. She tried to ignore the faint mocking smile that was in them, and looked beyond; but there was nothing. It was like staring through panes of glass at a dark night.

"Otto, I want you to try to remember something; it's not going to be very nice for you, but it's really very important to me; will you help me?"

"If I can."

"It was a car you hit, wasn't it?"

"Yes, for sure."

"What happened just before?"

"I don't remember; one moment I was in the car, the next I was outside."

"Please try."

"I had a hangover; the party was a good party; I don't know about Fabian." He smirked.

"Why are you smiling?"

"He scored with the host's daughter; spent the night with her." He shook his head. "Incredible, you know, he was always scoring with girls."

"But never keeping them?"

He looked at her, then looked away. "It wasn't important."

"Not to you; what about to him?"

Otto shrugged. "Your son was a bastard to women, Mrs. Hightower; better to leave it at that."

"What do you mean?"

He shook his head.

"Does it really matter, now that he's—" She paused. "Can't you tell me?"

He smiled strangely. "It's not important, really it's not important." He stirred his coffee. "We drove, we were just talking; I was in the front passenger seat, Charles and

Henry were in the back; for some reason I hadn't put my seat belt on, the catch in the Volkswagen is awkward, you know. It was dawn, we had our lights on; Fabian was talking to Charles, looking around; suddenly I saw these lights in front of us, coming straight at us, high up; I thought it was a truck."

"What?" Alex heard herself shout the word out involuntarily; she felt herself shaking, trembling in disbelief, confusion; she felt giddy, saw the floor slope suddenly away from her, as if she were in a boat hit by wash, and had to hold on to both arms to prevent herself falling sideways from the chair. "A truck?"

"It was an old Citroën apparently, big upright; we were sitting in the Volkswagen, low down. It looked like a truck. Fabian must have thought so too. He shouted out 'Truck!' After that, I was lying on grass, on mud—I don't really remember."

The chair felt like a seesaw; it swayed from side to side as if it had a life of its own; she fought it, leaned against it, and watched his eyes all the time, those eyes that were like the night.

"I'm afraid it does not tell you much."

"Sometimes," she said distantly, vaguely conscious of the curious flutter in her stomach, "one doesn't need to be told much."

17

The house looked fresh and clean. Mimsa had left one of her usual indecipherable notes: "Dere Misy Higtow, dun al jobbs. Don got no more clenning for winnow stuff. Got probblims in dounstair toilee, paper no stick wall. See yoo tummorro."

She frowned, and made a note on the shopping pad. She hesitated outside the downstairs lavatory, then went up to Fabian's room. Mimsa had left everything as it was, as she had told her. She picked up his diary, sat down on the bed and took out the postcard she had taken from Carrie's mother, and the letter Carrie had written to Fabian, which she opened out and pressed flat. Then she laid the postcard beside it and began to compare the handwriting, going through each letter of the alphabet in turn.

She began to feel chilly as she worked, and sensed the temperature dropping. She stood up and left the room without looking up at the portrait, went downstairs into the drawing room and sat beside the phone. She picked up the receiver, hesitated and dropped it back on the rest. She stared again at the letter and the postcard, then picked up the receiver again and dialed Philip Main.

"I'm sorry," she said, "if I was a bit abrupt last night."

"No, gosh, quite understand—I behaved—"

"No, you didn't, you were nice and kind."

"Did you go to—today?"

"Yes."

"I see." He sounded disapproving.

"That's why I'm calling you. I want to talk to you about it. I wondered if you were doing anything this evening."

"Oh, nothing important; only about to prove conclusively the origins of man."

"I'm sorry."

"It's waited two billion years, I don't suppose one more night's really here nor there."

"Want to try another of my frozen dinners?"

There was a silence. He coughed and sounded uncomfortable. "I—er—I'd rather take you out somewhere. Nothing to do with the cooking, you understand. Think it's good for you to get out."

"Want me to meet you somewhere?"

"No, gosh, no; I'll pick you up—I'll wait outside and hoot."

"You are allowed in," she said, smiling.

"It's—er—jolly difficult to park outside sometimes."

He sounded evasive, and it puzzled her; she shrugged. "Fine. What time?"

"About an hour?"

"I'll be ready." She replaced the receiver, then slipped the postcard and letter underneath the phone, and carefully placed it on top to weigh them down.

The restaurant was small and simple, with an empty Monday evening air about it. Candles burned optimistically on each of the bare wooden tables and the staff hovered earnestly, as if to assure them that they hadn't made a mistake in coming here, that they were not normally empty like this.

"If you stand at the bottom of a mine shaft in the middle of the day and look up at the sky, you can see

Venus. It's up there, all the time. In the fifteenth century sailors used to navigate by it."

"Did they have mine shafts on their ships?"

Main smiled wistfully. "Didn't need to, girl." He tapped his eyes. "They could see it, just by looking."

"So why can't we?"

"Evolution; we've moved on; our senses are getting dulled; we have computers to navigate for us now."

"So we can't see Venus because of pollution in the sky?"

"No, good Lord, no; we can't see it because we don't know how to see it anymore; perhaps primitive man in the jungle in other countries can still see it, but if we had the sensitivity to see it, we'd be blinded by the dazzle of electric lights."

"So evolution isn't always too smart."

He swirled his wineglass and stared down at the table. "It gets the job done," he said defensively.

"With every generation our senses get dulled?"

"Old senses get dulled; new senses develop." He paused. "There's a certain irrational streak."

"What do you think is irrational?"

"Man's ability to run fast; getting faster every generation. No one had run a four-minute mile until 1954; now people do it in three minutes fifty. And yet, we don't even need to run at all these days." He shrugged.

"I thought that was because the athletes take drugs?"

"In part; only in part; evolution has something to do with it."

"So our legs should be getting shorter?"

"And our arms; don't need them. All we're going to need is fingers to push buttons."

"So, in thirty-two million years' time we'll just be bodies with fingers and feet, all looking like potato men?"

He scrabbled in his pocket and pulled out his cigarettes. "So, you went to your medium."

She nodded, and took the cigarette he offered. "Mr.

Ford has given me rather a lot to think about. He claimed to have got through to Fabian; he was describing the accident." She lit the cigarette from the candle, looked around to see if any waiter was listening and leaned across the table. "He said that someone in the car was shouting out that a truck was coming straight at them."

"Could have picked that up from the papers—or telepathically from you."

She shook her head. "He was killed by a car, not by a truck; there was no truck."

Main looked puzzled. "It said in the paper—"

"That's the point," she interrupted. "That's the whole point! It said in the papers that it was a truck, so I was convinced he had read the papers, and put two and two together. I went to Cambridge this afternoon and had a chat with Otto, the boy who survived. I asked him to tell me what happened just before the accident. He said that they'd seen what they thought was a truck coming, and that Fabian had shouted out that there was a truck!" She drank some wine and drew heavily on her cigarette, then stared hard back at him.

He shrugged. "Could be telepathy: you picked the message up from Fabian just before the accident, in your subconscious, but it did not register, then Ford picked it up from you." He shrugged again. "That's rather a complex way of looking at things. Or—"

"Or Ford is genuine?"

"I don't know about that. Remarkable."

A waiter appeared. "Was it the pigeon for you, madam?"

"No, me."

Alex waited in silence until the food had been served, then leaned forward again. "Do you know where I could find a handwriting expert?"

"Handwriting?"

"Yes. I don't know what they're called—the sort of

person the police would use to see if something was forged."

"There's a chap I've used from time to time in my research; thought I'd have a go at disproving the Dead Sea Scrolls." He smiled wryly.

"To annoy your father?"

He looked pensive. "No, a long time after—" He paused and stared sternly at his pigeon, as if it had committed a misdemeanor.

"Looks very nice," she said.

"Dead rat," he said.

"What?"

"Dead rat," he repeated.

"Dead rat?"

"Yes. Had a name like Dead Rat. Derat, Durat, Dendret. Dendret he was called."

"Is there anything that you don't know?" She smiled.

"I don't know why I ordered pigeon; I just remembered I can't stand the stuff."

"I'll swap with you."

"No, no, good Lord, no. A chap's got to accept the consequences of his actions." He gave her a strange look, which for an instant disturbed her.

"You don't have to be a martyr anymore these days, we've evolved past that."

"Touché," he said, prodding the pigeon dubiously with his fork.

She felt comfortable with all the junk in the Volvo around her, her feet nestling in an undergrowth of papers, parking tickets, cassettes. The car had a homey, lived-in feeling, like an old boat. "Do you ever clean your car out?"

"No, gosh, no. Usually change it when the ashtray gets full."

She smiled, and stared at the ashtray, jammed open, crammed with dried-out butts. "What do you call full?"

The wipers smeared the rainwater across the screen,

splaying out the lights of London in front of her like a kaleidoscope.

"Does it bother you, going back to the house on your own?"

She shrugged. "No. I've got used to it; Fabian only came down in the holidays."

"Would you ever like to have any more children?"

She shook her head. "I'm too old, too set in my ways."

"How old are you?"

"Ancient." She smiled. "Sometimes I feel very ancient."

She watched the whites, oranges, reds, exploding and sliding away in front of her eyes, heard the roar of the engine, felt the force of braking, heard the sluicing of the tires cease suddenly. The wipers clacked in front of her, clack, clack, clack, almost in tune with the rattle of a taxi engine and the beat of the music from a disco nearby; clack, clack, two tiny instruments in the orchestra of the London night.

"I can't have any more children," she said. "We had—" She paused; the knowledge was still painful, perhaps now more so than it ever used to be; she ran her tongue along her lower lip and watched the show.

He double-parked outside her house and kept the engine running. "Thanks for the meal," she said. "Would you like to come in?"

She noticed a strange expression flicker across his face for an instant, almost of fear, she thought.

"I'd better get back to work."

"Tonight?"

"A chap can't keep the world waiting forever."

"Nor his agent."

"No. Gosh, no."

"Look—would you mind just coming in for a second, so I can show you the postcard, see what you think?"

Again she saw that same flicker across his face and

this time there was no doubting the fear that was there. She stared at him, feeling uncomfortable herself now, wondering what was disturbing him, what had been able to break through the seemingly impenetrable defenses that he carried around with him, like a shell.

He stared through the windscreen for a moment, saying nothing, then pushed the gear lever into reverse with a strange, resigned motion, as if conceding defeat, and turned to look over his shoulder.

He seemed to be having difficulty climbing the steps, as if pushing against some unseen force. She watched him hesitantly; it was as if he were wading through deep water.

He stopped as they reached the front door, and swayed, putting his hand on to the door frame for support. His face went sheet white, and he began to sweat. He closed his eyes tightly, and she looked at him, afraid.

"Philip? What's the matter?"

He looked up, rivers of sweat torrenting down his face. "Fine," he said. "Fine. I'm fine. It's going; I'll be all right."

"What, Philip?"

"It's all right." He looked at her nervously. "It's all right. Fine." He smiled.

The smell hit them as they walked in through the front door. A vile, hideous stench. Alex gagged, turned around, and gulped in lungfuls of air from the street. Main put his hand over his nose, and looked around silently.

"What is it?" She turned on the hall light; everything looked normal. "It's like a dog—"

He shook his head. "No, not a dog."

She went into the kitchen with her handkerchief over her nose. "Not in here," she said, lifting it away. "Hardly smells at all in here."

Main came down the stairs. "No smell upstairs either."

She went back into the hallway, where the stench was far worse, then outside and stood on the doorstep and sniffed the wet night air. "It's inside, Philip," she said. "Maybe it's a dead mouse or something?" She looked at him, and saw him staring around wide-eyed, his face sheet white. "Philip? Why don't you sit down? I'll open the windows." She went into the drawing room and turned on the light; she felt her eyes pulled sharply down to the floor.

Lying there, as if they had been flung, were the postcard and the letter from Carrie.

The wall sloped sharply away from her. For an instant she had to bend her legs under the pressure, and then there was nothing beneath her at all, and she found herself running across the floor and crashing into the wall. She put her arms up for support and the wall seemed to push her away; she tottered back a few steps and fell over.

"Alex? Are you all right?"

She stared up giddily and saw Main staring down; it was almost as if she were watching everything from a distance, that she could see herself lying on the floor, looking up at Main. She heard a voice, and it took a moment to recognize it as her own. "I—I must have tripped."

She saw a hand floating in the air; it gripped hers, pulled her up; she watched herself put her arms around Main, then suddenly, quite vividly, felt the crumpled softness of his jacket and the warmth of his chest. She hugged hard and felt his strong back muscles. "On the floor," she said. "They were under the telephone when I went out, weighed down; someone's moved them."

She felt his firm hands on her back, trembling; or was it she who was trembling, she wondered.

"Calm down, girl, calm down."

She could tell from his tone that he was struggling to suppress the anxiety in his voice. What's the matter with you, she wanted to say. What the hell's the matter with you? She stared at him. "Just another of those tricks of my mind?"

He looked down at his battered brown brogues, and coughed. His voice went into a quiet whisper, as if he was talking to himself. "No, good Lord, no, it's not a trick." He looked up at the ceiling and around the walls, pensively, still ruffled by anxiety. He sniffed again. "Drains, most likely."

"I'm sorry," she said, bending down and picking up the card and letter. "Do you want some coffee?"

"Could I have a drop of whiskey?"

"Help yourself; I'll put some coffee on." She went out of the room.

Main walked to the cabinet and poured himself a large whiskey. Then he picked up the card and letter and walked over to an armchair. He sniffed again and winced, looking up at the ceiling, then sat down slowly. He held the whiskey under his nose and sniffed it gratefully, then closed his eyes tight.

"Our Father," he said, "which art in Heaven, hallowed be Thy Name. Thy Kingdom come—"

"Philip? Are you asleep?"

He opened his eyes with a start, and felt his cheeks reddening. "Hmmm," he replied, fumbling for his cigarettes.

"What do you think?"

"Think?"

"About the letter?"

He looked down at the letter and read it carefully. He shrugged. "Seems pretty definite. What does she mean, 'weird'?"

"Not the content," she said. "The handwriting. Look at the postcard."

"It's a little different," he said. "Might have been written balanced on her knees, or when she was stoned; looks basically the same."

"But your friend Dead Rat would be able to tell?"

"Dendret?"

Alex saw his head suddenly whiplash around, as if trying to catch sight of something behind his shoulder, staring wildly. "Are you OK?"

"What?"

She sat down on the arm of the chair and shivered. "I don't think I can keep the windows open forever; they don't seem to be making much difference."

"Much difference?"

She put her hand on his forehead. It was damp and cold. "Do you want to lie down?"

He stared blankly ahead, across the top of his whiskey, and said nothing. Alex went out to pour her coffee; when she came back in, he was still sitting there. The smell in the room was venomous.

She sat down beside him again, on the arm of his chair, and saw the sweat again on his face. "We'd be better in the kitchen—it's fine in there." She looked at him, unsure that he had heard, and put her hand on his forehead again; she wondered for a terrible moment if he had had a stroke.

"I don't belong here," he said suddenly. "I'm not wanted here."

"Do you want me to call a doctor?" she said, becoming alarmed at his incoherence. She waved her fingers in front of his eyes, looking for a flicker of movement, but there was none. "Philip, do you want me to call a doctor?" She waited. "Can you hear me?"

"Hello, Mother."

The words were gentle, crystal clear, as if Fabian were standing right beside her.

She whirled around, stared out at the hallway, then at the open windows. She ran over to them and looked out. The street was empty, nothing out there except the dark and the parked cars and the rain.

She had not imagined it.

She stared at Main, who was now trembling violently.

"Mother."

The words had come from Main.

She watched him shaking, breathing heavily, and sensed the room getting colder. She saw the sweat running down his face, and watched him clenching his knuckles, so tight she thought his hands would break.

She stayed watching him.

Mother.

The word rang around inside her.

Suddenly Main sprang to his feet, pushed his arms away from his body and shouted in his own voice, "No, I say, no!" He stared around the room as if lost, confused, breathing deeply, then stared at Alex with eyes filled with terror, eyes that scarcely recognized her. "I—must—go," he said slowly, hesitating after each word. "I—must—go—now. I should not have come."

"What's happening, Philip, please tell me."

He stared fearfully around the room with the same expression on his face that she had seen on Iris Tremayne's, then he walked determinedly out into the hallway.

"Stay and talk to me."

"Come with me."

She shook her head.

"I'll wait for you in the car."

"Dendret," she said. "Where do I find Dendret?"

He opened the front door and went outside, a complete stranger suddenly.

"Philip!" She heard her own voice, shrill, afraid, like the call of a lost chick. She turned and looked around the hall. She grabbed her bag, her coat and her keys, closed the door and ran down to the pavement.

Main was sitting in the Volvo in a thick cloud of cigarette smoke; as she slammed the door, he started the engine and drove off.

"Philip, I want to stay here."

He ignored her and turned left onto the King's Road. She looked at his face, which was expressionless. He was driving fast and she was being thrown around in her seat. The seat belt warning light was flashing and clicking like a furious insect and she tried to ignore it. He said nothing until they were inside his flat.

He gave Alex a brandy and sat down with his whiskey, stared at the floor then let out a low whistle. Alex sniffed the brandy and drank some; she felt it burning deep inside her stomach, clutched the huge balloon tightly with both hands and drank again gratefully.

"What happened?"

He whistled again and pulled out his cigarettes.

"Was that Fabian speaking, or you?"

He offered her the pack, still without saying anything, and she shook her head, pulling one of her own out.

"You don't want to admit it, do you?" She watched his face redden as the torment built up inside him, and wished for a moment that she, too, had said nothing. "I'm sorry."

She heard the click of his lighter and watched him stare at the tiny flame that was dancing in the draft; he stared at it intensely as if it were a genie he had summoned up to help him.

"Very unusual," he said suddenly.

Alex noticed for the first time how tired he was looking; his skin seemed to be hanging limply from his face, like a flannel on a washing line, everything wrung out of it.

"What do you mean?"

He shrugged and said nothing.

"Do you remember, in your last book, something you wrote?"

He drew hard on his cigarette and stared out into space. Alex shuddered; for an instant as the smoke drifted around him, he reminded her of a picture she had once seen of sallow ghouls in an opium den.

"You said that we are all prisoners of our genes."

There was no flicker of response.

"You said that we cannot fight the programs we are born with, and we cannot change them; the only liberty we have is to disagree with them."

Slowly he nodded his head.

"That they were chosen for us at the moment of conception, random pickings from the selection of genes in the father's sperm and the mother's egg. In that split second is determined everything that is to be inherited or left out from each parent. Right?"

He turned and looked vaguely in her direction.

"You've inherited your father's powers, and you don't want to admit it."

He looked away from her again and into space.

"Please explain it to me, Philip; please explain what happened."

"Just a theory, that's all," he said without looking at her. "Just a theory, girl. There's no proof."

"Not in genetic engineering?"

"That's a different sphere."

"But I'm right, aren't I?"

He stared down at the floor. "Maybe," he said quietly. "But it is considered unlikely. The color of your hair is transmitted in genes, the shape of your nose. Pyschic power is something different—" He shrugged. "It's meant to be a gift."

"Intelligence isn't passed on in genes?"

"Yes, of course it is."

"I always thought intelligence was considered a gift."

"Not at all."

"What about behavior? Is that passed on in genes?"

"To an extent."

"So why not psychic powers?"

He stared at her for a moment, then looked away.

"Why didn't you want to come into the house? What happened?"

"It's all hokum, girl; I don't know where these spirits, voices, manifestations, whatever come from. We can only see a very narrow band of light waves, hear a narrow band of sound waves. Perhaps when we die we leave behind us imprints in other waves outside these, and some people are able to tune into them and pick them up. It doesn't mean they are still alive somewhere else, doesn't mean that at all."

"What does it mean?"

"That they've left an imprint, like a photograph. The trick is being able to see it." He tapped his head. "We probably all have the power, but most of us don't know how to use it; some do and keep quiet all their lives; some become mediums; it's a good con." He looked at her, color beginning to return to his face. "I didn't want to con you."

"Con me?"

He thought carefully before speaking. "I had a feeling I might pick Fabian up; what good would it do you? Raking it all up, giving you some false hope that he's out there somewhere."

She stared at him, leaned forward and crushed out her cigarette, startled at how fast she had smoked it. "You're lying, Philip," she said.

"I'm not lying, girl. I'm just trying to put it into plain English."

"If that's all it was, you wouldn't have been so frightened. You were terrified about something. About what?"

He shook his head. "You're imagining it; that's what happens when people dabble in this."

"Philip." She looked at him. "Please look at me. You're my friend. Do you seriously expect me to believe that if there is such a thing as an imprint that can be left behind, that after twenty-one years, all that is left of Fabian are two words? 'Hello, Mother'? Stop being evasive and tell me the truth."

He picked up his whiskey glass and studied it; he swirled the whiskey around, sniffed it testily, then studied the glass again carefully, as if searching for a hidden hallmark. He spoke without looking at her. "It's possible there's a presence in your house; a malevolent one."

Something wet and slimy trickled down her spine. She shivered, and drank some more brandy; it tasted like dry ice. She pulled the glass away sharply, her mouth burning, stared around the room, closed her eyes and tried to clear her mind. "Surely, if there's a presence, it's Fabian?"

"Those who—believe in this are of the opinion that evil can be a very mischievous thing: that it can prey on the victims of grief, take advantage of their weakness, and their blindness to the truth."

"What are you saying?"

"Rogue spirits, girl. One of them might be conning you now; trying to pretend he's your son."

She stared at him for a long time in silence, trembling, despair soaking through her; she stared at him as if he were an outcrop of land to which she was moored; the last piece of land on earth.

"Why?" she said finally, helplessly.

"Spirits sometimes try to come back."

"Do they succeed?"

"There is evidence that they can possess people, and influence them. For good and—for bad." He smiled wryly.

Alex shook her head. "You amaze me; you're so cynical, and yet—I don't know—you know so much more, don't you; you're like a stage sometimes, with a hundred backdrops."

He smiled. "No, good Lord, no." He shook his head. "Don't overestimate me, girl."

"Why do they try to come back?"

He twisted his glass around in his hand, then looked at Alex. He looked away, around the room, then back at his glass, twisting it again. Finally he looked up at her, his face heavy with doubt. The words came out slowly, as if dragged against some tremendous inner reluctance. "Because they have unfinished business."

18

Arthur Dendret had a sharp pointed beard and a sharp pointed head; he moved around his office in short clockwork-like stages, as if he had been preprogrammed.

Every inch of the available floor and shelving space of the cramped office was covered with untidy bundles of documents, and equally untidy stacks of reference books, and the walls were hung with cold, lifeless prints of Regency Terraces, which revealed nothing about him. In contrast to his own size, his desk was vast and almost completely empty. The only relief on the acreage of flat green leather was a neat blotter, a magnifying glass and a framed photograph of a stern woman.

"Please, sit down." He pulled off his gold half-rimmed glasses, peered accusingly at them and then replaced them. He laid both hands on the blotter, squinted at Alex and gave a wide, almost imbecilic grin.

She stared at his brightly checked suit, and his drab woolen tie, the color of slime. "Philip Main gave me your name."

"Ah, yes." His face screwed up like a sponge; he blinked furiously, and raised an arm in the air as if hailing a taxi. "Dead Sea Scrolls. Very interesting. Thought he might have been on to something for a time, but of course it ended up at a blind alley; always does with the Scrolls, don't you think?"

Alex smiled politely. "I'm afraid I wouldn't know."

"No, well, he's a determined chap. Still—" He leaned back and looked expectantly at her.

Alex opened her handbag and laid the postcard and the letter on the wilderness of his desktop. He stared at them for a moment, opened his drawer and pulled out a pair of tweezers. In turn he picked each one up and placed it down in front of him. "Not Dead Sea Scrolls, these," he said, "not Dead Sea Scrolls at all." He grinned, then chuckled, his shoulders moving up and down several times as if pulled by strings. He turned the postcard over with the tweezers. "Ah, Boston, Cambridge, MIT, know this view well. Had a flat tire on this bridge once; not a good place to have a flat; not a good country to have a flat in, America; not in a Peugeot anyway."

Alex stared at him curiously.

He pointed his index finger upward. "They have these spikes they put through the wheel, to get the tire off; you can't do it on a Peugeot." He turned the postcard back over. "What can I do for you?"

"I want to know if the person who wrote the letter is the same person who wrote the postcard."

Dendret picked up the magnifying glass and studied several lines of the letter carefully, then leaned over slightly and studied the postcard. As he read, his lips pursed and the action elongated his nose. He reminded Alex of a rather aggressive rodent.

Quite decisively, he put down the glass and leaned back in his chair; he looked up at the ceiling, closed his eyes for a second then opened them again and stared directly at Alex. "No, not at all. The writing on the postcard's a very poor imitation of the writing on the letter; there are eight points of difference clearly visible, just through the glass. The *t* bars for instance." He shook his head. "No, quite different. The spacing; pressure, slant, the loops—look at the loops! There really is no comparison to be had."

He looked irritated, thought Alex, as if he had been expecting a glass of fine claret and only been given house wine. He picked the tweezers up and placed the items in front of her, without attempting to hide his disdain.

"I—er—I'm sorry," she said. "As a layman, I—"

"No, of course, you wouldn't." His tone had become almost belligerent. He took a deep breath and stared for a moment at the photograph of the stern woman; it seemed to calm him down very slightly. He no longer stared at Alex, but through her. "Frankly, I would have thought a child of six could have told those weren't the same."

"Unfortunately," said Alex, equally acidly, "I don't have a child of six."

Dendret produced an invoice pad from his drawer, and pulled out a gold pen from his pocket. He wrote on the pad, then turned it upside down on to his clean blotter. "That will be thirty pounds."

Alex looked down at the imprint of the writing on the blotter, then at the crisp white piece of paper that he put down in front of her, using his fingers this time, not the tweezers.

She paid him in cash, and he slipped the notes possessively into his wallet, like a rat storing away food, she thought.

"Do give my regards to Mr. Main."

She sat in her car and stared at the postcard with a heavy heart. She read it for the hundredth time: "Hi Mum, This is a really friendly place, lots of things happening, met some great people. Will write again soon. Love C."

She looked at the postmark. The word "Boston" was just discernible. She tried to concentrate; whom did she know in Boston? Or had been to Boston? Or anywhere in the States? Who had posted it? And the others? Who? Fabian? He'd never been to America, so far as she knew.

She drove straight to Cornwall Gardens, and rang Morgan Ford's bell. A woman's voice crackled through the entryphone, and the latch released with a loud buzz.

She walked nervously up the stairs, and Ford's door was opened by a cluttered-looking girl with thick-lensed glasses and a thatch of floppy hair that covered most of the rest of her face; she reminded Alex of an Old English Sheepdog.

"Ah-ah," said the girl, "Mrs. Willigham? Mr. Ford won't keep you a moment."

Alex shook her head. "No, I don't have an appointment. I wondered if it was possible to see Mr. Ford just for a quick moment."

The girl smiled nervously. "I think it would be best to —ah—make an appointment." She shifted her weight from one foot to the other then back again while her head nodded up and down.

"I saw him yesterday, you see. It's just something I want to ask him—it's very important."

The shifting of the girl's weight increased in tempo. "I'll speak to him for you," she said earnestly but dubiously. "Ah—ah—what did you say your name was?"

"Mrs. Hightower."

The girl nodded her head again and marched off in great long ungainly strides, her body stooped forward. Alex looked around the corridor; it was narrow and drab, with a gaudy red carpet and rough white rendering on the walls; it gave no clue at all as to the almost baroque magnificence of the drawing room it led to.

The girl clumped back toward her, clutching a large diary. "I'm afraid Mr. Ford doesn't remember you at all."

"But it was only yesterday!"

The girl shook her head. "That's what he said."

"It must be in your book, surely?"

The girl opened the diary. "What time was it?"

"Half past ten."

"No." She shook her head. "We had a Mrs. Johnson then."

Alex felt herself blushing. She stared at the thick lenses: it was like looking at the girl's eyes through the wrong end of a telescope. "Ah, yes, of course; I gave my maiden name."

"Mrs. Shoona Johnson?" said the girl dubiously.

"Yes."

"One moment." She trotted off again. This time Morgan Ford himself followed her out. He looked up at Alex, and smiled politely. "Ah yes, you came—wasn't it yesterday?"

Alex nodded, and looked at his tiny pink hands and the enormous rhinestone ring. He was in a different gray suit today, a snappier one, with a louder tie and gray shoes with large gold buckles. Yesterday he had looked like an insurance salesman; today he looked more like a game show host. "I'm sorry to barge in on you," she said, "but I need to talk to you very urgently."

He looked at his watch, and she saw the faint flicker of irritation on his face, which he managed to keep from his voice. "I can give you just a couple of minutes, until my appointment arrives; I musn't keep people waiting, you see," he said kindly.

The cats were still on sentry duty by the gas log fire, and watched her suspiciously.

"Perhaps you could remind me," he said.

"My son was killed in a road accident in France; when a driver drove the wrong side of the autoroute."

"It does ring a bell." He nodded to himself. "You must forgive me—I see so many people."

"You got very excited yesterday."

He frowned. "I did?"

For a moment she wanted to shout at him, clout him on the ear. Then despair took over and the anger slipped away. "It's no good," she said, "if you can't remember what happened; I wanted to ask you about something my son said."

"Please—sit down."

Alex sat in the same chair and saw the tom approaching her, slowly, walking in a wide arc.

Ford smiled at her with a slightly distant look in his eyes. "Perhaps if you gave me something close to you, a bracelet or a watch?"

"I gave you my watch yesterday."

"That would be the best then."

She nodded and unclipped the clasp.

He sat down beside her, and held the watch out. "Ah yes," he said, "ah yes. Very strong feelings." He shook his head. "Incredible; remarkable. What is it you want to know?"

"I was rude to you yesterday, because I didn't believe what you told me. Certain things have happened since then." She looked at him carefully, searching for something shifty in his face, for a flicker, a blush, for the hint of something uncomfortable. But all she saw was a polite smile. "You told me that my son, Fabian, wanted to come back; what did you mean?"

Ford looked at her. "There are feelings coming through that are immensely strong. There is a spirit here who is earthbound, presumably your son, but there are so many other things going on, much conflict, I sense a girl, I'm sorry, there isn't time now, but we must do something. He is earthbound, confused; we must do something for him."

"What do you mean, earthbound?" She heard the buzzer ring in the hallway.

"That he hasn't gone over. It's a common occurrence, I'm afraid, in a sudden death, like an accident or a murder; the spirit needs to be helped over. He may not be aware that he has died, you see." He smiled.

"There's nothing"—she paused—"nothing malevolent?"

He smiled and handed her back the watch. "There's evil everywhere; but we protect ourselves against it. Simple procedures—there is no need to worry—providing we conduct everything properly." He looked at her and she tried to read his expression.

Without warning, the cat jumped into her lap, and she felt her heart miss a beat.

"The environment is very important. You see, an earthbound spirit gets lost very easily; nothing is familiar; he tries to talk to people and wonders why they don't answer back." Ford smiled. "He has no energy, because he has no body to give him energy. We have a circle, and the circle creates energy, like a beacon. He can find his way to the circle, then we can bring in spirit guides who can take him off, over to the other side."

"Do you mean a séance?"

Ford winced. "Circle is better; I think séance has a rather vulgar tone to it; seaside gypsy ladies and all that." He smiled again.

"I know you're in a hurry—I'll be quick. You said yesterday that a girl was coming through, someone called Carrie. Can you remember anything about that?"

He shrugged. "There were so many channels yesterday, all trying to come through, so much confusion."

"It's very important."

"I'm sure it will all become clear when we start the circle. Now, we need somewhere suitable, somewhere familiar to your son; in your home would be best, if you have no objections?"

Alex shook her head.

"What about your husband?"

"We're separated."

He nodded. "Was your son fond of your husband?"

"Yes."

"Then I would like your husband to be there. We need people to give the power; it's very important to have some people close to him. Are there any brothers or sisters?"

Alex shook her head.

"Do you have any other relatives?"

"No." She paused. "My husband's very skeptical, I'm afraid."

"So are you." He smiled, a warm kind smile. "It is very important. A father can give you so much energy in a situation like this."

Alex stared at him hesitantly, but said nothing.

"Also, if you have any other friends, people that knew him, who would be prepared to come, it would be helpful. I can bring people, you see, but it is much better if there are others that knew him."

"How many others?"

"At least two others. We must have a minimum of five, preferably more. Now, let's make a date.The evening would be best; do you have a room without windows?"

"I have a photographic darkroom."

"Perfect."

"No, I'm sorry, it wouldn't be big enough."

"Any room would do, perhaps his own bedroom would be best; but it's a room you should not use for anything else as long as the circle continues. You must make sure the windows are well sealed, so that no light can come in, no light at all, do you understand?"

"Yes."

"And you must eat nothing for six hours before. No one must."

"Six hours?"

"And everyone must have a bath before and wear clean clothes. These are my rules and they must be obeyed."

Alex listened to the gentle lilt of his voice and frowned at the detail; why did these people have to be so obsessed with ritual, she wondered. Why couldn't they just get on with it?

"You must clean the room thoroughly, vacuum very carefully. Evil attaches to dirt, you see, the dirt in the room, on our bodies, the waste products in our systems; we must give evil the least possible chance." He stood up and she followed him down the corridor; the new arrival was nowhere to be seen. Who was it, Alex wondered. What did they look like? Why had they come?

"Margaret!" said Ford loudly. "Could I have the diary?"

The secretary trotted obediently out of a door and handed the book to him. "A Tuesday or a Thursday would be best," he said. "Those are the nights when circles meet around the world and generate psychic energy. You must keep the same day each week clear for several weeks ahead. It may be immediate, it may take a while; continuity is essential. Now, today is Tuesday; no, there wouldn't be enough time. How about this Thursday? Could you manage that?"

She nodded. "Somehow."

He showed her out himself. "You must persuade your husband," he said. "It really is most important."

"Yes."

She tried once more to read his face. It seemed that there was something beyond that gentle smile; something that he knew and did not want to tell.

19

"I believe everyone is wonderful and has something special to offer the world." The woman whispered the words in an awestruck Californian accent, as if her personal discovery was a secret she wished to keep from the three million radio listeners. Alex wondered if she was holding the interviewer's hands and staring into her eyes. "Tibetans will tell people if they are troubled to go and walk under pines, they've been doing if for fifteen hundred years."

"Gosh!" said the interviewer.

"Crap," said Alex, leaning forward and snapping off the radio. The world was full of people who'd discovered the secret of life, who saw it lying in undigested lumps of sweetcorn in their stools; Christ, did you have to stare down lavatories or walk under pines to cope with life? Lucky for them that they had the time. Lucky for them that they had nothing better to do.

She swung the Mercedes off the road and on to the rough cart track, through the gateposts with the small hand-painted sign that read CHATEAU HIGHTOWER, and smiled. At least David had never lost his sense of humor; nor, she thought fondly, his patience. He should have divorced her and found another woman by now, someone who would love him, make him happy. He deserved that; but right now she was glad he hadn't.

After a few hundred yards the track, as usual, turned into a quagmire, and the car lurched and bumped through the gates of the pig farm with its appalling stench; muddy water splashed on to the windscreen and she put the wipers on. A filthy dog ran out of an outhouse and barked at her. She passed the pens and the farmhouse, and drove through another gate, past another sign marked CHATEAU HIGHTOWER, with an arrow underneath it. She could see the small cluster of buildings a mile or so down to her right, nestling in the valley of the South Downs, the fields of vines staked out, and sheep scattered incongruously on the slopes around, like white bushes.

As she drove down the steep hill, the lake came into view on the left, a weird lifeless expanse of water with a strange man-made island in the center. The estate agent's blurb had described it as a unique medieval pond believed to contain rare carp; it had excited David at the time more than the buildings. Carp, she thought, there were people who believed eating carp was the secret to eternal youth.

She passed the huge open-sided barn that contained a rusting tractor and a pyramid of manure, and pulled up in the muddy courtyard in front of the ramshackle flint cottage that was David's home and, for a brief time, until the isolation and the cold had finally become too much, had been hers also.

It had been a long time since she had been down here and little had changed. The stable block on the far side of the courtyard still looked as if it was about to collapse, in spite of the freshly painted sign on the wall which read CHATEAU HIGHTOWER RECEPTION. She smiled again; the absurd grandeur of the name always made her smile. A mud-spattered Collie loped out of a doorway and looked at her dozily.

"Hello, Vendage," she said.

The dog managed a single flick of its tail, then dipped its nose and sniffed something on the ground. She walked past David's Land Rover over to the stables, opened the reception door, and looked in. It was a cold, musty room, with a stone floor and an old kitchen table with an even older cash register perched on top. Two half-empty bottles with Chateau Hightower labels stood there, their corks sticking out of their necks like ill-fitting top hats. The rest of the room was piled high with white boxes, all with Chateau Hightower stenciled in green. She went out and the door swung shut behind her with a loud bang.

She walked the length of the courtyard to a tall flint barn at the end, which looked as if it might once have been a chapel, and went in. It was dank and cold, with a stale vinous smell like an empty pub.

Her husband was standing down at the far end between two massive plastic vats, deep in thought. She walked past a shiny red grape-crushing machine, past a row of smaller plastic vats, and a large glass jar filled with an opaque liquid. He raised a wineglass to his nose, sniffed thoughtfully, then tipped the contents into a drain cut into the center of the floor.

"Hello, David," she said.

He looked up with a start. "Good God!" He smiled and scratched his beard. "You gave me a fright!"

"I'm sorry."

He walked toward her, his arms open; he was wearing a grimy denim jacket and tattered cotton trousers. She felt the prickle of his beard against her face and the cold wetness of his lips.

"Aren't you frozen in that?"

"Is it cold? I hadn't noticed."

She looked down at his feet. "I thought farmers wore boots—not bedroom slippers."

"I'm not a farmer," he said with a hurt expression. "I'm a chatelain."

She smiled. "I'm sorry, I forgot."

"Anyway, they keep my feet warm. Here, I want you to taste this." He walked over to one of the giant vats and half filled the glass from a tap on the side. "Forget the color, it's very young; it'll clarify."

She looked dubiously at the murky gray liquid, then sniffed it; there was a soft, flowery smell.

"Good nose, eh?"

She nodded.

"It'll get stronger. But not bad, eh?"

She tasted the wine and winced at the coldness. Dutifully, she swilled it around in her mouth, looking at him for instructions as to whether to swallow it or spit it out. She saw the desperate eagerness in his eyes, like a child waiting for praise. In contrast to its nose, the wine had a dull steely taste; something almost buttery. She swallowed, wondering if it was the right thing to do. "Hmmm," she said pensively. She saw the enthusiasm waver on his face and doubt appear. "It's very nice. Very nice."

Happiness flooded across him, and he rubbed his hands together gleefully. "I think I've cracked it, don't you?"

"All your wines are very nice, David."

He shook his head. "Everything I've done to date has been rubbish, a con, a copy of something else; second-rate Alsace. I've tried to copy Breaky Bottom, St. Cuthman's and everything else that I thought was good." He shook his head and clapped his hands. "Originality. I want to create a great English wine, something distinctive, unique." He formed a circle between his forefinger and his thumb. "And limit the production; that's the secret. They'll be queueing all the way to the road for it."

"If they can stand the smell of pigs."

He looked hurt and she was sorry she had made the remark.

"Did you—did you really like it?" he said.

She nodded.

"It's got a long way to go yet; you realize what it is, don't you?"

"Yes," she lied, giving him a reassuring smile.

He looked relieved. "I knew you would; at least if you picked up nothing else from being married to me, you learned your wines."

She smiled again, reassuringly.

"I think Fabian would have been proud of this. He came down for the vendage last year; he helped pick these grapes. It's going to be very special, isn't it?"

She nodded.

"Chardonnay!" he exclaimed, looking up at the ceiling; he repeated the word loudly, clearly, like a Bible thumper in the pulpit. "Chardonnay!" The word echoed around the cold damp barn, and his teeth shone maniacally through his beard.

Alex shuddered; he seemed such a stranger suddenly.

"Montrachet, Corton Charlemagne!" He kissed the tips of his fingers.

"I need to talk to you," she said.

"I could make twenty-five thousand bottles this year; that's not bad, is it?"

"I need to talk to you, David."

He held out his hands. "Look, look at these."

She stared at the grime in his nails and in the pores of the skin.

"I used to have them manicured in London, didn't I? Do you remember?"

She nodded.

"My hands were beautiful—it's just everything I did with them was crap. Now they're filthy, ugly, but with them I create great beauty. Isn't that wine wonderful?"

"Yes; I hope it does very well for you. Can we go in the house and talk?"

"Sure." He took the glass from her and walked toward the door; he stopped and patted a huge stainless steel trough. "For fermentation," he said proudly. "No other winery in England has one like this." He looked up at Alex, and she stared into his sad brown eyes. This was the world he'd rejected London for, the life he'd rejected his

big salary and fast cars and smart suits and expensive
manicures to live; to do his own thing: this cold dingy
building with its sour smell and strange machines, the
rows of vines and the sheep and the solitude.

"Are you happy?" she said.

"I'm doing what I want."

"But are you happy?"

He shrugged and walked on. She followed him out of
the building into the bright daylight, across the yard with
the smell of mud and dog and manure, and ducked after
him through the low doorway into the cottage.

He filled the kettle from the tap in the stone sink and
put it on the stove. Alex sat down at the pine table and
instinctively brushed some breadcrumbs into the palm of
her hand.

"Do you want anything to eat?"

She shook her head, and emptied the crumbs into the
large brown paper bag that was the waste bin.

"It's nice seeing you. You haven't been down for a
long time."

She looked at the heap of plates and dishes piled
around the drying rack, and smiled. "You ought to get a
dishwasher."

He shook his head. "No good for wineglasses; leaves a
deposit."

"You make it hard."

He shrugged. "Not much else to do when it's dark;
might as well wash the dishes."

The kettle made a faint-hearted hiss, like a sigh, she
thought. "I went to a medium."

He wiped a mug carefully with a dishcloth and looked
at her. "And?"

"He got in touch with Fabian."

David put the mug down and pulled a tobacco tin out
of his pocket.

"I know what your feelings are on the subject, but

there are some things that have been happening—some very strange things."

"What sort of things?"

Alex stared at an old wooden clock on a shelf. Four-fifteen. "Is that the time?" she said weakly, looking at her own watch for confirmation.

"It's usually a few minutes fast."

"I was meant to be at Penguin at four." She shook her head.

David looked at her. "Important?"

She nodded. "It's taken a month to set it up."

"Can't someone else go for you?"

"No."

"I thought you had some good assistants."

"I do, but I have to be there myself for this one." She looked at her watch. "I'd be lucky to get there by six." She found herself blaming David; it was his fault that she had forgotten, that she was stuck down here, in this filthy kitchen, in the middle of bloody nowhere. His fault that she might have blown one of her best-ever deals. "Can I use your phone?" she said lamely.

"You don't need to ask; you own half of it."

"I don't want a lecture," she snapped, "I just want to use the bloody—" She paused, bit her lip; there was no point in getting mad; no point in trying to blame David, or anyone else.

"You were pretty convincing."

"I think I've salvaged it." She dug her hands into her coat pocket. The boots were slightly too big and her feet slipped about inside them; she wondered whose they were.

The track squelched and moved beneath the weight of their feet as they walked along below the fields of vines; endless rows of thin gnarled branches, unrelieved by any greenery or flowers, they stood like a regiment of skeletons at the gates to Hades. Alex shuddered, worried by the horrific thoughts that had been coming into her mind recently. She slipped, and grabbed on to David's arm; it was rigid, powerful, and his strength surprised her; she had forgotten how strong he was.

"OK?"

"Fine."

"Finished pruning on Sunday," he said proudly. "Three months, almost to the day."

"Good," she said enthusiastically, assuming that it was. The afternoon light was fading, and the air was turning sharp. She heard the bleat of a sheep, and a light aircraft droned high above them.

"You think I'm cracking up, don't you?" she said.

"No, I don't think that," he said, looking annoyed suddenly. "How the hell did the sheep get up there—look." He pointed, and Alex followed the line of his finger up the hillside beyond the vineyard.

"Doesn't Vendage keep them under control?"

"Bloody dog's not interested in sheep; all he wants to do is sleep and chase rabbits."

"There must be something wrong with his genes."

David looked at her oddly, then up at his vineyard again. "Bloody things. Must be another hole in the fence." He shook his head. "I think you're under a lot of strain and it's showing, isn't it? You've always been superefficient; that's how you've succeeded. You'd never have forgotten an appointment in the past. Roses in windscreens, in bowls. There are a lot of red roses in the world, Alex. Nice to think they're a message from Fabian, but it's a little improbable. You're clutching at coincidences, putting a meaning to them, and screwing yourself up in the process."

"I am not screwing myself up," she said angrily.

At the end of the vineyard the track forked. "Shall we walk around the lake?"

"Sure," she said.

They walked through a short wood and came out on to the bank of the lake. Alex stared at it and felt unsettled;

she had never felt comfortable with it, and now it had a
sinister, almost menacing feel. Medieval pond: the estate
agent's description had never left her mind since she had
first read the blurb. She wondered if it had ever been
drained, and what secrets were buried at the bottom of it.
She smelled the flat stagnant smell, saw the thick reeds,
like dead men's fingers, and the strange octagonal concrete
island a hundred yards out in the middle. There was a
tunnel under the lake; you could walk through it, and
come up on the island; halfway along the tunnel, there was
a ballroom, at the bottom of the lake. The agent had taken
them there once, hastily. It had been built at the end of the
last century by an eccentric engineer who had had something to do with designing the London Underground, according to the agent. Now it wasn't considered safe anymore.

She shuddered at the memory of the place; they had
gone in through a wooden door in the bushes somewhere
near where they were now, into this strange concrete
bunker, dark and cobwebby, with a horrible dank smell.
Then down a stone staircase under the ground, with a steel
door at the bottom, like the door to a fallout shelter, or a
bank vault, with a huge wheel that had to be turned. A
watertight door, the agent had said, some precaution about
flooding. The agent had unwound the wheel and pushed
the door open, into the pitch black tunnel with another
identical door thirty or forty yards ahead. She remembered
another huge wheel on the wall, and a battery of smaller
wheels, and the agent warning them never to touch these,
because they would flood the tunnel. They had opened the
second steel door, and seen the tunnel stretching on ahead,
with a faint glow of light at the end, which was the ballroom. They'd walked down to it, a vast room with a
domed glass roof covered in slime and tendrils of weed, the
occasional dark shape of a fish just distinguishable from
the murky water. On the far side of the ballroom, there
was another steel door, which led farther down the tunnel

and up to the island. There had been an ominous puddle of water on the floor, and the agent had looked up nervously and declared that the roof could cave in at any time. That was four years ago.

"Remember going into that ballroom?" she said to David.

He nodded.

"Is it still standing?"

"I've been meaning to have a look; I'll go out in the boat with a snorkel one day and see if it's still there."

"You could go down the tunnel."

He shook his head. "Too dangerous; if there's a leak and one of the sections has filled up, you'd be drowned if you opened the door. Fabian used to be obsessed by the place; I gave him quite a blasting last year when I caught him going down there." He shrugged. "It's a pity; it would have been a good place for a party."

"I thought you didn't like parties anymore."

"It would go with my chatelain image, don't you think? Launching the new vintage with a party under the lake?"

She smiled.

He pulled his tobacco tin out and pried off the lid. "Look, Alex, I didn't mean what I said as a criticism. I'm very fond of you still; I always will be—that's my problem and I have to cope with it. Fabian's dead. Mediums are charlatans. They'll take your money for as long as you'll pay them." He rubbed the cigarette tightly between his fingers, then put it between his lips; they stopped and he clacked his lighter; Alex smelled the sweet smoke for an instant. "How did the medium know the truth about the truck?"

"He didn't. He read in the papers that it was a truck, which you knew was wrong; by a sheer fluke the boys in the car thought it was a truck, and that makes you think the medium is a genius. Anyway, you gave a false name— there probably was someone called Johnson whose son was killed by a truck; there are hundreds killed on the roads every week. Think about it."

"He didn't say that it was a truck. He said that Fabian was saying it was a truck."

"Look, see what we're doing; raking it all up again." He shook his head. "Your medium chap, Ford, or whatever his name is, told you that he was in touch with Fabian?"

Alex nodded.

"So what you're implying is that Fabian's lived on—is still living on, since the accident, albeit in another world—the spirit world, or whatever?"

She nodded again.

"So surely he would have realized after the accident that he was mistaken, that it was a car not a truck? Why didn't he tell the medium?"

She stared ahead across the water and tried to block out his words. A ripple appeared suddenly and she wondered if it was a fish. She felt tired and drained, as if all the energy had been vacuumed out of her body, and she was left weighed down by a coat of heavy lifeless flesh. "How do you explain Philip Main?" she said, but there was no fight left in her words.

"Your hearing Fabian's voice coming from him?"

"Yes."

"He's probably acting; maybe he's a good actor."

"Why should he do that?"

"To make you think you need to go to a medium. Next you'll find he'll be recommending someone—and taking a percentage. You're very naïve sometimes, darling; you're brilliant at your work, but you can be very naïve in other things."

"It happened with you, too, David—that night at the house, when I asked you to leave. It was as if you'd—you'd changed into him. I heard his voice, coming from you. I *saw* him."

He shrugged. "The mind can play strange tricks."

They stood in silence for a moment. "I'm cold," she said. "I'd like to go back now."

They turned around and walked in silence. There was a loud plop near them.

"A fish!" said David.

"It sounded big."

He nodded, and smiled sadly. "Fabian would have made a much better fisherman than me; he had more patience."

"It's funny how you can see different sides of your own child; I never thought he was patient; he used to fly into the most frightful tantrums when he was younger, if he didn't get what he wanted immediately. Dreadful, it used to frighten me."

"He had a good nose for wine. I think he could have gone a long way in wine, if he'd wanted." He noticed the scorn on Alex's face. "A growth industry," he said defensively. "When he was last down here, only a few weeks ago, he tasted the Chardonnay; got it right away. That's pretty good."

"A few weeks ago?"

"Yes."

"He told me he hadn't been down since before Christmas."

David smiled apologetically. "Perhaps he didn't want to offend you, make you—I don't know—jealous or something." He shrugged. "He'd been coming down a lot just lately, particularly since Christmas."

Alex felt uncomfortable and wasn't sure why. "What was he doing?"

"Helping me a bit with the pruning. He really seemed to be getting quite interested in the place. I got the feeling he was thinking of joining me here after Cambridge. Of course it wouldn't have been practical, not at the moment anyway, because of the money. A couple of years, though, and we could be in profit."

"Did he come alone?"

"Yes. I'm sorry—you're not upset are you?"

"No, no of course not; I'm pleased that you were such good friends; it's nice."

"I wish I'd got to know him better really; he was very deep. I used to watch him sitting out there on the island, fishing for hours on end, and wonder what he was thinking."

"What do you think about when you're fishing?"

He shrugged. "You, I suppose."

"Me?" She smiled.

He relit his cigarette. "The happy times we had together. When we first met. How I can win you back." He turned and looked at her, and for a moment then they stopped walking and stared at each other; then Alex looked down at the ground.

"It's really turning cold," she said, starting to walk on again.

"Do you have to go back to London tonight?"

"Why?"

"I'd like you to stay and have dinner. Or we could go out. We were going to have a date this week."

"Haven't you got some bird turning up?"

"Bird? No, crikey, no."

"The one that owns these boots?" She saw him go red.

"I don't know whose those are," he muttered awkwardly. "I think we inherited them with the house."

She smiled. "I don't mind if you—you know—"

He shook his head. "Are you going to stay?"

"I'll have supper, then I must get back."

"Stay down tonight, unwind; you look so tensed up— I'll sleep in the spare room—you can have my room—it's nice and warm."

"I'll see," she said.

They went into the tiny drawing room, and Alex kept her coat on while David lit the fire. "Only use this room when I have visitors, otherwise I live in the kitchen."

"I'm happy in the kitchen."

"No, it's cozy here once it warms up. You used to like this room."

She nodded and stared around at the photographs, at the old battered furniture, and the elderly Bang and Olufsen music center. She remembered the day they bought it; she had been knocked out by the design of the thing. How large and clumsy it looked now. There was a picture of Fabian on a tricycle, and a very recent black-and-white close-up, with a penetrating stare in his eyes that unsettled her, made her turn away. She watched the flames dancing in the grate, and savored the smell of the smoke.

"Give it a few minutes and it'll be nice and snug. Put some music on if you like." David started to walk out of the room.

"What sort of music do you listen to these days?"

He shrugged. "Mostly Beethoven." He looked at her. "Why are you smiling?"

"Nothing."

He went through into the kitchen and Alex followed him, smiling again to herself.

"I just find that amusing, I suppose. I tried to teach you to appreciate classical music and you wouldn't have it; you said it made you feel too old. You'd never listen to anything but pop."

"I quite liked jazz," he said, defensively.

"It's funny, isn't it, how we all change."

"Have you changed?" he said, running the tap and washing his hands.

"Yes."

"I don't think you have."

"I used to be frivolous, like you; now I'm serious and so are you."

"At least we've changed together."

I wish we had, she thought sadly.

* * *

They sat at the kitchen table, facing each other across
a candle flickering in a saucer, and David ladled out the
stew.

"It doesn't bother you, that it's your own sheep?"

"No. Probably would have done when I lived in London. The country changes your attitudes."

She dipped her fork into her plate, blew on the end
then tasted it. "Good; very good."

He shrugged and looked proud.

"There's another reason why I want to see the medium again, David."

"Potatoes?"

She nodded. "I think Fabian may have—"

"Carrots?"

"Thanks."

"May have what?"

"You know the girl, Carrie, he was going out with?"

"Yes."

"She ditched him after Christmas."

"Did she? He never mentioned it."

"He did to me. He told me he'd ditched her—probably just his pride."

"No one likes admitting they've been ditched."

"No. But I thought she should be told, you know—"

"Of course."

"I went to see her mother; the mother hasn't seen her
for a long time; she said she was in the States and showed
me some postcards, recent ones, that Carrie had written."

David poured some wine.

"When I was going through Fabian's things, I found
some identical postcards, and a letter from Carrie in which
she told him she didn't want to see him again. I thought it
rather odd that he should have the same postcards—what
did he want with blank postcards—all from Boston?"

He shrugged.

"I'd pinched one of the postcards from Carrie's

mother, and I compared the handwriting with her letter; it didn't look quite the same, so I took them along to a hand-writing expert."

"A graphologist?"

"Yes. I was trying to remember the word." She stared at him. "David, the postcard Carrie sent to her mother from Boston, postmarked seven days ago, wasn't written by Carrie. It was written by Fabian."

He sat down and stared at her through the steam of the stew and the flickering light. "Are you absolutely sure?"

"Yes."

He shook his head. "What are you saying?"

Alex shrugged.

"Are you trying to say that he is still alive?"

"You went to France."

He swallowed and went white, nodding slowly. "So what's it all about?"

"That's why I went to see the medium."

He was silent for a long time, while the food cooled in front of him. "I'm sure there's an explanation," he said finally. "Probably a very simple one."

"We have a choice, don't we. Either a medium, or the police."

"Or we could do nothing."

Alex shook her head. "No, we can't."

20

She vacuumed Fabian's room herself, drew the curtains and taped them all the way around against the wall. Then she turned out the light and stood in the pitch dark. She felt a chill like a cold draft down her neck and began to tremble. She fumbled for the light switch and couldn't find it. She heard the scraping of her hand against the flat wall. The switch had gone. No. She felt the crack of the door, heard the clunk as she rubbed against the handle, saw the faintest glow of light through the curtains, heard her own heavy breathing.

She found the switch and snapped on the light, sighing with relief, too scared to look at Fabian's portrait on the wall.

The room had a strange emptiness without the bed, which Mimsa had helped her to move out in the morning, and she stared at the six empty chairs, wondering how Ford would want them arranged. There was so much she should have asked him, she realized, as she unplugged the Hoover and carried it downstairs.

It was six o'clock. She wondered whether to put peanuts out; were they allowed to drink? To smoke? The house had a cheerless, expectant feel. Could she put music on, she wondered.

The doorbell rang and she went down. David stood

there in a somber suit and dark tie and for a moment she hardly recognized him.

"Hi," he said.

She blinked. "You came!"

"I said I would."

"Thank you." She leaned forward and kissed him lightly. "I—I thought you might not. You're looking very smart."

"I wasn't sure what to wear."

They went through to the drawing room. "Would you like a drink?"

"Am I allowed one?"

She smiled nervously. "I don't know. I think I need one."

He pulled out his tin of tobacco. "Is it all right if—?"

She shrugged.

"I don't think Fabian would mind."

"Oh sod it, let's have a drink." She poured out two generous whiskeys. They clinked glasses.

"Cheers," he said.

She smiled nervously.

"Who's coming?"

"Sandy."

"Sandy? That loony."

"She's the only person—friend—I could think of who wouldn't think we were bonkers."

They sat down and she watched David roll a cigarette.

"Thanks for Tuesday night."

"It was nice having you down."

"It can't have been very comfy for you; that room was never warm."

"I was fine. Having you in the house warmed it up. It gets lonely down there at nights."

"I thought you enjoyed that."

He shrugged. "We make our beds, we have to lie in them."

She smiled again, trying to think of something else to say; it was like making small talk with a stranger. She drank some whiskey and felt more confident. She looked up at the wall. "You never took that picture of the horse."

"It looks good where it is, I don't mind; anyhow, the damned thing never brought me much luck." He lit his cigarette and took a long pull on his whiskey. "Seven o'clock?"

She nodded.

He checked his watch. "Been doing any more photography?"

She shook her head. "Not since—"

He smiled and shook his head. "What did you do last night?"

"Stayed at the office till about eleven, then brought a pile of work home. I didn't sleep much—I couldn't—I was thinking about this evening all the time."

"Don't expect too much."

She smiled wearily then looked up at the ceiling. She heard the beating of her own heart, as loud as war drums, she thought, and wondered if David could hear it too. The doorbell rang, a long positive ring, so long it became almost aggressive. She saw David start to get up. "I'll go," she said.

A tall meek-looking man in his early sixties stood there; he had gray hair cropped to a close stubble, and his ears, which were too large, looked as if they had been stuck on as an afterthought. He was far too thin, she thought.

"Oh, er, is Mr. Ford here?" He stooped, as if embarrassed about his height, and spoke in a timid voice that was scarcely louder than a whisper.

"He should be here any minute."

"Ah. I'll wait outside then."

"You're very welcome to come in."

The man smiled. "Thank you. I'm here for the circle, you see, tonight."

Alex nodded, closed the door behind him, and

-ushered him into the drawing room. "This is my husband, David." She looked at the man's creased brown polyester suit and noticed he had huge feet.

"How do you do," said David, standing up. "David Hightower."

"Pleased to meet you." He raised a hand nervously forward then withdrew it again before David had had time to shake it. "Milsom."

"Come for the er—?"

Milsom nodded.

"Would you like a drink?" said Alex.

The man looked around hesitantly. "An orange juice, if you have one, please."

Alex went out of the room. "What do you—do?" she heard David say. She paused in the hallway.

"I'm with the Post Office."

"Ah. What do you do for them?"

"I deliver letters."

"Ah. A postman?"

"Yes, yes."

"Ah." She heard David pause. "Interesting."

"Yes."

There was a silence. She went into the kitchen and poured out an orange juice. When she returned to the drawing room, they were still standing facing each other, both staring at the ground in silence.

"Mr. Milsom's a postman," said David brightly.

"Really?" She handed Milsom his drink. "You're a friend of Morgan Ford?"

Milsom went red. "Well, colleague, really; I help out sometimes." He went even redder, and tapped his throat. "Sometimes the spirits speak through me, you see." He gave a nervous, embarrassed laugh.

Alex caught David's eye and saw him fight the smirk off his face.

"Ah," said David.

The doorbell rang again and Alex escaped, relieved,

to answer it. Morgan Ford, Sandy, and a young man she had never seen before were standing there.

"Darling!" said Sandy, her jet black haystack of hair wilder than ever, a purple cloak billowing around her. "You never told me it was Morgan Ford—we just met here on the doorstep! This is the finest medium in the country. Why didn't you tell me? How did you persuade him to come?"

Ford stood quietly like a man standing in his own shadow, holding an enormous tape recorder. He looked even smaller out of his own environment, Alex thought.

"Hello, Mrs. Hightower." He smiled politely, and she shook his tiny hand, feeling the sharp edges of the rhinestone ring. "May I introduce Steven Orme."

"How do you do." She held out her hand, and shook his; it felt cold and bony and had no energy in it, as if it were completely detached from him. Orme was in his early twenties, with slicked-back hair and a large gold earring in one ear. He had an elongated deadpan face and cold half-closed eyes. A creep, she thought, and wondered if he was Ford's boyfriend.

"Please, come in."

"There's one other who should be arriving."

"I think he's already here."

Ford nodded.

They went through into the drawing room. "I wasn't sure," she said to Ford, "whether we are allowed to drink or smoke."

"It's best to avoid anything, if you can." He stared at David. "Good," he said. "This must be your husband?"

"Yes," said Alex.

"Excellent; perfect."

"Why?" said Alex curiously.

"He's exactly what I imagined; not psychic. It's important to have an earth, you see, like the ground wire in an electric plug. There should be one person in the circle who is not receptive; it helps a great deal in protecting the circle."

"So clever of you, darling, you couldn't have a better person," said Sandy, shedding her cloak and allowing a gossamer purple gown to unfurl around her.

Ford smiled modestly, or at least made a good pretense of modesty, thought Alex.

"Perhaps I could see the room, Mrs. Hightower?"

She led Ford upstairs. He was immaculately dressed in gray, as before. Everything about him looked freshly pressed; even his gray socks.

"Perfect," he said, laying down the cassette player. He looked up at the portrait. "Yes, exactly as I imagined him. It's good to have that. Yes, this is a good room, I can feel him here, he's comfortable here, he knows this room."

He walked around the room, looking at the posters on the wall, the telescope, and examined the curtains. "Is there a socket?"

She showed him.

"Saves the batteries." He smiled, uncoiling a wire from the player. "He's here already, you know, just waiting for us." He turned and smiled again, and Alex had a sudden urge to throw him and the rest of them out, now. He was annoying her, kneeling on the floor, fiddling with his cassette, too cheap to use his own batteries.

She looked at the portrait on the wall and Fabian stared back coldly, arrogantly; she thought of his charred corpse; and shuddered, and wondered.

"Are we doing the right thing?" she said suddenly.

"It's entirely up to you, Mrs. Hightower. If you don't want to go ahead, just say so, please. There's no point in proceeding unless you want to communicate with your son, no point at all." He pushed a switch on the player and she saw a green light come on. He stood up, pulled a red light bulb out of his pocket and looked around for a moment, then went to the bedside table and changed it over with the normal bulb. He switched it on and off a couple of times, to test it. "I'm ready," he said.

"Would you like me to fetch them?"

"Thank you."

She went down the stairs slowly, heard the stilted murmur of uncertain conversation and stopped, feeling a sense of dread. It wasn't right. Nothing was right. Iris Tremayne might have been loopy; Philip Main was eccentric, yes, but not loopy. Something had frightened him, frightened a man she had thought was beyond fear; something in this house. Was she going to be destroyed tonight? Made mad? She felt a cold draft again, down her neck. It wasn't too late, she thought, she could stop it now.

Sandy came out into the hall. "Must just nip to the loo, darling."

"Under the stairs," said Alex.

"Won't be a sec."

"Sandy," she said, walking down the rest of the stairs. "Have you seen Iris Tremayne recently?"

Sandy looked at her oddly. "No, darling."

She was lying.

Alex walked into the drawing room trembling. Why had Sandy lied? She picked up a pack of cigarettes and shook one out; her hands were shaking so much, she couldn't open her lighter. David suddenly stood in front of her holding a match. She inhaled the smoke and then took another deep drag. "I think we're ready," she said. "Would you all like to come upstairs?"

She stubbed out the cigarette reluctantly and led them into the hallway. There was a dreadful scream, the sound of the toilet flushing, and Sandy burst out of the door, her face white. Everyone stared at her. She looked around wildly and patted her chest. "I'm sorry," she said. "The wallpaper—some of it fell on to me."

"We've got a problem with dampness," said Alex, falteringly.

"It gave me such a fright!"

Alex went to the lavatory and opened the door. There was a crack as she did so and the last remaining sheet of paper curled away from the wall and fell down on to the seat. She slammed the door shut and turned to face the others, who were standing silently, watching. "Dampness," she said, trying to smile, and pointed a finger up the stairs.

Ford had arranged the chairs in a tight circle. He placed Alex on his right and asked the others to sit down as they liked. He closed the door firmly, with finality, and stood in front of it. "I think I'm right that there are some of you here who have never sat in a circle before?" He looked at David, then at Alex. They both nodded.

"We never know if anything will happen, so we have to be patient. It's a good night tonight, clear, there should not be too much interference. Does anyone have any objections to my leading tonight's circle?" He looked around. "Good." He spoke gently, but authoritatively. "You must all do exactly what I say; if I feel things are getting out of hand in any way, I will stop it." He looked around and everyone nodded.

Alex felt slightly absurd, sitting in the bedroom, surrounded by these strange, earnest people. She was glad David was with her and she wished she had more friends around; she felt vulnerable and very scared. She looked up at Fabian's portrait. "Don't harm me, darling," she said silently.

"We conduct our circles in three stages. We begin with prayers, to protect the circle against evil spirits and simply mischievous spirits. Then we go into meditation. After that we will try to communicate directly with the spirits. We would like to communicate with Fabian, and we believe he would like to communicate with us; we will try to give him energy." He looked at Alex and then at David. "You see, spirits have no energy of their own—but it is possible for them to use the energy we create in our circles to speak, and sometimes even to appear." He smiled and clasped his

hands gently together, like a master giving a lesson to
school children, thought Alex. "If you want to speak, or
ask questions at any stage, please do so."

"What do you mean, evil?" said David.

"What we are doing is trying to open up channels for
the spirits to come through. We want to communicate with
good spirits, but in opening channels, in giving our energy
for spirit use, we are exposing ourselves to misuse. There
are evil spirits around, evil forces that try to come in
through these channels, make use of the energy. That is
why we protect our circle by prayer, and why I must stop
it instantly if I sense the forces of evil."

"What happens if evil comes through?" said David.

Ford smiled. "Usually it is mischievous spirits more
than evil ones; they play pranks, try to confuse us, try to
get their own messages through—strangers to us who
would like to communicate with the earth plane—get messages through to other carnates. But we will be protected;
the power of prayer is strong. This is why it is so dangerous for amateurs to tamper with the spirit world, for people to play dangerous games with Ouija boards." He
smiled again. "Are we ready?" He looked pointedly at
Alex and she nodded.

Ford switched off the light and the room was plunged
into darkness. Alex felt calm. Suddenly the room seemed
warm and friendly; it was going to be all right. She cupped
her hands together and leaned forward.

"Dear God," said Ford's gentle assured Welsh lilt.
"We pray to you that you will look after our circle and that
we shall come to no harm."

She closed her eyes out of respect and felt faintly silly.

"Guide us safely throughout this evening."

The prayers continued for an eternity, it seemed. Ford
asked for healing for people whose names she had never
heard of, for peace in the world, for someone called Mrs.
Ebron's leg to get better quickly.

Finally they stopped and the room was very still. She

heard a siren a long way off in the distance, and then it was gone; even the traffic seemed still. She thought again of the terror in Sandy's scream. What was going on in that lavatory, she wondered, opening her eyes and looking nervously around. She could see shadows, silhouettes. She looked toward the window and saw a faint streak of light down one side. She hoped the room was dark enough. The silence continued; she wondered if Fabian was watching them and tried to imagine him, but could feel nothing.

There was a click, and she suddenly heard "Spring" from Vivaldi's *Four Seasons,* light, sad, airy. "We'll begin our meditation now," said Ford gently. "I want you to close your eyes and imagine you are walking on soft grass in a field. It's a warm spring day, a clear sky, you feel the sun warming the air, feel the grass soft and springy beneath your feet. It's good to walk on, you're enjoying walking, breathing in the air, cool and fresh, the start of a fine day. The field is gently sloping up a hillside; you walk across it, imagine the grass beneath your feet, the sky above you. Now you see a path in front of you."

Alex thought of a field at David's vineyard, tried to imagine it, as Ford said, tried to feel the grass beneath her feet, tried to stop feeling self-conscious and go with his words, relax with his soothing voice.

"Go along the path, it's nice to be walking along a firm path again, enjoy it. You can see a white gate ahead of you now; open the gate and go through and you can see a river, a wide gently flowing river, with trees and rushes and lilies. It is peaceful, so peaceful. There's a bridge across the river, you can see it clearly." Alex thought of a river she had once known, with an old stone bridge arched across it, crumbling.

"You can see people on the far side, standing there. Your friends, waiting to greet you. Cross over the bridge now, go to them, greet them, hug them, spend time with them. Don't be afraid, go, enjoy, be happy with them."

Alex saw white ghosts on the far bank, swaying and

opening their arms; she saw the slits which were their eyes, like the painting of the three phantoms she had seen on Ford's wall, and she hesitated. She saw Philip Main standing among them in a shabby corduroy suit, shrugging, then she saw Ford standing there. What friends does he mean, she wondered. Living or dead? She stepped on to the bridge and the ghosts swayed toward her, stretched out their arms, like faceless monks with cowls over their heads. Main and Ford disappeared. Then she saw Fabian standing among them, looking away from her, his head bowed as if he were ashamed.

She felt herself hurrying anxiously; she stumbled on a loose brick, and when she looked up, the ghosts had closed ranks and he had disappeared. She stood among them, staring into their cowled hoods, into voids. "Fabian?" she said, trembling. She pushed her way among them and saw one, taller than the rest, Fabian's height, facing away from her. "Fabian?" She tapped him on the shoulder. "Darling?"

Slowly he turned around. Inside the cowled hood was a charred skull that stared at her helplessly, with an almost apologetic look.

She felt herself about to scream and sat upright with a start, opened her eyes and looked around. Where was she? Where the hell was she? She heard her own breathing; it was the middle of the night, surely? Had she imagined it all? Weren't they having a séance? Where was everyone? She felt sweat pouring down her, and she looked around, trying to see in the dark. She saw a faint streak of light; was that the curtain? The streak of light she had seen before? She wanted to call out, say something, but she was afraid of speaking to an empty room. Weren't there people here? Surely they hadn't left her alone? But why couldn't she hear them?

There was a tinkle of music and the strains of Vivaldi's "Summer" filled the room; the speakers were slightly tinny and she could hear the hiss of the tape. She

breathed out slowly, relief flooding through her. Baloney.
It was a con; hypnotism; a cheap trick dressed up in an
elaborate production. She closed her eyes, thought again of
the charred skull and shuddered. She opened her eyes and
looked around, restless; her backside was stiff in the chair
and she wanted to move, but was afraid to break the silence. She could sense David now, restless too; what must
he be thinking?

She heard the shuffle of a foot on the carpet, the creak
of a spring, the rustle of fabric; she smelled Sandy's pungent perfume. What was she meant to do now? Would
Fabian suddenly appear? She looked around again at the
dark shapes; what were they all doing? Were they in hypnotic trances? Asleep? Or sitting there in the dark, thinking, like her?

She closed her eyes again, and tried to concentrate on
the river. But it had gone and, instead, she saw David's
lake, the medieval pond, the expanse of flat black water
with its fringe of reeds like dead men's fingers, and the
crumbling octagonal island in the middle.

She tried to imagine a bridge across to it, but no
bridge would come, only the tunnel underneath. She
thought of the entrance, like the steps down to an air raid
shelter, overgrown with grass and weeds. She saw the rotting oak door, turned the key, stiff in the rusting lock, and
pushed the door open. She felt it scrape across the concrete, warped and sagging on its hinges, heard it clacking
like the laughter of crows as it vibrated. She could smell
the must and the damp and could hear, a long way off, the
echo of dripping water. It was cold in here, so cold. Gingerly she walked forward, and down, listening to the echo
of her own footsteps, and the splashes of dripping water
like pistol shots.

She came to the inner door, unlocked that, and
walked into the dark passageway, her feet squelching on
the unseen floor, wondering whether she was treading on
frogs or toads or just water and slime. Deep under the lake

now, she came to the next door, which led into the domed ballroom, a heavy steel watertight door, the door David said she must never open. If there was a leak in the ballroom, and it had flooded, then opening this door . . . She unwound the huge handle, like a steering wheel, four, five, six turns, and the door swung open, outward, as if she had been expected.

She stood back blinking in surprise, and stared around the huge domed room. It was snug, warm, cosy. Up in the ceiling, through the glass roof, carp and trout swam around, lazing, playing in warm pools of light. There was soft carpeting on the floor and fireplace burning cheerfully. A woman stood there in a nursemaid's outfit; she stooped down, lifted a thin charred branch out of the fire with her bare hands, and held it high above her, a tiny gnarled object with burned twigs coming from it. The twigs began to move, at first as if in a breeze, but then they took on a life of their own and became little pink arms; tiny fingers curled and opened and she heard a baby cry.

"Don't cry; you're going to see Mummy now." The nursemaid carried the baby across toward her with a smile, and Alex shuddered as she realized how like Iris Tremayne the woman looked.

Then she felt the weight of the baby in her arms, saw the pinkness of his hands and his legs, and looked down at his face.

A charred skull stared back.

A dim red light came on, and she blinked, startled. The music had stopped, she realized. She saw Ford standing by the door, and she looked at Steven Orme, Milsom, then at Sandy, who smiled reassuringly. She avoided David.

"How did everyone get on?" asked Ford. "That was a long meditation—I felt it was going well, so I didn't interrupt."

Alex looked at her watch. Ten to eight; it had been over half an hour. Impossible. She steeled up her courage and looked at David; his head was bent over, his ear pressed to his jacket, and he had a strange preoccupied expression on his face.

"Sandy," said Ford in his gentle voice. "How did it go for you?"

"Incredible, Morgan. I saw Jesus."

Ford inclined his head slightly and smiled.

"He was standing in front of me with a basket; he told me I must try to develop my healing and he showed me how to do several things that have been confusing me."

Ford looked at Sandy, puzzled.

"I sensed Jesus was in here too," said Steven Orme, in an enthusiastic, nasally voice. "I felt him come in."

They're all bloody bonkers, thought Alex.

"I think," said Orme, "that he may have come in to protect the circle. What do you think, Morgan?"

"Sandy's healing is very important; he may have felt it was necessary to come and see her." He looked at Milsom. "Arthur?"

"My wife," said Milsom, his gruff voice tinged with a boyish excitement. "Always pop over and see her when I can."

"How was she?"

"Fine; she was showing me what she's doing. She's working on a project with some others, building this huge column of light, you see."

"Ah, yes," said Ford, nodding. Alex watched him, wondering what she should say.

"And Mr. Hightower?" asked Ford.

"Think I fell asleep," said David.

"Very easy," said Ford dismissively. Alex felt Ford's eyes on her. "Would you like to tell us what you saw, Mrs. Hightower?"

Alex looked at David and regretted it. Don't be conned, he was saying; don't be a fool.

"I saw Fabian," she said, and was reassured by the approving look in Ford's eyes.

"Yes, I thought you would; I thought he would be there. I could sense him very strongly; he's around now. I think we're going to be in touch tonight; it's very strong."

"His face was all burned and charred, like a skull."

Ford nodded. "It is natural in meditation for the subliminal to play a part. You are projecting to him from the earth plane. The image you have is his carnate one, and it is inevitable that is how you will see him. Later, when he comes through to you, he will project his incarnate body, and that will be as you would like to remember him."

"He was running away from me." She felt herself blush, feeling ridiculous; she glanced at David, saw him trying to say something with his eyes, some warning, but she looked away before the message could get through.

"Probably your subliminal again, your fear of losing him forever. This will pass after your first communication; after that, you will be able to join him in your meditation whenever you like, and I think you'll find he'll he very helpful to you." Ford smiled again and walked over to the tape recorder. He knelt down, ejected the tape and turned it over.

Alex looked around the room and felt herself trembling again. Fabian's portrait looked sterner than ever in the red lighting and Orme's cruel cold face unsettled her. She looked at Milsom, and he smiled cheerfully back.

"You may hear a strange voice, Mrs. Hightower," said Ford. "I have a guide, called Herbert Lengeur—he was a doctor in Vienna in the 1880s; a nice chap; he moved to Paris in the '90s. He looked after Oscar Wilde for a time."

She stared at him; he said it casually, as if it were normal. She was too nervous to ask him what he meant.

"Is everyone ready to go on? I sense strong influences tonight; you must all remember to do what I say, it's very important. All right?" He stared at Alex, and Alex stared back.

She shivered and felt a deep sense of dread. She did

not want to go any further, did not want him to turn out the light.

There was a loud click, and a weird drumbeat came out of the player, at a quick tempo that seemed to be increasing all the time.

Then the light went out.

She sensed him almost immediately, as clearly as if he had opened the door and slammed it shut behind him. He was in the room, standing behind her, watching.

She felt the shivers racing down her arms. She saw a shadow cross the room, she was certain, something darker than the dark, and she wanted the light on, wanted to touch someone. But she dared not move, dared not give away to her son, to his strange penetrating gaze, that she could feel, that she was frightened. *This is what you want, darling, isn't it? That was the reason for all the signs you gave me; we're here now, for you. Be kind, please be kind.*

God, she thought suddenly, it all seemed so long ago now. So long ago that he had been alive and everything had been normal.

There was a mournful hideous wail, like the cry of a vixen in the night, separate from the beat of the drums and way above it; it came from someone in the circle around her. She heard it again. Lower, slower, it dissolved into a ghastly choking sound, as if someone was trying to breathe through a broken throat. Who had made it, she wondered. Ford? Milsom? Orme? Sandy? It was impossible to tell.

"Mother."

Fabian's voice, weak and frightened. There was a click and the music stopped.

"Mother." Not one shadow of a doubt; it was her son speaking. She felt cold, the room was turning to ice, felt herself shaking so much she could hardly bear to sit still.

"Darling?" she said nervously, out loud. "Hello, darling."

She heard the hideous choking sound again, then suddenly a single dreadful piercing scream, a young woman's scream, the most pitiful frightened scream she had ever heard; she thought it would echo around the room forever.

Oh, Christ, please stop this, she thought, *please stop it now.*

"Who is there?" She heard Ford's voice, calm, assured.

A voice replied with a heavy Germanic accent; the voice was cultured and had completely different intonations from anyone in the room. "This is Herbert. There is a young man here who would like to speak with his mother."

"Please tell him we are waiting for him. He has already started to come through."

Alex stared at Ford through the dark. He had heard Fabian too. It wasn't a trick of her imagination. There was no way that his voice had been faked. She tried to feel excited, to put away the fear, but the dread and the cold encircled her; it was impossible, surely, she thought, for anyone to feel so alone in a room full of people? And yet, she knew, as she felt the force of the cold and the fear, like hands on her shoulders, that she might have been the only person left in the world.

"He is needing some energy." The Germanic accent was almost chiding.

"I want everyone to hold hands," said Ford. "We will allow our energy to surge through us, to give power to the spirit."

Alex felt her hand seized; Ford's tiny hand was so warm it felt as if it was burning her. The rhinestone cut into her skin, but she did not dare change the position. She pushed out her right hand and felt a limp, bony hand; who was that on her right, she tried to remember. Milsom. The hand responded tentatively.

"Feel the power," said Ford. "Let it surge, let it surge!"

She sensed Ford and Milsom rocking backward and forward, and rocked with them. Then suddenly they stopped; Ford's hand closed tight over hers, a clamp, and he had become immovable, like stone.

"Mother!"

Fabian's voice hung in the air.

She heard the strange choking again and realized it was coming from Milsom. She looked at him, tried to see something of him then suddenly she heard Carrie's voice from directly opposite her, where Orme was sitting.

"Don't let him, Mrs. Hightower."

Pitiful, frightened, the words, unmistakably Carrie's, pierced the air like a knife scraped against marble.

"There seems to be a young woman coming through our channel," said Ford patiently.

"There is no young woman," said the German voice.

"Who is there?" said Ford calmly. "Please tell us your name?"

There was a ferocious snarl, which made Ford and Milsom both jump, almost jerking Alex's arms out of their sockets.

She felt a cold draft of air blowing down the back of her neck spreading out over her shoulders and down her body.

"Please help me, Mother." Fabian's voice came through again.

He sounded so close, she felt she could reach out and touch him. She stared around the darkness. "Where are you, darling?"

A strange deep nasal voice suddenly snarled back. "Don't listen to the little bastard."

She jumped again, shaking, staring wildly around at the dark.

"Who are you, please?" she heard Ford say, still calm. "Kindly tell us your name, or else leave the medium at once, in the name of God."

"Mother!" shouted Fabian desperately.

The deep voice snarled again in the dark: "I'm his father."

Alex's head was swimming; she swayed, felt the grips of Ford's and Milsom's hands.

"No," said Ford. "His father is here in the room with us."

"Mother," Fabian's voice whimpered again.

"Please stop this," said Alex. "I want to stop."

"There is a rogue spirit who is interfering," said Herbert Lengeur's cultured Germanic accent suddenly, calmly. "It is trying to make mischief."

"Rubbish. Don't listen to him. I'm his father," the voice snarled back.

"The spirit's father is here with us; please leave us, whoever you are," said Ford, his voice growing sterner.

"My name is John Bosley. I am the boy's father."

The voice boomed, echoing around the room.

Alex tried to free her hands from Milsom and Ford, but could not. "Oh God, please stop this." She was shaking uncontrollably and felt as if she was going to vomit at any moment. "Morgan, please stop this!" she shouted.

"Darling?" She heard David's voice, anxious, soft. "Are you all right, darling."

"I want to stop. Please ask them to stop."

"Mother!" Fabian screamed again. "Carrie!"

She curled up in the chair, tried to free her arms, tried to tuck her head under her arms. "Help me," she said. "Help me."

Then she heard Carrie's voice again, quietly imploring. "Please don't let him, Mrs. Hightower."

"Don't let him what?" she said weakly. "Tell me. Don't let him what?"

"May 4, Mother." She heard Fabian's voice, different now, gently, confiding, just as he had always sounded. "They're going to let me out on May 4."

"Out of where, darling?" she said weakly. "Out of where?"

There was a long silence and she found herself becoming conscious of the room again, of the creaking of chairs, of breathing and the rustle of clothes. Ford's grip relaxed on her hand, then let go completely.

She sensed that Fabian had gone, as definitely as he had arrived. There was nothing in the room anymore, except the darkness and the silence. She freed her right hand from Milsom and gingerly touched her face with her fingers; it was soaking wet.

"Mr. Ford," she heard David say. "I think you should stop; my wife is frightened."

There was no response; she looked around, tried to see the silhouettes, but could see nothing; she felt her heart thumping so hard it was making her chest ache. "David?" she whispered.

"Are you all right, darling?"

"I'm—" She paused. "I'm OK."

There was a long pause, then she heard Ford's voice, gentle again. "The spirits have gone."

She heard the creak of a chair, the sound of feet on the carpet, and then the light came on and she closed her eyes against the brightness. When she opened them again, Ford was standing by the door, his head bowed slightly, deep in thought.

She looked around the room; nothing had changed, nothing had moved. Still trembling, she wondered what she had expected to see, then sank back in her chair, totally drained. Opposite her, Orme was slumped at a hideously contorted angle across the arm of his chair. His mouth was open and his chin pushed forward like a beached fish; his eyes, wide open, stared up at the ceiling. For a moment she thought he was dead. Then he moaned softly and rolled back into the chair.

Milsom was leaning forward with his hands clasped and resting on his knees. Sandy was lying back in her chair, dabbing her forehead with a handkerchief.

Alex glanced nervously at David, who had his hand inside his jacket and was looking suspiciously at everyone.

She stared at Ford. "What happened?" she said.

Ford looked strangely back at her and said nothing.

"Please tell me," she said, trembling. "Please tell me what happened." She looked across at Orme again, then at Milsom, then Sandy. Everyone was strange, so strange. She stared at Fabian's portrait on the wall and at the cold brass telescope underneath the window. She thought how stark the room felt without the bed, how cold and flat the lighting seemed, how normal the room suddenly seemed again. Had she been in a trance, she wondered. Yes, perhaps that was it, all a weird dream. She relaxed very slightly, and looked at the people again. *Why won't anyone look at me?* She stared at Milsom, at Sandy, at David. *Look at me someone, please. Smile at me, tell me it was all a bad dream; tell me that you've all been sitting here and no one saw anything. Please, please tell me.*

The fear slowly subsided and was replaced with a flatness. Was that it, she thought. Just voices? Where was the ectoplasm? The specters? Green slime hurtling from people's mouths? Levitations?

David was fiddling around inside his jacket again. *Am I still alive,* she wondered, suddenly. *Is that why they're not looking at me?* Panic gripped her. *Can't they see me? I've died, that's what's happened, I've died. Look at me, please David. What are you doing?* Suddenly her hands touched something in her lap, something hard and prickly which made a crackling sound like parchment, and she recoiled in shock. It felt like a huge dead insect. She tried to move her hands away, but they were entangled in it, and she felt the skin on her fingers tearing. She stared around wide-eyed, shaking wildly, too afraid to look down. *What is it, what the hell is it?*

She looked again at David for help, but he was still concentrating on his jacket. She felt a sharp pain in her finger, like a bite, that made her cry out in pain, and she had to look down. For a moment she stared in disbelief. Then she let out a scream which filled the room.

It was not an insect but a small shriveled rose, black and charred.

21

Alex opened her eyes and focused hazily on the portrait of the horse on the wall. Somewhere in the distance she heard the murmur of voices. She looked around, puzzled, trying to get her bearings. Surely she had been in Fabian's room? Now she was downstairs in the drawing room. There had been people all around, but now she could see only two, David and Morgan Ford, and they seemed a long way away, so far they might have been in another room, or even in another house.

"I never said goodbye to anyone."

They didn't notice her.

"Your conjuring tricks might be fine for little old ladies," she heard David say.

"Apports are common occurrences, Mr. Hightower."

What time was it, she wondered. How long had she been here on the sofa? What had happened to everyone else?

"You really mean that roses can dematerialize, travel across time and space and rematerialize?" said David.

"Many things happen in the spirit world that cannot be explained in ordinary terms. Apports are messages from the departed to their loved ones; their only way of offering tangible proof."

"What sort of proof is a burned rose?"

"I never said goodbye to anyone," she said again. Still they did not notice her.

"We know only very little about the spirit world; we are learning all the time."

"By experimentation on people when they are at their weakest?"

"I would never allow anyone into a circle who I felt was not strong enough."

"My wife wasn't. Look what happened to her."

"She'll be fine; she's just very tired. Giving power is very draining. It's very soon, you see, very soon after the bereavement. It's best normally to leave these things for a few months, at least."

"So why didn't you?" said David.

"It was important."

There was a long silence. "What do you mean?"

"There is a mischievous spirit around."

"No," said Alex suddenly, loudly. "No, there isn't."

She saw them turn and look down in her direction, as if they were trying to confirm a distant landmark.

"How are you feeling, darling?" said David tenderly.

She saw him lean over her, saw the tangle of his beard and his eyes peering down at her in turn, first one then the other.

"Would you like me to call the doctor?"

"She's calming down now," said Ford. "In another half an hour she'll be fine. Apports do cause great emotional stress."

"Apports," said David. Alex heard the crackle, like parchment, and saw David turn a blackened object around in his hand. "Just a rose, an old dead rose plucked off someone's bonfire, that you or one of your accomplices dropped in her lap while we were holding hands in the dark. Someone with a very sick sense of humor."

"David," said Alex. "Please, don't be angry."

"I'm not angry, darling. I'm sure Mr. Ford meant

well. Perhaps people are comforted by these things; you obviously weren't. Try and sleep some more."

"I'd like a cigarette," she said, sitting up on the sofa. The room seemed to slip sideways, and for a moment she was looking down at the wall; then it righted itself with a heave that churned her stomach.

"Don't sit up just yet, darling. Wait a few minutes."

"It wasn't how I thought it would be," she said, and looked up at Ford.

"It never is," said Ford gently, and smiled.

"Fabian was so clear."

"What do you mean?" said David.

"Fabian."

"Fabian?" he echoed blankly.

"Fabian; surely you heard him?"

She watched the puzzlement on David's face, saw him turn to Ford and then look back at her again. "Heard him?"

"Yes. And Carrie. And—" She paused and went red.

"Nothing happened, darling, you must have imagined it." Again he looked at Ford, and she saw Ford turn dismissively away from him to look back at her.

"Fabian spoke to me," she said.

"Well, he didn't speak to me. The only person who spoke was Mr. Ford. And those two odd chaps; one sounded as if he was being sick, and the other as if he was being strangled."

Alex felt frightened again suddenly, frightened and isolated. "You mean you heard nothing?"

"He wouldn't, Mrs. Hightower," said Ford reassuringly. "He is not a sensitive." Ford coughed and turned to David. "But your role was essential; there was mischief around tonight. You kept us earthed; without you we would have achieved far less."

"Achieved?" said David incredulously. "What on earth did you achieve?"

"I think you should ask your wife that," said Ford.

Alex saw David staring at her.

"David," she said, feeling herself blushing, "would you mind terribly if I had a word in private with Mr. Ford?"

David looked at her, then at Ford.

"Perhaps you could make us a cup of tea?"

He stood up awkwardly and rubbed his beard. "Yes— I'll—" He looked around, put his hand in his jacket pocket and took it out again. "I'll go and put the kettle on." He walked out of the room and Alex heard the click of the door closing. She stood up and the floor tilted away from her. She swayed, then felt steadier, and walked across to the drinks cabinet.

"Are you feeling better now, Alex?"

She took a cigarette out of the box, noticing that it was the first time Ford called her by her Christian name.

"Thank you. I think so. There's been rather a lot to take in." Her eye caught the rose David had left on a side table; she wandered over and touched it gently. "Did Fabian really send this?"

"Something happened to it. Someone burned it on the way."

"A spirit?"

"Yes," he said quietly.

"He often brought me roses; perhaps he was bringing me one back from France and it got burned in the accident. Could that be it?"

Ford nodded. "It's a possibility." He frowned.

"But you don't think so."

"There were other spirits around tonight, making mischief. Herbert, my guide, warned us."

"What do you mean?"

"When we hold circles, we are opening channels for communications from the spirit world. I can never know who is going to come through. We hoped tonight it was going to be Fabian, but often others come through; sometimes evil spirits will try to influence the circle, and try to manifest."

"Evil spirits?"

Ford nodded. "Evil spirits can be very cunning. Good mimics. Take on a departed person's characteristics. Voice. Mannerisms. Appearance. They try to use the energy we create in the circles."

"Why?"

"For their own purposes."

"Do you believe in evil?"

Ford was silent for a moment. "Of course. The positive and the negative, Mrs. Hightower. All existence, both here and in the spirit world, is a balance between the two."

"And one of these—evil—spirits might have burned the rose?"

"It's possible. There was much that happened tonight that I do not understand."

"So it wasn't successful?"

"I don't know. Our intention was to rescue Fabian, free him from the earth plane. But there was too much interference, too much confusion. I cannot be sure that he has gone over." She saw him shake his head.

"Interference from the girl, you mean?"

Ford nodded. "Partly."

Alex lit her cigarette and sat down again on the sofa. "She came through before, in the sitting room in your house. A girl called Carrie whom Fabian used to go out with."

Ford nodded. "But this man claiming to be Fabian's father?" He stared at Alex. "John Bosley, or something like that? I don't understand why he came through; but sometimes these mischief makers do."

Alex felt her face burning again. "Have you ever had any experiences," she said, "of spirits who want to come back?"

"To human form?"

She nodded.

"You mean possession?"

"I'm not sure what it's called. Someone who wants to come back because they have unfinished business."

Ford glanced at his watch. "Many spirits are confused after death—the earthbound ones; often they do not realize they are dead; it is only when they try to talk to their loved ones and their friends and they discover no one can see them, no one can hear them, that they start to realize what has happened. Until that point many of them try to carry on as before, turning up to work, imagining they are doing everything they used to do before they departed."

"Has anyone ever succeeded?" she said.

"In carrying on with their work?"

She nodded.

"Yes."

"How do they do it?"

"They use the physical mind and body of someone living. They take them over—so that person becomes a host body. That's what we know as the state of possession." He smiled. "There are well-documented instances of spirits continuing their work through influencing living persons. There have been cases of surgeons, painters—and composers. Mozart was composing at four years old; it is very likely that he was under the influence of a spirit."

"What about evil?"

"Hitler," said Ford. "There is no proof, but much evidence that Hitler—and several other members of the Third Reich—were possessed by evil spirits, which would account for their actions."

"When I came to see you and we had our sitting, you told me at the end that Fabian wanted to come back. Is that what you meant? That he had unfinished business?"

Ford looked nervous suddenly. He wasn't comfortable with this subject. She wondered if it was out of his depth. "Unfinished business?"

"Yes."

Ford smiled. "What sort of business do you think?"

Alex looked down at the carpet. "It seems so strange, talking about him as if he's—" She paused then stood up abruptly, walked across the room and tapped the ash from her cigarette into the wastepaper basket.

"As if he's still alive?"

She nodded.

Ford smiled mysteriously. "You're a very sensible lady; perhaps too sensible."

"What on earth do you mean?"

Ford shook his head and smiled again.

"I don't understand."

"I think one day you will."

His face darkened and she felt uncomfortable again.

"We should have another circle, next Thursday."

"No."

"It's important; for your son."

"I found it too frightening."

"The first time is. But things are not resolved." He looked anxiously around the room. "You will feel better when they are."

"I can't imagine ever feeling better."

"No," he said. "You won't as long as the spirit is around. When we have helped the spirit across, then you will have peace and the healing will start."

"Don't you think perhaps I've just been raking things up; that it would be better to leave them as they are?"

"You must think of your son."

She stared at him, again trying to figure him out. Was it all a con, as David had insinuated? Had she been hypnotized, imagined everything? No, the voices had been too clear, too real, surely. And yet a small piece of doubt nagged at her. It was, after all, in Ford's interest to go on for as long as he could spin it out, for as long as he could give work to his strange colleagues with their gold earrings and their big feet. "I also have to think of my husband."

"Because he is skeptical?"

"There's another reason." She paced around the room

then sat down again. "This man who came through, claiming to be Fabian's father—"

"The mischievous spirit?"

Alex shook her head. "No, not necessarily a mischievous spirit." She paused. "David is not Fabian's father."

Ford stared at her, searching, and looked down at his fingernails, checking his immaculate manicure. Something was disturbing him, she thought. The revelation should have clarified things for him, but it seemed to have made them worse. "Bosley, wasn't it—a name like that?" he said.

"I wouldn't know who he was."

She saw Ford look at her oddly, and she smiled awkwardly. "I don't mean it like that," she said. "We couldn't have children, you see." She felt herself blushing. "My husband's sperm count was too low."

"You had a donor?"

"Not exactly—well, sort of." She sighed and inhaled deeply. "I didn't want to have artificial insemination—some stranger's sperm—I wanted to have David's child. We were put in touch with a specialist who was experimenting at the time, mixing one's husband's sperm with a donor sperm, a high-motility sperm, they called it."

She smiled sadly. "That way you were supposed never to know whether it was your husband or—" She trailed off.

"And now you think that—?"

She blushed. "David's always been convinced Fabian was his, which is good. But I've always known he wasn't."

"How?"

She felt herself going even redder. "It wasn't working. The specialist told me he felt David's sperm was too hostile—I never quite understood—something in the chemistry wasn't right. I asked the specialist to let me have it neat—without David knowing."

Ford nodded. "Genes are important to the spirit world, you see," he said. "The blueprint for character. We know that they are essential to the carnate mind and body, that they shape and control everything, but I believe they are just as important to the discarnate state."

"That we take our genes with us?"

"The part that relates to our character."

"So Fabian has found his real father now?"

"It's a possibility."

She shook her head. "I don't want David to know. He was so proud of Fabian. I don't want his pride to be taken too."

Ford nodded. "I understand. But your husband is not what we call a 'sensitive.' He won't pick it up from the spirit; he won't know unless you tell him."

She sank her face in her hands. "Oh God, I feel so confused, so confused and frightened."

"Alex," said Ford gently. "There is a terrible conflict going on between your son and his real father. It is something we must try to resolve, because it could harm your son—and it could harm you."

"How do you mean?"

"There is a very strong dark force present; I have been trying to play it down, not to frighten you, but I have never in my life experienced anything stronger. Your husband reckons I am a charlatan; you, I think, believe me, although you have doubts. To prove my sincerity, I am prepared to waive all my fees, but you in turn must do exactly what I say. Do you understand?"

She shook her head. "No," she said. "I don't want to go on."

"Alex," he said gently, "you cannot turn the spirit world on and off at the touch of a button or at the twist of a tap. These things have to be seen through, or else they will see it through themselves."

Alex felt an ice-cold shiver again, felt a draft blowing down inside her blouse, a hideous damp cold wind that made her blouse stick to her skin, as if she had just put it on sopping wet.

"Is there any way you can find out the real identity of your son's father?"

"I went to a man in Wimpole Street. A specialist in infertility. Saffier. Dr. Saffier. He used sperm from donors —he told me they were very careful in matching up the donors—features—" She paused. "Hair color, eyes, that sort of thing."

"And he helped you."

"Yes."

"I think you should go and see him. Try and find out more about this John Bosley."

"I don't even know if he's still alive."

"It's very important," said Ford.

"Why?"

"You'll understand."

The door opened and David came in. "Do you take milk, Mr. Ford?"

Ford stood up. "I'm sorry, I'm very late. I must be on my way."

"Do you want a broomstick, or did you bring your own?" said David, smiling.

Ford stood up and smiled politely back. "Oh, I don't need things like that; I'll just dematerialize in front of your eyes, if I may."

22

The Land Rover lurched, jolted and slithered on the muddy track. Alex smelled the stench of the pigs, saw several rabbits staring into the headlights, twitching; they turned and fled away through the fencing and into the fields.

It was a clear night; she could see the stars, the half-moon and the dark contours of the land like a never-ending shadow.

"Thanks for letting me come down."

"Don't be silly."

"I didn't want to stay in the house tonight."

"I'm not surprised. That chap, what's-his-name, Ford, has scared you silly with his tricks."

She stared through the windscreen, across the spare wheel. The nose of the Land Rover dipped and she could see the sheen of the lake, almost as if it were glowing from some light inside it. Medieval pond. She shuddered; why could she never get those words out of her mind, why did they always sound so sinister? She thought of ancient carp, hundreds of years old, menacingly guarding the deeps. She tried to look away from the lake, but her eyes were drawn there as if it were a magnet.

"He wasn't what I'd imagined," he said.

"What do you mean?"

"Well—he had a bit of a sense of humor really; I

never thought of people like that having a sense of humor —always thought they were deadly serious. He looked more like an insurance salesman than a medium."

She smiled. "That's what I thought when I saw him. Apparently he has a very fine reputation."

David stopped the Land Rover sharply, yanked on the hand brake and peered out of his side window.

Alex looked at him anxiously. "What's the matter?"

He raised a finger and continued staring. She listened to the beat of the engine, like a heart racing, looked around and felt vulnerable, afraid, wanted to get to the farmhouse, not be stopped out here in the dark, beside the lake and the fields.

"Buggers," he said.

"What is it?"

"Some sheep have got through into the vineyard— I've got my Chardonnay in that one; I don't want them in there."

She felt the relief surging through her.

"I'll have to sort that fence out in the morning."

"You don't mind if I borrow the Land Rover tomorrow?"

"It's not much fun grinding it up to London—you'd be better to take the train from Lewes."

She nodded.

"But just do whatever you like; I want you to rest, relax, get strong again."

She smiled and rested her arm along the back of his seat. She wanted to hug him, squeeze him, but no, she knew, deep down, it was bad enough what she was doing to him already. She didn't want to open all the old wounds again; it wasn't fair to him, or to herself, she realized as an afterthought.

She sat down at the kitchen table and watched David opening a bottle of his own wine. Vendage padded into the room, looked around and padded out again.

"You really did what he said and didn't eat for six hours before?"

She nodded. "Not since breakfast. And you?"

"I usually only eat twice these days, breakfast and dinner." He opened the fridge. "Like an omelette?"

"I'm surprised you don't have your own hens; you always wanted to in London."

"That was for the novelty of keeping them in London; they wouldn't be such a novelty out here."

She smiled.

"Anyway, wine and eggs don't go that brilliantly together."

"Even if you were to bring the hens up on Chardonnay vines?"

He put a handful of eggs down on the draining board.

"What were you doing during the séance—the circle, David?"

He looked at her and went red. "Doing?"

"You seemed to be fiddling around a lot."

He grinned and patted his chest. Carefully, he removed his jacket to reveal a tape recorder strapped to his chest. "It's all there. We'll see which one of us is right." He unbuckled the straps, pressed the rewind button and put the machine down on the table in front of Alex. She heard the shuffling whirr and looked up at him.

"Do you think that was wise?"

"What do you mean?"

"It might have put the spirits off."

"No one said that tape recorders were banned."

"I think you might have told me."

"If I had, you wouldn't have allowed it." He filled her glass, then frowned as the wine settled and clarified. He raised the glass by the stem and turned it around under the light bulb. "Color's good," he said.

"Very clear."

"Not too watery, you don't think?"

"No."

"Just a hint of yellow, isn't there?" he said excitedly. "The last lot came out a bit greeny."

"What do you do? Put coloring in?"

He frowned at her disapprovingly. "Never; not me. It's the skins of the grapes that give the color: depends how long you leave them in the must."

Alex sniffed the wine. It had a tart, slightly oily smell at first, and she puckered her nose; on the second sniff, she detected a faint sweet scent of grapes.

"Still very young," he said defensively.

"You must be careful not to make them too sophisticated, David. The majority of people aren't connoisseurs—they just want something that tastes pleasant."

"Bugger the majority; they can have their Blue Nun and Hirondelle. God, you don't understand, do you? It's greatness I want; the great English wine."

She sipped and closed her eyes and swilled the wine noisily around in her mouth, hoping that was what he wanted. It was sharp and stung her palate, making her wince; then she swallowed and felt it slide down her throat; as it hit her empty churned-up stomach, she flinched. "Good," she said, opening her eyes again. "Good, but a little sharp."

There was a loud click from the tape recorder. David leaned down and pushed the play button. There was a cacophony of sound and he turned down the volume. "I didn't bother with all the prayers and stuff," he said.

She heard Vivaldi's "Spring," tinkling, pretty, sadness tinged with optimism. ". . . feel the grass soft and springy beneath your feet," said Ford's voice. ". . . You can see a white gate ahead of you . . ."

"I'll run through this bit," said David, pushing the fast-forward. Alex sat watching the machine, afraid. She heard the weird drumbeat, then the mournful hideous wail, like the cry of a vixen; slowly it dissolved into a ghastly choking sound. She felt a prickly cold seeping down her spine as she waited for the words to come.

But the choking faded into a quiet crackle of static.

Frowning, David twiddled with the knobs, turning the volume up and down, but there was nothing but crackle. He ran it forward a few seconds and tried again; still the static. He stared dubiously at Alex.

"What's the matter?" she said.

"I think he's jammed it."

"Jammed?"

"Your friend; I think he must have brought a jamming device with him."

"Why should he have done that?"

"For precisely this reason."

He advanced the tape on fast-forward and the crackle continued, snapping, popping, hissing. Then, suddenly, they heard high-pitched voices, like chipmunks. David slammed his thumb down on the stop button and wound the tape back a short way. Then he pushed the start button again:

"Are you all right, darling?" It was his own voice. He stared knowingly at Alex.

"I'm—OK," said Alex's voice.

There was a pause and then she heard Ford. "The spirits have gone."

David switched off the machine.

"Don't spirits and electricity have something to do with each other?" said Alex, trembling, conscious of sounding slightly ridiculous.

"A con, darling."

She shook her head.

"All a con."

She shook her head again. "I wish you were right."

Alex slept with the light on in the lumpy double bed. Throughout the night her waking thoughts and her sleeping thoughts were peppered with wails and screams and Fabian's voice. Every time she lapsed into a doze she woke again, hearing him close, right beside her. She felt the sweat pouring from her and sipped water from the glass on the bedside table, afraid in case she should finish it before dawn, too afraid to go out of the room for more.

The night outside was full of sounds; an owl's hoot echoed across the water. The medieval pond. She dozed and heard the sound of carp swimming, strange echoing bleeps, ripples of water, saw one larger than the rest racing to the surface, crashing upward between the weeds, and its face came out into the daylight, a hideous burned human face, and she screamed wildly.

There was a gentle knock on her door. "Darling, are you all right?"

She closed her eyes and tried to go back to sleep. "Yes, I'm fine, thank you."

She heard him wander around and felt safer. She heard him go downstairs, heard a tap in the kitchen, the clank of a door opening and closing. The noises outside were different now. Birds were singing; it was peaceful and she opened her eyes and saw that the morning had come.

David was already at work in his winery. She pushed open the heavy door and walked into the huge flint barn. How could he put up with the smell all day, the stale dull acidy smell of yesterday's party?

There was a massive block and tackle hanging from a central beam, above a huge plastic vat in the middle of the floor. David was standing on top of the vat, adjusting the rope.

"I'm ready," she shouted up to him.

"I'll come down!"

She watched him shin down the precarious ladder. "What are you doing?"

"A new vat—only had it delivered yesterday. I want to move it over slightly. You're welcome to stay tonight, too; stay for the weekend, at least."

"Thanks. Do you mind if I see how I feel?"

"If you're definitely coming back, you might as well take the Land Rover and leave it at the station."

"You'll be stranded if I don't."

He turned and gave his winery a loving glance, as if he could hardly bring himself to leave it, even for a few minutes. "I'll be OK."

"You're lucky," she said, "having something you're so passionate about."

"You have too."

She shook her head. "I've hardly been in the office since—" She shrugged. "I suppose there are times in life when certain things become unimportant."

"Do you think your clients would agree with you?"

She looked away and blushed guiltily.

23

It felt comfortable to be in the bustle of London, to travel on the underground amid the surge of the commuters. London had a good feeling on Fridays. You could see it in their faces, in their slightly brighter clothes and in the carryalls and suitcases some of them carried, stuffed with green boots and baggy pullovers.

She walked down Wimpole Street. It had been a long time since she had last been here, she thought, and nothing in the street seemed to have changed.

She could not remember Saffier's number, but she knew the house by heart; over a dozen visits before he'd hit the jackpot. Over a dozen visits, clutching David's hand, trying to ignore his sheepish expression and feeling the little plastic vial wedged inside her blouse between her breasts to keep it warm.

She could still remember which button to push, the second from the top. "R. Beard FRCS, MRCOG," it said. She scanned the rest of the names. D. B. Stewart, B. Kirkland, M. J. Sword-Daniels. No Saffier. She stood back and double-checked, then rang the bell marked Beard and waited.

There was a sharp buzz and the latch clicked open. She pushed the door and went in. The hallway was painted a brighter color, but otherwise was exactly as she remembered it. She climbed the stairs and pushed open the door.

A smart beanpole of a girl looked up from her desk and stared at her from under her neat straw fringe. "I wonder if you can help me," said Alex. "I'm looking for Dr. Saffier."

The girl opened her lips and spoke in an unintelligible voice that sounded like a distant racing car; she tossed her fringe, which promptly fell back into place.

"Pardon?" said Alex, leaning forward, trying to tune in her hearing.

"Years," she picked up. "Gosh," she also managed to decipher.

"Do you have any idea where he might have gone to?"

The door behind the girl opened and a gentle-looking man in a dark suit that was too large for him came out. "Have you forgotten my coffee, Lucy?" The girl turned around and made a sound like a bunch of racing cars negotiating a hairpin turn.

The man ran a huge hairy hand over the back of his head and stared at Alex with wide blue eyes. "Julian Saffier," he said in a soft, husky voice, and shook his head. "He left here a long time ago—I've been here fourteen years."

"Would you know if he's still alive?"

He raised his eyebrows. "Used to be in the press a lot —haven't seen anything about him for a long time. Infertility?" The man looked at her quizzically.

Alex nodded.

"I have a feeling he bought a place somewhere in Surrey, set up a clinic down there. I may be wrong."

"It's very important that I get in touch with him."

The man smiled. "I'll look him up in the Register for you." He went into his office and came out holding a heavy red book and leafed through it. "No, not in here." He looked thoughtful, then turned to his secretary. "See if you can get me Douglas Kerr."

"Yah, OK," Alex deciphered, and watched her tap

some numbers out on the phone as elegantly as if she were playing a piano. She looked around. There was a framed picture of a yacht under full sail on the wall; a large expensive yacht, with *Houdini* emblazoned on its side.

"Are you an old friend of, er?"

She shook her head. "I was a patient."

"Ah. Clever man, I believe."

"Are you in the same line?"

"Well—not really—I'm a conventional gynecologist."

Alex nodded. Several racing cars accelerated down a long straightaway and the beanpole thrust the receiver at him.

"Hello," he said, "Douglas? Bob Beard here. Yes, fine, and you? Yes, Felicity's fine too; had a hole-in-one last week, would you believe? Yes . . . at the Dyke. Listen, must be brief. Tell me, does the name 'Saffier' ring any bells?"

Alex watched him nervously.

"Julian Saffier?" He turned to Alex.

Alex nodded. "Yes."

"Yes, that's the one." He paused. "Yes, infertility . . . about eighty? Maybe; yes, I suppose he would. I just wondered, on the off-chance, whether you knew him? Similar line of work . . . yes, I thought you did." He paused. "No, no, nothing like that—just someone wants his address." Again he paused. "Guildford? Yes, I thought it was somewhere around there. Any idea who might have his address? I've tried the Register." He frowned. "Good Lord; was he? How long ago? I see, that would explain it. Listen, thanks very much, talk to you soon."

He turned to Alex, clasping his two huge hands together. "He was struck off the Medical Register, I'm afraid," he said, almost apologetically.

"Struck off?"

He nodded and smiled awkwardly.

What for? she wondered, feeling very uncomfortable. What for? "I don't suppose you know why?"

He shook his head. "I'm sorry, no, I don't." He looked at his watch.

"I've taken enough of your time, thank you."

He smiled. "You might find him in the phone book, or Directory Enquiries. But I don't know if he's still alive even."

She could hear the vacuuming from the street as she climbed out of the taxi. Mimsa's vacuuming always had a particularly frenetic quality to it, as if she were trying to catch the dust before it hid.

The house felt light, airy, safe. The smell of laundry, the grinding of the Hoover and the grunting of Mimsa reassured her. Normality. Perhaps David was right. Perhaps.

"Ah, Missy Eyetoya. Much messing in toilet. Is a no paper on wall."

"I know, Mimsa." She nodded. "There's a problem with dampness."

"I getty fixed for you. My humsbund, he good fixing toilet paper."

"Thanks, Mimsa, but don't worry." She recoiled at the memory of the last time Mimsa's husband had come to fix something. She took the small pile of mail on the hall table, went through to the drawing room, picked up the phone and dialed Directory Enquiries. "Mimsa!" she shouted. "What did you do with that rose that was on the side table?"

"I putty in garbage."

"Could you get it out?"

"Eh?"

"Enquiries. Which town, please?"

"Guildford," she said, sifting through the envelopes. One, a fat buff envelope, was postmarked Cambridge. Then she heard the operator's voice and her heart leapt. Saffier was listed. She scrawled the address on the back of the buff envelope, her hand shaking so much that she

could hardly read her writing. "Thank you," she said
weakly, and glanced at her watch. Eleven o'clock.

She tore open the envelope; there was a compliments
slip from the Bursar's Office and several letters addressed
to Fabian at Cambridge. She glanced through them: an
American Express bill, a bank statement, a large envelope
marked PRIZE DRAW PRIORITY and an airmail letter from
the United States, postmarked Boston, Mass. Fabian's
name and address were typed on the front by a dot matrix
printer. Inside was a letter, similarly typed, and two sheets
of computer printout.

The paper was headed in block capitals: NEW EN-
GLAND BUREAU. In smaller letters underneath were the
words: Office rentals—weekly, daily, hourly. Secretarial
services. Accommodation addresses. Confidentiality assured.

The letter read simply:

Dear Customer,
We have now dispatched the last postcard,
and await your further instructions. Please find
enclosed your statement for the quarter ending
March 31st, and your invoice for the next quarter should you wish to continue with our services.

Faithfully yours,
Melanie Hart,
Executive Administrator.

Alex felt herself going white. She read the letter
through again and began to shiver; the room was turning
cold and something seemed to be turning her inside out.
She looked at the statement. A list of mailing dates. She
studied the dates. They were all a fortnight apart. Something rang a bell about the timing, and she frowned. Two
weeks apart. She opened her handbag and pulled out Carrie's letter and the postcard. She studied the postmark

date. March fourteenth. She looked at the statement, ran her eyes down the list of dates. And saw it. March fourteenth. The asterisks, she realized; the asterisks in his diary; two weeks apart. Numbly, she took out her cigarette lighter, walked over to the fireplace, lit both the letters, the printouts, the postcard and the envelopes and dropped them into the grate.

"You want light fire? I light for you."

She turned and saw Mimsa standing in the doorway. "No, it's fine, thanks, Mimsa."

"Cold in 'ere. Sheesh, it cold." Mimsa rubbed her hands and frowned. Then she held her hands up to Alex. "Been in garbage cans, both garbage cans. Ees not there."

"Who's not there?"

"Rose."

"Rose?" Then she remembered and began trembling. "Not there? What do you mean? You said you put it there." She watched the last corner of the paper go brown, blacken and then erupt into flame.

Mimsa shrugged.

She felt her muscles tensing, saw Mimsa only dimly, as if she were staring at her from a long way away. "When did you put it there?"

Mimsa shrugged again. "I don know. Hour ago?"

"Have they been emptied today?"

"No, dey don come today."

"I'll have a look."

Mimsa followed her out, protesting. "What you want get dirty for? It no good rose, finish."

Alex turned the cans on their sides, and tipped the contents out on to the pavement. A wine bottle rolled past her and into the gutter. She knelt in the stench and the gunge, peering into the empty tins, shaking them, checking the cartons, poking her fingers through the fluff and the rotten fruit and the plastic bags and the dust. Mimsa watched her for a moment, as if she were mad, and then dutifully joined her. "Ees better get fresh roses."

Alex stared at the rubbish on the pavement and inside the dark empty cans.

"Maybe someone took," said Mimsa.

"Maybe," said Alex as she began to put everything back in. She looked around nervously at the quiet street. "Maybe."

24

Alex floored the accelerator, felt the clunk of the kickdown and heard the aggressive bellow of the engine as the Mercedes surged forward past the line of traffic. She cut sharply in front of a Granada, which hooted angrily at her. New England Bureau. The charred rose. She wondered if the world had finally gone completely mad. Perhaps we have moved nearer to the moon, she thought, or Jupiter, or perhaps they have moved nearer to us? What was going on? What the hell was going on?

She turned the Mercedes off the Guildford bypass on to the narrow country lane. The road became dark, shrouded with overhanging trees which blotted out the afternoon sun. It wound up a steep hill, under a stone bridge, then dropped down sharply into a small village, which seemed to consist of a couple of houses, a pub and a gas station.

A youth by the pumps gave her the directions and she found the entrance half a mile farther on, marked by a large white sign almost hidden by shrubbery, which read WITLEY GROVE. She drove through two tall stone pillars, each topped with a black cast-iron falcon, over a cattle grid and down a long potholed tarmac drive between two fenced-in fields.

Rounding a bend, she saw a sprawling Victorian Gothic mansion, wildly asymmetrical, with stark red-brick walls and steeply pitched half-timbered roofs, like witches' hats, she thought.

Several cars were parked in front of the house, and she was relieved by the sign of life. She climbed out of the Mercedes, feeling butterflies in her stomach, and glanced uncomfortably at the house. It was stark, bare, an institution, not a home. She had the distinct feeling someone in the house was watching her, but glancing around at the dark leaded windows, she could see no sign of movement.

There was a black Daimler limousine outside the front door, the chauffeur sitting inside with his hat off, reading a newspaper. As she walked past it and up the steps to an imposing porch, she wondered who it belonged to. Some Arab client? She stared nervously at the small brass plaque beside the huge oak door: WITLEY GROVE CLINIC. Was he still practicing—in spite of having been—? Would she be able to see him, now, today, right away—or was some starchy secretary going to make her wait three months for an appointment? God, he used to have a real gorgon in London. She tried to remember Saffier himself, but his face was fuzzy. She remembered how much she had depended on him; hope when there had been no hope, when the doctors had told her to forget it, they could never have children, adopt. His memory was coming clearer now: the voice, the faint hint of an accent; permanent suntan, the stiff handsome face, a good-looking mid-European; a smoothie, with a sparkle in his eyes and short neat hair that had been dyed to match his face-lift; the smart suits and the ties that were too loud with the white shoes; he always wore white shoes. In a showroom she wouldn't have bought a used car from him; in Wimpole Street he was her god.

They'd sent him a present when Fabian was born: a case of champagne. She wondered whether Saffier would remember, whether that would stand her in good stead twenty-one years later. Would he allow her to see the records? Did he still have them? She leaned forward to press the bell, but at that moment the front door swung open. She looked up and to her amazement saw Otto staring down at her.

She stood back, blinking, confused, and tried to focus. She saw the raked-back hair, the lacerations, the welts, the pockmarks, the hooked nose, the mocking eyes.

"Hello, Mrs. Hightower," he said. "Won't you come in?"

I'm going mad, she thought. I'm going mad. Somehow I have driven to Cambridge by mistake, come to Otto's room. She glanced over her shoulder. The driveway was still there, the chauffeur in the Daimler turning the page of his paper. Am I in the middle of Cambridge? Are there fields in the middle of Cambridge?

She followed him into the huge dark hallway and gazed in amazement at the ornate carved oak staircase with hideous gargoyles on the newel posts. No, this is not his room; surely his room didn't look like this? A suit of armor stood stiffly on guard at the bottom of the stairs and she looked away from the dark eye slits of the visor, shuddering; suits of armor had always frightened her.

"You didn't make the service," he said.

In a room nearby she could hear the hubbub of voices. She could smell sherry, cigar smoke. Was it a dining hall? Had she come to a Cambridge dining hall?

"The service?" she echoed blankly. Otto was looking smart, oddly smart, in a dark gray suit and black knitted tie. "Have you been to church, Otto?"

The eyes. *Oh, God, stop smiling, stop looking like that.*

A woman appeared in front of her, small, in a black-and-white outfit, carrying something. "Dry or medium, madam?"

"Dry, please, thank you."

Alex took the glass, felt its weight, felt it gone suddenly. There was a noise, a long way away, a distant tinkle.

"Don't worry, madam, I'll get a cloth, please take another one."

She took the glass, clutched it in both hands, holding it to her body as if it was a newborn infant.

Otto smiled, his knowing smile. "Of course. I thought you would be there."

Riddles. Riddles were everywhere; the world was becoming a riddle. She sipped the sherry, dry, nutty, it warmed her stomach; she sipped again and realized she had drained the glass. "I don't understand."

Stop smiling; for Christ's sake, stop smiling. Think; be rational; calm down. "I—I thought this was Dr. Saffier's house."

"It was." The answer came back straight at her, like a hard-hit ball.

"I—" She stared at her empty glass and smiled nervously. "I'm just a bit surprised to see you."

The two eyes stared knowingly, smiling, mocking.

She stumbled, trying to find the words, trying to put them together. "Do you know where—where—?" She looked at the black tie again. Black tie; dark suit. Black tie. "Where Dr. Saffier has moved to?"

The eyes smiled back, laughing at her, and his mouth joined them silently. "Yes, sure, of course."

"I—er—didn't know you knew him."

"I know lots of people, Mrs. Hightower."

"Another sherry, madam?"

She took the glass from the tray, holding it tightly, and put her empty one down.

"Would you like to meet some of them?"

"Some of whom?"

"Dr. Saffier's relatives. Dr. Saffier's friends."

"Well"—she shrugged, puzzled—"yes—I suppose—"

But he had already turned and was walking down the corridor toward the room full of people.

It was a huge paneled room, the walls hung with massive oil canvases, ancestral portraits, hunting scenes, naked cherubs, all larger than life, and she hesitated in the doorway, staring at the pall of smoke, the men in their sober, formal suits, the women in dark dresses, wearing hats, veils, the waitress with her tray of drinks weaving her way through them like a native in a jungle.

"This is Dr. Saffier's brother," said Otto, leading her to a group of three people.

A frail, elderly man, white haired, with a skinny, almost skeletal face, held out a hand heavily marked with liver spots. His grip was much firmer than she had expected. "How do you do?" he said in a cultured voice with the tiniest trace of a mid-European accent.

"Alex Hightower," she said, thinking how different from his brother he looked, yet how similar he sounded.

He nodded pensively, with a sad expression. "You were a friend of my brother's?"

Were? Were? She saw that he, too, was wearing a black tie; and the man next to him. "Er—no—I was a patient of his—a long time ago—he helped me a lot."

"He helped many people." He shook his head. "And then they did that to him."

She was conscious of the other man and the elderly woman standing beside them, whose conversation Otto had interrupted, and glanced at them. They both nodded and smiled.

"My sister," said Saffier's brother. "And my brother-in-law, Mr. and Mrs. Templeman."

"How do you do?" said Alex.

They both smiled again, but said nothing.

It was beginning to sink in. It was a wake. There had been a funeral. Whose? Whose? Panic was beginning to grip her. Not Saffier, please not.

"It was all a setup," said the woman indignantly, in an accent far more guttural than her brother's. "The Establishment wanted to get him, and that was their way of doing it."

"Absolutely." Saffier's brother nodded and looked at Alex again. "Never recovered from that, you know; that's what did it. I saw him last week—the day before he died.

Destroyed, you know; he was destroyed. A brilliant man, brilliant. He helped so many people. So many letters, you know, so many."

The three of them stood silently, nodding their heads sadly, like puppets. She felt trapped suddenly, cornered, and wanted to get away, outside, wanted air.

"He carried on working, of course," said his brother. "Wasn't allowed to call himself Doctor, anymore—but they couldn't stop his clinic. Do you know what he did? He bought a doctorate by mail order from America. By mail order! So he could call himself Doctor again; they couldn't stop him!" He chuckled and looked at his sister and brother-in-law, who smiled. Then he began nodding again.

Mail order, thought Alex. The New England Bureau. There was a heavy silence; Alex stared at them awkwardly, feeling like an imposter. "Would you excuse me just a moment?" she said, backing away from them. She turned and walked back into the hallway, feeling the tears streaming down her cheeks. She stopped and wiped her eyes, dabbing them gently.

"Leaving already?" She heard Otto's voice, and turned around.

"I have to get back to London."

He smiled, the knowing smile again, she thought. "With your business unfinished?"

She blushed. What did Otto know? How much did he know? What the hell was he doing here? "Are you related to Dr. Saffier, Otto?"

He stared at her silently, and she felt his eyes raking her, boring into her, and she felt herself turning cold, bitterly cold, as if she wasn't in the presence of a human being at all, but of a ghost. A menacing, evil ghost. "Just a pupil," he said, so quietly she was not sure what he had said.

"Pardon?"

"A pupil." The stare; the smile; saying, *You idiot, you fool, surely you knew that?*

"A pupil," she echoed helplessly.

"I wrote a thesis on him—on his work."

"I—I thought you were studying chemistry."

"Yes. His work was chemistry; chemistry and biology." He smiled and stared mockingly. "Biology and chemistry are very intertwined, Mrs. Hightower—I think you understand that more than most people."

She felt herself reddening even more. How much do you know, she wanted to say, feeling her embarrassment beginning to turn to anger; *how much do you know, you bastard?*

He turned away from her, looked around the hall and studied the suit of armor at the bottom of the stairs. Then suddenly he spun around and stared hard at her. "I know why you have come here."

She was startled by his words and by his movement; she tried to compose herself, tried to stare him back and show nothing. "Do you?" she said acidly. "Do you really?"

"Oh yes." He smiled. "I can help you. I know where the files are. I know where all of them are." He turned away again, and began to walk across the hall toward a corridor.

She felt the anger draining away and helplessness replacing it. Limply, she followed him.

The drawer slid open silently and stopped with a sharp metallic clang.

"Tell me, Otto," she said, "why was Dr. Saffier struck off?"

He stared inside the drawer at the files. "He interfered with young boys in a public lavatory."

She reeled as the words sank in, then watched his face, to see if it was a joke, something from his odd sense of humor. But there was nothing; a fact, that was all.

Did he interfere with you too, you bastard, she wondered.

"No," he said, turning to face her.

"Pardon?" she said, feeling a flush sweeping through her that was both cold and hot at the same time.

"No, he did not interfere with me."

She stared at him, feeling her head hot, so hot it was sweating. How? Had it shown in her face? Or had he picked it out of her mind?

She looked around the dank cellar, lit by one naked bulb, at the shadows that danced menacingly against the walls each time she or Otto moved, at the old green filing cabinets that stood in a row in the middle of the room like sentinels. What did they contain, she wondered. What secrets were there that should have been in the Public Records Office? What secrets were there that Saffier had not taken with him to the grave? This strange, brilliant man who interfered with boys. Public lavatories? Surely he had style? Surely he could have at least—? Frightened, she stared up at the stairs they had come down, up at the door at the top which Otto had closed and locked from the inside.

Otto ran his fingers through the files with a sharp clacking that echoed around, then stopped. He pulled out a slim green file and held it up to the light, studied it for a moment, then walked across the cellar floor to a metal table directly beneath the light bulb. He laid it down, nodded at her then stood back.

Holding her breath, Alex walked over to the table and looked down; she saw the name typed on the index tab: "Hightower, Mrs. A." Nervously she lifted the flap. There was a sheaf of graph paper and several index cards held together with a paper clip.

She felt her face go red as she looked at the graphs and remembered. Temperature charts, with the likeliest days of each month circled in black. God, what they'd gone through. She looked at the top index card. Her date

of birth. David's date of birth. His sperm count. Then a list
of dates, with tiny illegible handwriting in faded ink beside
each one. Her heart began to sink. Nothing. There was
nothing here. Nothing that was going to help.

And then she saw it.

She began to tremble as she read, and then re-read,
the tiny slanting handwriting beneath the date on the last
card: "J. T. Bosley."

She heard again the echo of the sharp nasal voice. *My
name is John Bosley. I'm the boy's father.*

She tried to hold the card, but her hand was shaking
wildly. She looked around and saw strange shapes flickering in the shadows, flickering among the filing cabinets and
along the walls that seemed to stretch away into the dark
forever.

She saw Otto's face; the smile. The smile. Otto walked
to another filing cabinet, opened the drawer, pulled out
another file, carried it to the table as if it were a priceless
jewel and laid it down. Again he stood back and folded his
arms behind him.

The tab was marked simply: "Donors."

Inside was a thick sheaf of computer printouts.
Names in alphabetical order, pages and pages. On the
fourth page she found it: "Bosley. John Terence. Guy's
Hospital, Lon. Date of Birth: 27/4/46." He would have
been twenty-one then, she thought. It was followed by several lines of minute detail: the color and texture of his hair,
size of forehead, color of eyes, exact length and shape of
his nose, mouth, chin, teeth, neck, his build. She shivered.
It could have been a description of Fabian.

At the end of his section were the words "Donations
used. 1 time. Ref. Hightower, Mrs. A."

She turned and looked at Otto.

"Have you seen enough?" he said.

"Is there any more?" she said weakly, trembling.

He smiled again; that hideous knowing smile; the
mocking eyes. "Not down here."

"So where?"

"That depends on what you want to know."

"Don't play games with me, please, Otto."

"I don't play games."

"Who was John Bosley? What was he like? How did he die?"

"He's a doctor. But I don't think he died."

Alex shuddered as the snarling in the séance came back. Bosley's words. *Don't let the little bastard . . .* "Yes; he's dead; I know that."

Otto looked at her scornfully and shook his head. "He didn't die."

"How do you know?" she demanded, feeling her temper flaring.

"I already told you. I know a lot of things."

"Well this is one that you don't."

He smiled. "Would you like his address?"

She looked, hesitantly. Something; there was something in the way he spoke. "What is it?"

"It's easy to remember. Dover Ward, Kent House, Broadmoor."

"He's a staff doctor there?"

"Oh no, Mrs. Hightower." Otto smiled. "He's an inmate."

The words sank in slowly. Inmate. Inmate. She wanted to escape from here, be somewhere, anywhere, alone. She wanted to be away from the eyes, from the smile, from the pleasure that was in that smile. Inmate. Public lavatories. What had Saffier been up to? How much damage had he done, to her, to others? Christ, what the hell had he been playing at? Impregnating her with the sperm from a criminal lunatic. "What—why—was—is he there, Otto?"

Otto shrugged. "Murder; I don't remember how many."

"Who—how—?" She wanted to sit down, wanted

desperately to sit; she leaned against the table, let it take her weight, tried to think clearly. "Who did he murder?"

Otto shrugged, and smiled. "Women."

"Did Fabian know?" She stared at the floor.

"Yes."

"You told him?"

"A son has a right to know who his parents are."

She felt a flash of rage, but bit her lip, somehow contained it.

"I showed him the file."

Alex glared at Otto. "And you thought you were being frightfully clever?"

"Your son was kind to his father, Mrs. Hightower. Kinder than you will ever know."

What did he mean? A knife. It was as if he had a knife inside her and kept on twisting it. "He was a very kind boy," she said helplessly.

Otto glanced up at the door and smiled again. "Shall we go back and join the party?"

25

She drove up the hill through the messy High Street of the village; an uneasy blend of neat Victorian red-brick houses and modern urban sprawl. Plenty of money. How did they feel, she wondered, living here, so close?

The sign was like any other road sign, small, unobtrusive: BROADMOOR. 1/2 MILE.

She felt her pulse racing as she turned off into a much steeper road. It did not feel right, it was too quiet, too residential. She wondered whether she had misread the direction. She saw an elderly man weeding the front garden of his bungalow and she stopped the Mercedes. Then she hesitated for a moment, embarrassed suddenly, embarrassed to ask the way, embarrassed to admit to a stranger that she was going there.

"Is this the right road for Broadmoor?"

"Straight up; you'll see the sign."

She felt herself blushing under his gaze; what did he think her business was? Was there something wrong in going there? In merely being even associated with the place?

The sign rose up from behind a tall hedgerow. BROADMOOR HOSPITAL. PRIVATE. Gray with black and red lettering. She turned into a road with neatly trimmed grass verges. PRIVATE ROAD PATROLLED BY WARDENS.

A few hundred yards farther up the hill, she rounded a corner, and gasped. Christ. The massive buttressed red-brick wall and the huge Victorian red-brick institution rising up behind it, with the barred windows and the steep slate roof. More unfolded; it seemed to go on forever. A huge red-brick tower with guard rails, a weather vane and a massive radio aerial at the top and the wall, stretching away out of sight. The wall. She shivered. Bosley was in there somewhere. The father of her child.

There was a maze of roads and signs and triangles of neatly mown grass in front of her. STAFF CLUB, ACCESS TO MAIN GATE FOR COLLECTIONS, DELIVERIES & EMERGENCIES ONLY, CRICKET GROUND. Signs. Everywhere. Everything labeled. Was John Bosley labeled too? UPPER BROADMOOR ROAD, TERRACE, CHAPLAIN'S HILL, DRIVE CAREFULLY, SPEED CONTROLLED RAMPS. She looked around, bewildered, for the road name she had been given. Then she saw it, right beside her. Kentigern Road.

She followed along and it dipped down away from the wall, past a sloping lawn with two fir trees and a small statue of a winged angel. Salvation, she thought, staring at it, puzzled. Then she saw the house, Redwoods. A sizable modern brick house, standing back from the road behind another grass triangle, with a parking area in front of it.

The door opened before she had got out of her car and the chaplain stepped out, a sturdy middle-aged man with graying hair and a kindly face; he was dressed in conventional black, with a white Roman collar, and wore sandals, she noticed. His glasses were turning dark in the sunlight, blotting out his eyes.

"Mrs. Hightower?"

She nodded and his hand enveloped hers, warm, firm, comforting.

"You found it all right?"

"Thank you."

He looked at his watch. "I'm afraid we will have to be

brief—unfortunately one of our patients has had a sudden family bereavement and I must—"

"Of course," she said. "It's kind of you to see me at such short notice."

He led her through into a large drawing room with a pink carpet and pointed her to a sofa. He sat down in an armchair and put his feet up on a pink ottoman. She looked around the room. Everything was in soft pinks and browns; the colors were unobtrusive, like the furniture, but did not quite blend. The room felt oddly bare to Alex, lacking bits and pieces, ornaments, as if it had recently been burgled. There was a solitary Coalport statuette on the mantelpiece, a young courting couple, a framed photograph of a schoolboy on the wall and a television; but little else, nothing to dominate, nothing to distract from the presence of the man in the armchair opposite her. She wrung her hands together. "It's very kind of you to see me," she repeated.

He smiled benignly. "Not at all." He paused. "John Bosley?"

She nodded.

"Know him well."

"He really is still alive, is he?"

There was a strange flicker across his face. "He was yesterday, yes. Very much so."

"I wasn't sure—that was all."

"Oh yes, very much alive." He stood up. "I've just remembered—one moment." He went out of the room and she stared around again, at the television, then back at the statuette on the mantelpiece. Two young things from another century, elegant, in love, carefree. Carefree. Was there such a place, she wondered.

"I brought this—just to make sure." He walked back into the room and handed her a small black-and-white photograph.

She stared down. The photograph was shaking in her hands, shaking so much it was almost a blur. She saw a double portrait, one face-on, the other in profile, with a row of numbers printed beneath, a pale gaunt face; a shock of fair hair. And the eyes. The eyes. "Oh my God," she mouthed. "Fabian. It's just so incredibly like him." The photograph fell out of her hands into her lap. She tried to pick it up, but it danced in her trembling fingers then flipped on to the floor. She leaned over, feeling sick suddenly, violently sick, and put her hand in front of her mouth.

She breathed deeply and it passed. Then she looked at the chaplain again. He was back in his chair, smiling gently.

"Very difficult," he said gently. "Very difficult."

"The likeness," she said. "It's incredible."

He nodded; there was something about his expression that she thought was odd.

"You've never seen him before?"

She shook her head.

"Forgive me—I don't quite understand. You say he's the father of your—er—son?"

She nodded.

"But you've never seen him?"

She felt herself going red. "My husband was—er—is —infertile. I was inseminated by semen from a donor— John Bosley was the donor. It was all done through a specialist in London."

He nodded, frowning. "So you're not, strictly speaking, related?" He paused. "Well, I suppose you must be; an interesting one, that." He smiled, happier.

"Would it be possible to see him?"

"I'd have to get the governor's consent."

"I'd like to see him."

He smiled. "I don't know." He shook his head. "It may be opening a whole can of worms that's not good for his treatment. I can put your request forward—but I'm not optimistic. He's making progress, you see, but the treatment of schizophrenia is a very slow and difficult business, and he has, of course, already had a major setback."

"Am I allowed to know why he's here?"

He stood up again. "I brought the file—I think it's probably quite irregular—but under the circumstances—I'm sure we can make an exception."

She pushed the sheaf of stiff typewritten sheets back into the yellow envelope and wound the string back around the fastener.

"Oh—before you do that, we'd better put the photograph back."

"Photograph," she said mechanically. The blood was drained out of her and she felt exhausted. She unwound the string again, grateful to have something to do for a moment, to occupy her mind, anything. "Photograph," she said again.

"Mrs. Hightower, there's nowhere in the Bible," he said gently, "nowhere where it says that a person has to be a good person to be of value."

She stared at him blankly, seeing only the stark paper and the clinical black typing, and nodded, trying to fight back the tears. "If someone is mad," she said falteringly, feeling a tear running down her cheek, "if someone is mad, can he be absolved of blame?"

"God laid down the Ten Commandments. We cannot break them without responsibility. There is sin and there is responsibility, even in the mentally ill. Psychiatrists cannot wipe a slate clean. I cannot either." He smiled again and crossed his legs. "A person who has committed a crime when ill can only become better when he becomes aware of what he had done, when he can say, 'I was ill then, but now I feel I need to be forgiven.'"

"Has John Bosley said that?"

He shook his head. "I'm afraid he's confused, terribly confused."

"It seems very cruel," she said.

"Cruel?"

"Cruel of God to make that condition."

"We take the view, in the Church of England, that evil will not enter a person who will not receive it." He smiled. "Evil must be invited in—Satan must be invited by that person into his life. Satan will not come on his own."

She looked at him, chilled. "You're saying that John Bosley, in spite of his madness, is fundamentally evil?"

He lifted his arms, slowly, with a sad bemused expression on his face. "Perhaps not in spite of his madness—we must consider the possibility that the mental problems of someone who has committed a terrible crime are a symptom of their evil."

She shuddered. There was a long silence and she sensed him looking at his watch.

"Can schizophrenia be passed on—inherited?"

"There is a lot of evidence, yes. The Schizophrenics Society could give you information—they have been making some very interesting discoveries."

"So my son—?"

"It's a possibility to be aware of." He looked at his watch again. "Perhaps you could come back and we can have a longer chat?"

"Thank you. I'd like that."

He stood up and straightened his shirt.

"You said that there had been a setback in his treatment—what was that?"

His face reddened and he touched his hands together awkwardly. "Just a foolish incident," he said. "Very foolish."

"What happened? Did it have anything to do with my son?"

He looked again at his watch. "Nothing. It was nothing." He paused. "Perhaps you should know. Next time—I'll tell you next time—I'll have to think about it."

She stared. What was it? What the hell was it?

"You'll be able to find your way out all right? Back to the main road? Just turn right."

"Thank you, Father—er—Reverend—er—" she said.

He smiled. "Call me. I'm very busy for the next few weeks—perhaps in June sometime?"

"Thank you," she said. "You've been very kind." But his mind was somewhere else, somewhere a long way away.

26

"He wouldn't let me keep the photo."

Phillip Main leaned back with his feet on his desk. He crossed his legs, uncrossed them, and ground his heels into the pile of papers, then raised himself up on his elbows and shifted his weight in the armchair. He stared pensively at the phone. "Extraordinary, this man Bosley. Just left her?"

"Apparently."

"Chained her up in a cellar?"

Alex nodded, white-faced.

"And left her?"

"Yes."

"Without telling anyone?"

She said nothing.

"Did he have a grudge—against women?"

Alex turned her cigarette over in her fingers. "She'd jilted him."

"Extraordinary. Quite extraordinary. A doctor; must be an intelligent chap—you expect this sort of—in—" He opened his hands out. "People do extraordinary things."

"Why, Philip?"

The room darkened suddenly and she heard a spatter of rain outside. She thought of a cold cellar, a woman, chained, sitting, whimpering, shivering, and heard the drip of water. She shuddered.

Main pushed a cigarette through the fronds of his mustache and let it hang there, unlit. "What gave you the idea?"

"The idea?"

"To see the chaplain?"

She shrugged. "I don't know. I rang up Broadmoor to see if I could see Bosley." She smiled suddenly, weakly. "When they answered they sounded just like a hotel."

"And they wouldn't let you?"

"You have to write to the Board of Governors. I asked if there was anyone I could speak to." She shrugged. "They put me through to the chaplain."

Alex stared around the chaotic study, at Black, asleep on the sofa. His desk, worktable, filing cabinets, military chest and almost every inch of floor space were covered in piles of paper. An ancient electric typewriter was buried under it, and so were the printer, screen and keyboard of his computer. It was everywhere, like snow. "It reminds me of your car," she said.

"My car?"

"Your study. How do you work in here?"

"I manage."

She smiled. "I don't think I've ever been in one of my authors' studies before. It's quite an insight."

He looked around, nodding. "You haven't been in the office much."

"Are you keeping tabs on me?"

"No, good Lord, no. I think it's good that you're staying down with David."

"He's trying to keep me sane."

He fumbled with a box of matches. "Will you—" He sounded embarrassed. "Will you get back together?"

She shook her head.

He struck a match and lit his cigarette, looking at her quizzically. She blushed.

"He's being very kind to me; he has a lot of strength. I suppose I need him at the moment, and I wish I didn't; I don't want to hurt him again." She paused. "He deserves someone nicer than me."

"Gosh, don't underestimate yourself, girl."

She felt weepy and closed her eyes tightly for a moment, nodding her head. "I'm so frightened, Philip."

"What's David's view?"

She stared out through the window at the grimy rear wall of the house behind. "He wants me to see a psychiatrist."

Main shook his head. "No," he said. "Gosh, no."

"What do you think I should do? You're so full of contradictions, aren't you. I need help, Philip. I must have help." She looked at him again. "You said, last time we spoke, that sometimes spirits try to come back because they have unfinished business."

"It's a theory. Just a theory."

"Everything's just a bloody theory to you."

He looked hurt and stared around the room, helplessly.

"I'm sorry," she said. "I didn't mean to get angry. But all you ever do is give me theories; all everyone does is give me damned theories. Last night I had three hours of David's theory, how I'm emotionally disturbed, in need of psychiatric help. I had the curate's theory, a few days ago, that I'm in need of pastoral help. I have Morgan Ford's theory, about dark forces of evil. And I have you, going on about genes, what is it? That we are prisoners of our genes?" She leaned forward in the hard chair. "The chaplain talked about genes, too; that schizophrenia could be passed on. Ford talked about genes as well. He said they were important to the spirit world; something about them being the blueprint for character."

Main nodded slowly. "They are."

The phone rang. Main leaned over and picked up the receiver. "Hello?" he said thoughtfully.

Alex watched him. She felt safe here, safe with his clouds of smoke and his crumpled jacket and his solid furniture. Knowledge; he knew things, knew so much, had the answers to many mysteries. He was comfortable with life.

Except. She thought with a shudder of the last time he had sat in her drawing room.

He picked up a pen and scribbled on the back of the nearest sheet of paper. "Good Lord." He paused, then continued scribbling for a long time. "Right," he said finally. "Terrific. See you." He hung up and looked at Alex. There was something in his eyes, a heavy weight, hanging there awkwardly. "That was my—er—chum, the prison psychiatrist."

"Yes?"

He smoothed out his mustache with his fingers. "The one who used to work in Broadmoor."

"He came back quickly."

Main picked up the sheet of paper and looked at it, then peered at her with a worried expression.

"Did the chaplain say anything to you about"—he hesitated—"about Fabian visiting?"

She went white and shook her head. "Nothing, except—" She paused. "He was going to tell me about something, but didn't. He seemed to change his mind; it might have been because we were short of time—but I don't think so. I don't even know when he went."

"About a year ago. Sometime in early May, he thinks. There was quite a to-do, apparently." He crushed out his cigarette and shook another one out of the pack. "Quite a to-do." He glanced down at his notes, then struck a match and lit his cigarette.

She stared at his two black boots on the desk, and noticed the heels were scuffed down at the back.

"While the chaplain was away on holiday apparently. They have someone filling in—the vicar of Sandhurst—he is cleared for security—and his curates—" He turned his cigarette over in his hand. "Fabian got hold of some theology student, managed to pass him and some other chap off as curates from Sandhurst and got inside." He looked across at her.

She stared back at him puzzled. "Why?"

"They carried out an exorcism."

The room darkened suddenly and she felt afraid. "And what happened?"

"It wasn't discovered until too late."

"Too late?"

He shrugged.

"Don't you think," she said slowly, "that Fabian probably meant it kindly? That he thought he was doing the right thing. Wouldn't you try to help your father?"

The room was becoming cold, bitterly cold, and she could feel drafts all around her.

Black sat up on the sofa and gave a low rumbling growl.

Main drew hard on his cigarette.

She stared at him, afraid, terribly afraid. "He was a kind boy; I'm sure he would have tried to help him." She thought of a cold dark cellar, a woman, chained, sitting, whimpering, shivering, and heard the drip of water. "Who was there?"

"Fabian, the theology student chap called Andrew Castle and another chap from Cambridge, not a priest at all"—Philip leaned across to study his notes—"someone called Otto von Essenberg."

The room seemed to slip sideways. "Of course," she said bitterly, "Otto. Fabian followed him around like a lamb." She shook her head. "What happens at exorcisms?"

"They try to drive the demons—the evil spirits—out of the person."

"It sounds slightly barbaric."

"It is barbaric," he said, then raised his eyebrows mysteriously. "But sometimes the old remedies are best."

"Are you serious?"

"There is evidence, girl, it does seem to have worked sometimes."

"Did it work on Bosley?"

He glanced at his scrawled notes. "His personality changed—and remained changed. He was aggressive and cruel before—then he became very docile, confused."

"Isn't that his schizophrenia?"

He drew deeply again on his cigarette and said nothing.

"Don't you think, Philip?" she insisted. "Surely that could have been part of his condition?"

"Perhaps," he said distantly.

She shivered, and saw Philip watching her with a worried frown, saw him toy with his mustache. "I'm frightened, Philip." She closed her eyes. "Oh, God, Philip, help me."

"I did suggest that you leave it alone."

"No." She shook her head violently. "No!"

"It would have been better."

She looked up at him. "It's easy to say that. He's not your son."

Main stood up and laid his hand gently on her shoulder. "You'll be all right, girl, don't worry. Would you like some coffee?"

She nodded and closed her eyes; she heard him walk out into the hall and listened to the steady drip of the rain, echoing around the room, around her head, around a dark empty chamber.

"It's hot."

She looked up and took the mug carefully. A car hooted outside. Normality; there was a real world somewhere out there, with ordinary people doing ordinary things. She wanted to be out there among them.

"Does the date May 4 mean anything, Philip?"

"May 4?"

"Yes."

He shook his head.

"Do they have dates in the—the spirit world—days of the week, months, years—the same as we have?"

"I—" He paused. "I think the perspective on time is different. No one knows."

"What do you mean, different?"

"We have a clear image, of the past, the present, the future. Possibly, in the spirit world, these are—transcended."

"They can move backward and forward in time?"

He shrugged.

"See events that have not yet happened?"

"There are theories."

She sipped her coffee. "What am I going to do?" she said.

"Go away, have a holiday."

"You're not even trying to understand."

He smiled kindly. "I am, believe me."

"Nothing will change if I go away; it'll all be the same when I come back." She felt the fear and her helplessness overwhelm her.

He sank back down into the armchair. "Oh dear, girl," he said. "Oh dear."

She fumbled for her handkerchief as the tears streamed down her cheek, then she sniffed and blew her nose. "Otto said that Saffier didn't know."

"Didn't know?" said Philip, puzzled. "Didn't know what?"

"About Bosley. About his condition. Thought he was just a normal healthy student. None of this—it didn't happen until years after."

"How did he find out?"

"It was Otto who—" She paused suddenly, as if a curtain had come down inside her mind. "It was Otto," she repeated, the words sounding like an echo. "I—er— Bosley began dabbling—in the occult—after medical school. Looking into alternative medicine—became involved in black magic—Otto—I—told me—I—er—" But she had forgotten suddenly what she was going to say.

It seemed that the temperature in the room dropped

even further. She sipped her coffee and sniffed again. Philip lit another cigarette and snorted the smoke through his nostrils. She watched the steam rise from her coffee.

"If an exorcism is successful, Philip, what happens to the spirit—the demon—whatever it is that's driven out?" She shuddered as a cold chill eddied through her.

He tested his coffee with his finger and stared thoughtfully at it. "It has to find a new host."

"Someone with the same genetic makeup?"

"It's a possibility." He tested his coffee again. "There's a scene in the Bible—Jesus casting out devils—sent them into swine."

"I didn't see any pigs at Broadmoor."

He stared at her and she felt her face reddening; she felt his gaze penetrating through, inside, deep into the innermost sanctum of her mind. He understood.

"Perhaps, girl," he said.

"It might explain a lot of things, Philip."

"Perhaps," he said. "It's a job to know."

"Everything's a bloody job to know."

He nodded, looking worried again. "You should be careful of your medium," he said suddenly.

She looked at him. "Why?"

"Sometimes they can be dangerous."

She tried to read his face, but it was impossible. "What do you mean, dangerous?"

"Having a go at"—he paused—"at things even they are not sure about."

She blew her nose and sniffed again. "You know, don't you, Philip? You know it all."

He paused for a long time before answering. "No, I don't know." He shook his head slowly from side to side, then he stood up and walked over to his bookshelves and stared at the titles. "No, good Lord no, far from it."

There was a long silence. "Philip," she said finally, "last time we spoke, you said that sometimes spirits try to come back"—she felt acutely self-conscious saying the words—"because they have unfinished business. How would they do that?"

He spoke softly, almost apologetically. "The spiritualist view is that—that they would have to come back through someone."

"Through someone?"

"Someone carnate. Living."

"Possess them?"

Main nodded. "Discarnate spirits have no energy."

"So they would use a human's energy?"

"That is the spiritualist view."

"A host?"

He nodded.

"The same as a spirit that has been exorcised?"

He nodded again warily.

"How would they find someone?" she said, sensing a sudden dryness in her throat.

He shrugged. "The spirit would look for someone with a weakness."

"What do you mean, weakness?"

"Unguarded." He pushed his cigarette into his mouth and puffed furiously on it, then inhaled the smoke sharply with a hiss. She looked at him and saw that he was shaking, deeply distressed.

"Evil spirits are cunning. They can con people."

"Con?"

"It's been known."

"What sort of con?"

"Often they pretend to be someone else."

She felt the single shiver roller-coaster through her, like a tidal wave; it nearly swept her out of her chair.

"They pick on someone who is down; bereaved people make the easiest targets of all."

Stop looking at me, she thought; please stop looking at me like that. "No," she said, shaking her head. "No."

"They can be very clever. Far more clever than it is possible to imagine."

She shook her head. "How can you stop them?" she said, her voice barely even a whisper.

"As a scientist?" he said.

She shook her head. "No," she said, and her voice became bolder. "As a person honest with himself."

He looked at her, then away, down at the ground, and shifted his weight, embarrassed. He crushed out his cigarette and pulled out a fresh pack from under a deep layer of paper.

"There has only been one effective way through the ages." He looked at her, then turned his attention to opening the cigarette pack. "The power of prayer."

He looked relieved suddenly, she thought, as if he had overcome some deep inner conflict to get the words out.

"Prayer?"

"Hrrr."

"What sort of prayer?"

His face went red and he stared at the ground as if reading from a prompter's script. "Exorcism."

She began to shiver violently; the temperature in the room seemed to have dropped even further. "Is it cold in here?"

There was no answer.

"Philip?" She felt her voice quavering. "Philip?" She looked wildly from side to side then spun around; he was standing behind her, a gentle worried look in his eyes. "Is it cold in here?"

"I'll shut the window."

"No." She did not want it to be shut, did not want the outside world excluded. "Perhaps I've just got a chill."

She felt his strong hands squeeze her shoulders and she tried to stop shaking, but she couldn't. "I would do anything in the world to stop this nightmare."

"Then see a priest," he said quietly, squeezing her shoulders again. "It would be best for both of us."

27

She drove up the narrow road behind the Chelsea football ground, into a sprawling modern housing estate, and leaned over toward the passenger window, trying to read the numbers. She hoped he wouldn't mind being disturbed at lunchtime.

Number 38, like all the rest, was a small house with a prim front garden, and she was slightly embarrassed about parking the Mercedes outside. She walked down the short path and rang the doorbell. Please be in, she thought, please be in.

The curate came to the door in clean, neatly pressed jeans and an old pullover, holding a piece of Lego in his hand. He looked younger than she remembered.

"Hello," she said tentatively, then fumbled, wondering what to call him. Reverend? Mr.?

"John Allsop," he said helpfully, sensing her difficulty, and stared at her, trying to place her. There was a slight twitch of his right eye. "Mrs. Hightower, isn't it?"

She nodded.

"How nice to see you. How are you?"

The enthusiasm of his greeting stumped her and she was lost for words for a moment. "I'm fine," she said, nodding, then wondered why she had said that.

"Good." He rocked from foot to foot and stared at the piece of Lego in his hand; she wondered if he was about to throw it in the air, like a juggler. "Good," he said again.

"I wondered if it would be possible to have a word?"

"Of course, come in."

She followed him into the narrow hallway. The sitting room floor was covered in Lego bricks, with what looked like a half-built crane in their midst.

He smiled apologetically. "Dreadful stuff this, far too complicated for me. Gave it to my son for his birthday. Ever tried it?"

She shook her head. "Looks very good."

"I'm afraid that was my son, not me."

They went into a tiny study at the rear of the house and he pointed her to the one armchair. She sat down, looking around. The room was blandly furnished, and in contrast to Philip's study, immaculately tidy. There was a small homemade bookshelf, filled with religious reference books which looked as if they were dusted every day, and several fossils and fragments of pottery on a mantelpiece above an electric fire.

"Is that your hobby, archaeology?" she said.

"Yes." His face became animated. "Those are all from digs I've been on."

"Interesting," she said, hoping her voice reciprocated some measure of enthusiasm.

"How are you getting on? It was about ten days ago that I came to see you, wasn't it?"

She nodded. "Not very well, I'm afraid."

"It's a difficult time this. He was your only child, wasn't he?"

"Yes."

"And you have marriage difficulties too, I believe?"

"Yes."

"Sometimes," he said gently, "this sort of thing can bring people closer together."

She shook her head and smiled sadly. "We have a good relationship, but I'm afraid we won't ever get back together." She remembered suddenly that Allsop had told her that his own wife had died recently, and Alex blushed, not wanting to make him feel ill at ease. "How are you coping, bringing up your son?"

"All right," he said, and a sad look came across his face. "People think it must be easier for people like me, in the clergy, to cope with things; but we go through the same feelings too."

"You have your faith, though."

He smiled again. "That gets sorely tested at times. Especially when your son eats your sermon."

She grinned. "How is your book going?"

"Ah, you remembered. Slowly, I'm afraid."

"That's what my clients always say."

"It's difficult, applying oneself. I'm—ah—digressing." He looked at her questioningly.

"I don't know quite where to begin." She clasped her hands together and interlocked her fingers. "There are some very strange things that have been happening, and I'm frightened."

His eye twitched again. "What sort of things?"

"I'm not quite sure how to describe them. Weird things, things that there's not really any explanation for."

"Do you mean perhaps that your mind is playing tricks?"

"No, not tricks."

"Bereavement causes all sorts of tricks to be played on the mind."

She shook her head. "These aren't tricks. Really they aren't. I'm not a nervous person; I don't have a wild imagination." She looked at him and knotted her fingers even tighter. "There are some very strange things happening in my house, and I'm not the only one who thinks that." She looked at him and wished he was older; he looked so young, so green, she thought. "I've been advised"—she paused again, feeling slightly foolish under his concerned gaze—"that I ought to bring in an exorcist."

His eyes widened and she felt him staring at her for a long time.

"An exorcist?"

"You probably think I'm mad."

"No, I don't think that at all. But I think we should talk about these things that are frightening you, see if we can find a reason for them"—he paused—"and perhaps look at some alternative solutions."

"Would it be possible, do you think, for us to talk at my house?"

He looked hesitant. "Of course, if that would be easier for you. I'll have a look in my diary."

"Is there any chance that you could come now?"

He frowned at his watch. "I have to pick up my son from school at four." He looked at her again and his face mirrored her seriousness. "Yes, that would be all right."

She saw a parking spot a short way down from her house and slowed down.

"Very nice car," he said.

"It's only an old one," she said, and instantly regretted the patronizing tone of her voice. "Over twenty years old."

"I'm afraid the Church doesn't run to Mercedes cars."

She detected the note of envy. "They're a bit silly really. Very expensive to service."

"We all need our compensations," he said.

She looked at him; what were his compensations, she wondered. God? The fossils?

Mimsa had gone, leaving behind one of her usual barely decipherable notes. She switched the kettle on then went out into the hallway. The curate was pacing around the drawing room, looking up at the ceiling, frowning.

"White or black?"

"White, without, please."

She took the coffee in. "Must just pop to the loo. There's one just under the stairs, if you—?"

"Ah." He nodded politely.

As she climbed the stairs she realized that the house felt curiously hot, muggy, as if the heating had been left on all day. It felt even hotter upstairs. She tested the radiator on the landing; it was stone cold. She looked around uncomfortably, then went into her bedroom and walked into her bathroom. It felt like a sauna.

She stood at the basin washing her hands and examined her face in the mirror. It was wet with perspiration. She pressed her hand against her forehead, but it was cold, almost icily cold, she thought, and wondered if she was coming down with the flu. She dabbed her face gently with a towel, careful not to smudge her makeup, closed her eyes and patted the lids.

There was a sudden cold blast of air, as if a freezer door had opened, and she felt the presence of someone watching her. She opened her eyes slowly and looked in the mirror.

Fabian was standing, motionless, right behind her.

She was conscious of a terrible jerk inside her chest, as if she had pushed a finger into an electrical socket, and then her body was wracked with pins and needles, hurting her so much she wanted to cry out in pain.

As she turned around to face him she realized there was no air in the room. She could not breathe.

He stood there, wearing a white shirt and his favorite baggy sweater, solid, so solid it seemed she could reach out and touch him.

But there was no air.

He was smiling a strange unfamiliar wry smile, and there was something in the dark of his eyes that was mocking her, something she had never seen before in her son, something that was ringing a terrible bell.

She felt herself beginning to panic. The pain of the

pins and needles was unbearable; she was shaking, her lungs ached, and she felt violently sick.

Tricks of your mind, she heard the curate's voice echo. Tricks of your mind.

She swayed, beginning to black out, pushed her trembling hands out behind her and clutched the basin.

And then he was gone.

She staggered into her bedroom, gasping, looking wildly around. She ran, tripping down the stairs, and stood in the hallway gulping air, shivering and itching all over. She went through into the drawing room. Allsop was staring at his coffee with intense concentration. He looked up uneasily as she came in. "I thought you said you had only one son."

"Eh?" She blinked at him, unable to speak.

"The young man who just went up the stairs."

Why was he smiling? What did he think was so funny? Then she realized it wasn't a smile at all but his nervous twitch.

"Fair-haired?" she gulped.

"Yes," he said quietly.

"In a baggy sort of sweater?"

Again he nodded.

She clutched the arm of a chair for support, unable to stand anymore, sat down and closed her eyes. Then she opened them and stared at him again. "I don't have another son. That was Fabian."

She heard a sharp clack, followed by another, as his cup rattled in the saucer. She saw the spoon vibrating in his hand, rattling against the side of the cup as if he were playing a tiny musical instrument, and she saw the coffee slopping over the side.

"I see," he said finally, his right eye opening and closing. With great difficulty he put the cup and saucer down and looked around the room, clearly badly shaken, trying to compose himself. "Is that what you meant?"

Alex felt something soft and realized she was still

holding the towel. She began to fold it, pressing carefully along the creases. "Yes."

"There is no possibility of there being someone else in the house?"

"What do you mean?"

"Like a window cleaner or a plumber, someone like that?"

She shook her head.

"No," he said, opening and closing his mouth several times, like a goldfish, she thought.

"Do you understand now what I mean?"

He looked around the room again and then at her. "About an exorcism?"

"Can you help me?"

He cupped his hands together and gently rocked backward and forward in his chair. He looked into his hands, frowning in deep concentration. "There are alternatives to—er—exorcism, which have the same effect. Exorcism is seldom advisable; I'm afraid there is rather a lot of bureaucracy surrounding it these days. One has to present a case to the bishop and it's up to him to decide; it can take several weeks at the very least." He looked up at her, fearful. "You see, it's rather frowned upon these days; ordinary clergy like me are not allowed to perform the exorcism service."

"I can't wait several weeks," said Alex. "Please, you must do something."

"It could be very much longer in your case, under our current guidelines."

"What do you mean?"

"Permission would not normally be given after a bereavement for at least two years."

She thought again of the terror in the bathroom and felt overwhelmed with helplessness. "Two years?" she echoed weakly.

"I'm afraid the Church considers the balance of people's minds can be in a troubled state for a long time after bereavement. It is only if things continue after this period that the service of Deliverance can be considered."

"Deliverance?"

"The modern terminology." He smiled and she saw the twitch again. "The Church prefers the word 'Deliverance'—it sounds perhaps a little less dramatic."

"But surely," said Alex, "if it can be proven—you've just seen yourself."

"The Church has been aware for centuries that the state of possession is normally caused by mental illness and not by spirits. The Church of England leaders have become increasingly involved in psychology these days; there is a strong awareness that not all problems can be resolved by pastoral care alone. I suppose it is an effort by the Church to move with the times, to become more responsible. Frequently, the circumstances in which clergymen have diagnosed the need for exorcism and carried it out have turned out to be mental illness, and they have sometimes made matters worse."

"And you think I'm mentally ill?"

He looked at her, then around the room again. "No. I think that you may be right. There is a presence in this house. Something troubled. But I don't think an exorcism is necessary. We need to try to establish why the spirit is troubled, then perhaps we can lay it to rest." He rocked backward and forward again.

"I know why he is troubled."

Allsop looked at her, continuing to rock backward and forward. "Would you like to tell me?" he said gently.

She looked at him, then shook her head. "No. I can't."

"It would be helpful to know the reason."

She looked out the window, then suddenly at the hallway, convinced she saw something move. She listened hard, watching, but there was nothing more. She stared at the curate. "I think that he has unfinished business."

He stopped rocking, then started again. "I'm afraid most of us depart unprepared, with much that we have planned to do in life still undone."

She nodded.

"Is that what you mean?"

"No." She looked down at the towel, then at Allsop. "I think he wants to come back to kill someone."

She looked down again, unable to face his stare, unable to face the knowledge that he thought she was mad.

"I think a requiem mass would be the answer," she heard him say gently, quietly.

She looked up at him. "What do you mean?"

"We could hold a simple requiem mass service here in the house. I think you'd find that would lay everything to rest."

She felt uncomfortable, frightened by the words. "How—would—what—I'm not sure exactly what you mean."

"We could have it today, if you like, after I've collected my son. I'd just have a few things to bring." He looked at his watch. "About six o'clock, would that suit you?"

Could he help her, this solemn young man with his nervous twitch and his pristine jeans? Could he confound all that was going on with a few prayers? Or would the spirits laugh him out of the house?

"Fine," she heard herself say. "Thank you."

"What will you do until then?"

"Do?" her voice said.

"I think it would be best if you did not remain in the house this afternoon. Is there somewhere you could go? Some friend you could visit?"

"The office. I'll go to the office."

"Yes," he said. "A good idea. Try to concentrate on something different."

He stood up, glanced around nervously, and made his

way to the front door. He paused by the staircase and his eyes widened, filled with uncertainty.

She followed him out of the house without looking back.

28

"There's an Andrew Mallins on the line; he says he has an idea for a play he would like to discuss."

She shook her head. "No, Julie," she said into the intercom. "Not today."

"Do you want to speak to him at all?"

"Ask him to call me next week."

She stared hopelessly at her desk; Christ, how it had piled up. She looked at the wooden calendar: "Wed. May 3." The intercom buzzed again.

"There's a Mr. Prior on the line," said Julie.

"Mr. Prior? I don't know him."

Julie's voice dropped. "From the crematorium," she said sympathetically.

"OK."

Mr. Prior's tone was deferential but to the point. "I was wondering," he said, "if you have had time to consider what you would like to do with the ashes?"

She looked at the calendar again. May 3. The chill went through her. May 3. Tomorrow, she thought. Tomorrow. May 4. "The ashes?"

"Of course, we could scatter them for you, if you'd prefer."

"No," she said.

"We do offer several very nice options. Perhaps a rose bush? We could scatter them over it, or bury the ashes under. Not in the urn, of course; there's not really the room."

"No," she said absently, "of course not."

"There's no need to make a decision now—we will hold them for you for three months."

Urn, she thought. A small black plastic pot. God, if only it were that simple. May 4. May 4. Tomorrow.

"A carved plaque on the wall is very popular; of course, you do have to renew it every fifteen years."

"Of course."

"An entry in the Book of Remembrance is permanent; that's a once-only payment."

A small black pot filled with fine white powder. Her child.

"There are some spaces still available in the rockery—but they are a little inaccessible. I'm afraid there's a waiting list for the more popular sites."

May 4.

"Or, of course, you could have the urn; a lot of people do that now; scatter them in his favorite place. Very popular these days; no cost involved, you see."

Favorite place. Scatter them over the lake. She thought of holding the pot, unscrewing the lid, the ashes blowing in her face, and shuddered.

"Perhaps I could think it over," she said.

"Yes, there's no hurry, we hold them for three months before—er—disposing of them. Of course, we would notify you first."

"Of course."

May 4.

Philip Main was on the line. Did she want to speak to him? Where was the man from the crematorium, she thought, suddenly. Had she finished speaking with him? How had she left it with him?

"How are you?" he said softly.

"OK."

"Did you—?"

"Yes. This evening." She felt tears flooding into her eyes. "They're doing a requiem mass. He said an exorcism would take a long time to arrange—that they wouldn't do one so soon after— Oh God, Philip, I'm so frightened."

"It'll be all right."

She blew her nose. "Shall I call you afterward?"

"Yes, we'll have a drink."

She sniffed and felt good suddenly, felt good having him on the end of the phone, felt a great flood of warmth come down and through her. "I'd like that."

She managed to park right outside her house. It was quarter to six. She switched off the engine and closed her eyes. She heard footsteps and looked up with a start; a man was walking past with a Labrador on a leash; he glanced admiringly through the windscreen at her. She looked away blushing, and felt strangely cheered for a moment. Normality, there was still normality; normality was possible. She clenched the steering wheel tightly with both hands and peered out at her house, like a rabbit, she thought, a frightened rabbit in its hutch.

May 4.

What the hell did it mean? Why did it keep coming back into her head?

How could she be sitting in her car like this, a few feet from her front door, and not dare to go inside? Her house? Her home? She stared at the blue front door, and the white paintwork of the walls; looking a little tacky perhaps, could do with a repaint soon. She tried to remember when it had last been painted. Five years ago at least. God, it looked so solid, so normal, would it ever be normal again? Could she ever live there again?

She trembled. In the mirror she could see the curate and another man, both in black cassocks, walking down the street, lugging something between them; a brown vinyl carryall, she realized, as they came closer.

The other man was older than Allsop, in his early forties, she guessed.

She got out of the car.

"Ah, good," said Allsop, "you've just arrived. We were worrying that we were late. You know each other, of course, don't you?"

Alex smiled politely at the older man; he had a suave dry face, the face of a career clergyman, not a pastoral one. In a suit, instead of his cassock, he could have been a high-flying lawyer. "No," she said.

"Derek Matthews," said the man in a clipped voice, holding out his hand, unsmiling. "The Vicar of St. Mary's."

"Ah," she said, feeling the firm shake of his hand. "I'm afraid I've been a bit remiss in my church-going."

"Most people are, Mrs. Hightower," he said humorlessly.

"I hope you didn't mind—that we didn't ask you to take the funeral service—it was a friend of my husband's—who knew my son—our son—" She shrugged. "We thought it would be appropriate."

"Naturally."

"Shall we, ah—?" said Allsop.

"Yes." She was unsettled by Matthews. "Of course, please come in." She looked down at the carryall. It looked as if it might have contained sandwiches for a picnic. "It's a—very pretty church, St. Mary's."

"Not to the purist," said Matthews tersely. "It's an architectural disaster."

She closed the front door behind her. Matthews looked around dismissively.

"Would anyone like any—er—tea?"

"I think we'll proceed straight away," said Matthews, looking at his watch. "I have a meeting I must get to."

She looked at Allsop and he tried too late to avoid her eyes. He blushed. "I—er—I thought it might be helpful if

Derek was present; he has had much more experience in these things than I." His right eye twitched furiously.

"Yes, of course." She looked nervously at Matthews. "Which room should we use?" she said.

"The room in which the manifestation occurred," said Matthews curtly, as if he were addressing a hotel clerk.

"The manifestation has occurred in every room," she replied acidly.

"May I ask if you've been dabbling in the occult in here at all, Mrs. Hightower?"

"I don't dabble in anything." She was conscious of the anger rising in her voice.

"You've held no séance in here, nothing like that?"

Look, she wanted to say, I'm not at school. But she restrained herself, and nodded. "We held a circle here, last week." She felt her face redden, and stared apologetically at Allsop, feeling she had let him down.

"Then I think we should go to the room where you held it," said Matthews, becoming increasingly impatient.

"I'm sorry," she said, feeling foolish and helpless.

She led the way up the stairs; nothing was going to happen, she knew, nothing at all, and Matthews was going to think she was an even bigger fool.

Oh, God, she thought as she opened the door, feeling her face go red hot with embarrassment at the sight of the chairs, still arranged in a circle.

She sensed Matthews's glare and was unable to face him. She looked up at the portrait of Fabian, then at the curtains, the tape still holding them tightly to the wall.

"These practices are very dangerous, Mrs. Hightower," said Matthews.

"I know," she said lamely, like a schoolgirl, looking at the mortified expression on Allsop's face.

Allsop put the carryall on the floor, and something inside made a loud clank. Matthews knelt down and unzipped it. "We'll need a table; and we'll need some salt."

"Salt?" she said.

"Just ordinary salt. Have you a saltcellar?"

"I'll get one." Alex fetched a saltcellar from the kitchen, then went up into her bedroom. The room felt chillingly cold, and she was frightened to be separated from the others even for a moment. She grabbed the small table from the end of the bed and hurried back to Fabian's room.

"Thank you." Matthews took the table and the saltcellar from her as if they were toys he was confiscating from a child.

They set about their preparations as if they had rehearsed them beforehand. Allsop pushed three of the chairs away, while Matthews began to pull objects out of the carryall and lay them out on the table.

He carefully arranged two small candles like nightlights in the center, then a chalice, a bottle of wine and a silver tray. They worked silently, ignoring her, as if oblivious of her, as if, she thought uncomfortably, she did not count.

Matthews pulled out a silver stoup, and poured a small amount of water into it from a container, mouthing a silent prayer as he did so. Then he poured some salt in. He picked up the stoup and turned, staring past Alex. "Protect us, Oh Lord, we beseech you." He pulled a silver aspergillum out of the bag, dipped the head into the water, then stepped past Alex and flicked it hard at the wall. He turned and solemnly repeated the procedure at each of the other walls. Then he put the stoup and the aspergillum down, pulled a gold Dunhill from his pocket and lit the candles.

Allsop carefully poured the remaining water back into the container, and replaced the stoup in the carryall.

"Shall we begin?" said Matthews.

Alex sat facing the two clergymen.

"You are confirmed, I take it?" said Matthews.

Alex nodded.

"Let us pray," he said loudly, sternly, as if addressing a courtroom.

The curate pressed his hands neatly together and brought them up to his face.

It felt more like a school class than a religious service. Silently, she copied him, trembling with anger and humiliation.

"Listen to our prayers, Lord, as we humbly beg your mercy."

Did they know any more, these two? With their plastic bag and their ornate silverware? Did they know any more than Morgan Ford? Than Philip? Were they just a couple of well-meaning charlatans under a massive flag of convenience? Or did they carry the authority and the clout of the divine power, the power above all else? What power?

She leaned forward and closed her eyes, trying to concentrate, trying to feel the bond with the God she used to talk to when she was a little girl, the God who used to listen to her and protect her, and make everything all right.

"Listen to our prayers, Lord, as we humbly beg your mercy, that the soul of your servant Fabian, whom you have called from this life, may be brought by you to a place of peace and light, and so be enabled to share the life of all your saints. Through Christ our Lord."

"Amen," said Allsop.

"Amen," she echoed quietly, self-conscious about the sound of her voice.

"We pray you, Lord our God, to receive the soul of this your servant Fabian, for whom your blood was shed. Remember, Lord, that we are but dust and that man is like grass and the flower of the field."

Put some feeling into it, man, she wanted to shout out, put some bloody feeling into it. She opened her eyes, and watched him angrily through her cupped hands.

"Lord grant him everlasting rest." Matthews paused to look at his watch. "And let perpetual light shine upon him. Grant to your servant Fabian, Lord, a place of rest and pardon."

She looked up at Fabian's portrait, then closed her eyes and covered them again with her hands. What do you think of all this, darling? Do you mind? Do you understand?

"Oh God, it is your nature to have mercy and to spare. You have called to yourself your servant Fabian who believed in you and placed in you his hope"

Nothing. She could feel nothing except disbelief that this was all happening. She watched Allsop, hands piously together, eyes tightly closed. The room was feeling stuffy; she could smell the melting candlewax, and felt herself perspiring.

"Oh God, you measure the life and times of all men. While we grieve that your servant Fabian was with us for so short a time, we humbly pray you that he may enjoy eternal youth in the joy of your presence forever."

The candles flickered, throwing their shadows over Matthews's face, as if they were throwing back the holy water in disgust.

"Our brother was nourished by Christ's body, the bread of eternal life. May he rise again on the last day. Through Christ our Lord."

"Amen," said Allsop.

She couldn't bring herself to say anything.

There was a long silence.

The room was getting even hotter.

"Holy, holy, holy Lord, God of power and might, heaven and earth are full of your glory. Hosanna in the highest."

Matthews fixed his eyes on hers.

"Our Father, who art in heaven, Hallowed be thy name. Thy kingdom come. Thy will be done on earth as it is in Heaven. Give us this day our daily bread. And forgive our trespasses, as we forgive those who trespass against us. And lead us not into temptation, but deliver us from evil."

Matthews paused, then stared up, over her head, as if the words were too important to be addressed solely to her.

"For thine is the kingdom, the power and the glory, for ever and ever. Amen."

He stood up silently and turned to the table. He picked up the host, and broke a piece into the chalice.

"Lamb of God, you take away the sins of the world; have mercy on us." He turned, and stared directly at her. "May this mingling of the body and blood of our Lord Jesus Christ bring eternal life to us who receive it." He beckoned her.

Slowly she stood up and stepped falteringly forward. He signaled her to kneel, then held out a wafer.

"Take, eat," he said, staring past her again, as he placed the wafer in her cupped hand.

She tasted the dry sweetness, then felt the sharp cold rim of the chalice, and the sudden heady wetness of the wine.

"This is the blood of Christ."

She walked silently back to her chair, a dull metallic taste in her mouth.

"Lord God, your Son gave us the sacrament of his Body to support us in our last journey. Grant that our brother Fabian may take his seat with Christ at his eternal banquet: who lives and reigns for ever and ever."

"Amen," she whispered.

Allsop said nothing, and Matthews glared contemptuously at her, a little girl, not concentrating, speaking out of turn. She closed her eyes.

"Almighty God, you have destroyed death for us, through the dying of your son Jesus Christ."

The words began to echo in her head, like hammering.

"Through his lying in the tomb, and his glorious resurrection from the dead, you have sanctified the grave."

She heard the dripping of water, sharp, fierce drips, like shots. One hit her forehead, like a punch from a fist, then another. They ran down into her eyes, salty and stinging. She put her hand up to her forehead. But there was nothing there, nothing but the slight damp of her perspiration.

"Receive our prayers for those who have died with Christ, and been buried with Him, as with heaven-sent hope they await their resurrection. Grant, we pray you, God of the living and the dead, eternal rest for Fabian. Through Christ our Lord. Amen." He looked at his watch again.

"Amen," said Allsop.

Matthews knelt down and blew out the candles, then began to pack the items away in the bag.

Allsop opened his eyes, smiled gently at Alex, then stood up and helped him.

She sat watching them. Is that it, she wanted to say, is that it? But she doubted whether Matthews would have even bothered to reply.

They went down into the hallway, and she opened the front door for them. Matthews went outside, then turned to her. "I hope you'll consider very carefully before experimenting with the occult again, Mrs. Hightower."

She nodded sheepishly.

He turned away, and walked down the steps. Allsop picked up the bag and smiled at her. "I'll call you in a couple of days, to see how you're getting on."

"Thank you."

She closed the door gently and turned around.

Fabian was standing at the bottom of the staircase.

She smelled gasoline suddenly; the whole hallway seemed to be filled with fumes. Then Fabian began to move toward her, gliding silently, without moving his legs, until all she could see were his eyes, someone else's eyes, not her son's, cold malevolent eyes glaring hatred.

"No!" she screamed, closing her eyes, turning to the door, scrabbling blindly with the catch. She wrenched it open and stumbled out into the street. "Help me!"

But no words were coming out.

"Help me!"

Nothing.

"Oh God, stop, come back, please come back!"

She stared after them, helplessly. "Please help me," she whimpered. But the two clergymen were almost at the end of the street, bobbing along in their cassocks with the bag strung out between them, like a pair of Humpty-Dumpties off to a picnic.

29

She drove too fast through the gates, and hit the water-logged cart track with a thump that bottomed the suspension and jarred through the whole car. Muddy blobs of water spattered the windscreen, and she switched on the wipers, swerving to avoid a deep rut; the nose of the Mercedes dipped sharply, rose in the air then crashed down again with a bang that deflected it sideways, almost pushing the car into the fencing.

The wipers clawed at the windscreen, screeching like angry birds. She smelled the stench of pigs and saw a small dark object scurrying out of the dull beam of the headlights. The Mercedes bounced again and crashed down. Still she kept the accelerator hard on the floor.

Ahead, down to the left, through the muddy streaks and the rubber talons of the wipers, she could see the lake covered in a thin canopy of mist, like a shroud, she thought, and shuddered. It always looked its most sinister at twilight.

She saw David's Land Rover parked outside the house and pulled up beside it. She switched off the engine, closed her eyes and almost wept with relief. The engine made several loud ticking sounds, then pinged, registering its protest, the smell of hot oil overlaying the stench of the pigs. It ticked again, pinged again. Somewhere in the falling dark beyond her a sheep bleated.

She climbed out of the car and stood still, her legs trembling. There was another bleat, then the distant splash of a rising fish carried across the still air. She took a few faltering steps toward the house, then stopped, swaying, and nearly fell. She felt the crunch of mud beneath her feet, moved forward again, heard a plop and a squelching sound and felt her right shoe suddenly become very cold.

"Blast," she said, pulling her foot out carefully, trying not to leave her shoe behind in the puddle. The house was in darkness, but she saw a light shining behind the barn door and walked across the courtyard toward it.

David was standing with his back to her, staring up at the gantry he had rigged from the beam. The block and tackle hung down, swinging gently just above the large new vat, which was still in the middle of the floor.

"Hi," he said without turning around. "Have a good day?"

"No," she said quietly.

"This is a bugger this; a real bugger."

"How did you know it was me?"

He still didn't turn around. "The car. Can always recognize your car—although you were driving a bit faster than usual. It's a real bugger—what do you think?"

"About what?"

"I'm wondering if I might leave it where it is—do you think it looks odd?"

Alex stared at the rope. "It looks like gallows."

"Gallows?" He turned around, then leaned forward to look closer at her. "Christ, you look terrible."

She lowered her head and felt the tears welling; she sniffed.

"Come on," he said, gently putting an arm around her. "Let's get you a drink."

They sat down in the kitchen.

"I think that's nice," he said. "Your own personal service." He smiled. "Shows the Church is having to get

competitive. If the congregation won't come to the
Church, send the Church out to the congregation. Go do
battle with the pizzas and the Chinese take-aways and the
visiting masseuses. Dial-a-Service, eh? Communion delivered to your own home—and there's no collection box to
worry about. I assume there wasn't a collection?"

"No, there wasn't a collection."

"Wouldn't put it past the buggers."

"David," she said sharply.

"I'm sorry."

He picked his glass up by the stem and swirled the
wine around. "Getting better by the day this, you know."

Alex smiled and sipped her whiskey. "Good."

"So does this mean you'll be going back now?"

She detected the note of sadness in his voice and held
her glass tightly in her hands.

"I thought—you know—" he said, blushing, "we
seem to be getting on pretty well. I thought—maybe—
perhaps—"

She closed her eyes tightly, felt the tears welling
again, and sat, clenched up, shaking, rocking the chair
backward and forward. She sipped her whiskey again and
could taste the salt from her tears. She opened her eyes and
looked at him. "It's not over yet, David." A single violent
convulsion rippled through her body, jerking her so hard it
hurt. "It's only just beginning."

She felt his firm strong arm around her shoulder, his
rough fingers caressing her face.

"You're safe here, darling," he said. "I'll look after
you, don't worry. Don't go back to London for a while—
not until you—everything—has settled down."

She nodded; a huge single tear rolled down her cheek,
just as far as his finger, which stopped it like a dam.

She was woken by the sound of water dripping, sharp,
fierce drips, like shots from an airgun. One hit her forehead, like a punch from a fist, then another. Plop. Plang.

The sound echoed around the room, as if she were in a cave.

Her feet felt like ice. There was a bitter cold draft blowing on her face. Plang, she heard. She put her hand up to wipe away the water.

But her face was completely dry.

She frowned, felt her heart thumping, and thought again of Fabian's pitiful cry in the circle. "Help me, Mother."

And then the snarling voice: "Don't listen to the little bastard."

What's happening to you, darling? Please tell me. Please.

Plang. It stung, as hard as if she had been hit by a tennis ball; she felt the water roll down the side of her head, and again touched it with her fingers. Nothing.

And then suddenly she understood.

She closed her eyes, shivering. She knew what she had to do; but she did not know if she had the courage to do it.

There were two sharp pings from the drawing room clock. She heard a slithering sound, the rustle of fabric then a sharp intake of air. The window creaked, there was a sharp exhalation, then the sound of the curtains flapping and billowing.

Her heart slowed down; the wind; just the wind and the curtains. That was all. She smiled in relief and sank back into the soft pillow, felt her feet warming, her skin relaxing, the pain subsiding. There was a sharp, stabbing pain in her finger and her whole body convulsed. Agonizing pins and needles wracked her and she convulsed again. Equally suddenly, the pain subsided and she was left tingling all over, as if she had fallen into a bed of nettles.

Then a violent shock wave passed through her, flinging her up in the bed, sitting her upright against the headboard. She whimpered. Something was standing in front of her, by the foot of the bed. A shadow, darker than the dark.

"Today, Mother."

The voice was clear; so incredibly clear.

"What do you mean, darling?"

The tingling was going.

"Darling?"

She put her hand out toward the bedside table, scrabbling for the light switch. The light came on and she blinked, her eyes sore and stinging, blinked at the dark wardrobe at the end of the bed.

The curtain billowed wildly out into the room, as if someone was shaking it in anger, and she heard the whine of the wind as it gusted. She cupped her hands together and closed her eyes. "Oh God, please help me. Please give me the strength to cope. Please protect Fabian's spirit, and bless him, and let him rest peacefully. Please, dear God, don't let him—" She paused.

Someone was looking at her.

She opened her eyes, but there was nothing, nothing but the furniture and the restless curtains and the sounds of the wind in the night.

She was surprised to see David sitting in the kitchen when she came down in the morning.

"How did you sleep?"

"OK," she said. "I was kept awake a bit by the wind."

He looked out the window. "Seems to have blown itself out; going to be a fine day. Are you going to stay down today?"

She nodded.

"Good. Like some coffee?"

"Thanks."

He put the kettle on the burner.

"I thought you were usually at work by now."

"I'm expecting a phone call. Think I may have tied up something really good. This is the only phone that's working—I dropped the one in the office the other day and the bell doesn't ring."

"I'll stay in here, and call you." She smiled. "I can play at being your secretary."

"It's OK. I have some paperwork to catch up on—I'll do it in here."

Damn, she thought.

"Anyway, it's not often I'm lucky enough to have your company on a weekday."

Why don't you understand, she thought, oh, Christ, why don't you understand?

He frowned at her, and she smiled back reassuringly; then she glanced past him to the rusty key on the hook on the wall behind him.

"I think I'll go for a walk."

"It's gorgeous at this hour." He smiled. "One of the compensations. I'll have the coffee waiting for you. Oh—er could you keep an eye out for any sheep in the vines?"

She nodded and looked at her watch. "I'd better call the office when I get back."

"I'll do it for you. I'll tell them you're not well, won't be in for a couple of days."

"You always make things sound so simple," she said, conscious of the irritated tone of her voice. She smiled at him, trying to compensate. "Can you just walk away from your work here, for as long as you like?"

He shook his head.

"Nor can I."

"There are times when you just have to."

She sighed and went out into the morning air, into the stale stench of the pigs and fresh sweet scent of wet grass. There was a chill tang in the air and a translucence in the early morning sunlight, something watery, almost ethereal.

She walked up the track, away from the house, and forked off right toward the lake. The concrete island was visible only as a shadow through the shroud of mist which lay just above the water. Medieval pond. She shuddered, her nostrils filled with the stagnant smell. Not even the birds sang near this lake. She stopped and looked at the tiny track overgrown with brambles. She picked one stem up, carefully avoiding prickles, and it came away in her hand.

Someone had snapped it off and replaced it.

She stood still, frozen, and stared at it. She looked carefully on either side of her, then stared into the under-growth; she sensed someone behind her, and spun around, her heart racing. No one. Warily, she tested another stem; that, too, came away.

Whoever it was had done a good job. The path and the dry, rotting oak door, with its concrete surround, had been very carefully camouflaged.

She turned the handle and pushed, but it was locked. Again, she sensed someone behind her, and turned around, trembling. But there was nothing. She stood still for a long time, and listened. The only sounds were the throb of a tractor and the distant bleating of sheep.

She carefully replaced the brambles in front of the door, and across the path, then looked at her watch. Nine-fifteen. She turned and stared at the lake again, then walked slowly, reluctantly, back to the house.

David was sitting at the kitchen table, a crumpled cigarette in his mouth, surrounded by his paperwork; he appeared entrenched for the morning.

"Did you get your call?"

He shook his head. "Don't expect I'll hear till later."

Alex nodded, walked into the drawing room and sat down. It was dark in here, quiet.

Leave it alone, her instincts told her; leave it alone, forget it, walk away from it, go back to the curate. Tell him.

"If there's a leak and one of the sections has filled up, you'd be drowned if you opened the door."

"Don't let him, Mrs. Hightower."

"Mother."

"Don't listen to the little bastard."

"May 4."

May 4.

Today.

She stood up, restlessly, and walked over to the unlit fireplace. She held up the photograph of Fabian on his tricycle. Tiny little eyes stared innocently from his plump giggling face. You could only see it if you looked closely, so closely. She put it back slowly, heavily.

May 4.

Today.

"Today, Mother."

"Don't let him, Mrs. Hightower."

Carrie.

"They're going to let me out today, Mother."

She got up and walked through into the kitchen. David smiled up at her.

For Christ's sake, go out to your barn, go out somewhere, anywhere. Why do you have to pick this morning? Let me have that key. I must have it.

"We could go to a pub somewhere and have a nice lunch."

"A nice lunch?" she echoed blankly.

"A pub lunch. A real pub lunch. We haven't done that for years."

"We haven't?"

She was conscious of him staring at her.

"Alex? Are you OK?"

She stared blankly. His words echoed around in her head.

"OK? OK? OK?" She felt herself falling and grabbed the wall, but it slipped away from her. She heard the scrape of a chair, then felt the hard grip of his hand.

"Sit down . . . down . . . down . . ."

She felt the wooden chair creak slightly, saw the walls slip sideways and the ceiling dip suddenly, sharply. Then the whole room tilted on its side and the floor rushed up to her, punched her hard in the shoulder.

David was kneeling over her. She heard his voice,

somewhere, a long way away. "I'll call a doctor . . . doctor . . . doctor . . . doctor . . ."

She shook her head, and the ceiling seemed to spin around, as if it were attached to her head by a piece of string. She felt the hard wooden floorboard against the back of her head. "No," she said. "I'm fine. Really, I'll be fine."

She looked up at his face, straight into the curled barbs of his beard. "I'm fine." She stood up unsteadily, and looked around. The walls stayed where they were. She sat back in the chair. "Must be the strain," she said.

"You should have a holiday. We could go together somewhere—separate rooms—"

She smiled sadly. "I wish it were that simple."

The phone pinged, then rang. David watched it, let it ring several times. "Don't want to seem too keen." He smiled at her.

Answer it, for God's sake, answer it; I can't bear this. Please answer it.

He spoke briefly, curtly, then hung up and looked at her. "Not the one I was expecting." He looked at his watch.

Please ring soon. You must ring soon. You must.

By lunchtime he was bored with his paperwork. "I'd better get over to the winery," he said. "Just check everything's OK."

The barn, with its vats and strange machines and vinous smell. That was his happy hunting ground, she realized. He could not bear to be away from it, even for a few hours.

"I'll shout," she said.

"Butler. His name. Geoffrey Butler."

"Fine," she said. She watched him walk across the courtyard, then went into the hallway and opened the boot closet. She reached up to the top shelf and pulled down the large rubber flashlight. She switched it on, pointed it at her face and blinked at the brightness of its beam. She switched it off and put it back.

It was two more hours before Geoffrey Butler rang. A quarter past four. Two more hours of staring at the key, at the flashlight on the shelf beside it, two more hours of waiting, fidgeting the day away. May 4.

"Geoffrey Butler's on the line," she shouted finally through the winery door, then hurried back across the courtyard, terrified in case Geoffrey Butler might have changed his mind, might have hung up. "He'll be with you in a moment, Mr. Butler," she said, staring at the key, the key that was so nearly hers.

Oh God, please be quick. But no, he scrabbled among his sheets of paper, made notes, more notes. She could take the key now and go while he was concentrating on his call. But if he saw it was missing? Too much of a risk.

"Calcium carbonate," said David. "Chalk. Yes." He chuckled. "Yes, common chalk; reduces the acidity. No, that's right, just ordinary chalk. Anyhow everyone's into calcium these days—meant to be good for you. Yes, of course, well within the EEC prescribed measures."

Come on, come on.

Finally, he hung up; then he walked over to her, flung his arms around her neck and kissed both her cheeks with gusto. "I've got it," he said. "I've got it! It's going to be mega-huge!"

"Good."

"Geoffrey Butler. He's going to stock it permanently, put it on his lists."

"I'm very pleased."

"I tell you something, for him to like it, it must be good. We're going to go out tonight; celebrate. Fancy that?"

"Sure."

"Would you mind if I just went back to the winery for a bit—just got to try a few things out for him—would you mind terribly?"

"No," she said. "No, I wouldn't mind at all."

She watched through the window as he walked across the courtyard and into the winery, and was about to lean forward and take the key when she heard the sound of a car. A customer, or a tourist, she thought. Free tasting any time. Visitors welcome. Go away, she said to herself, go away, whoever the hell you are.

She left the key where it was; he would come running in here in a moment, for a corkscrew, or a couple of glasses, or some damn thing.

Angrily, she went through into the drawing room, sat down on the sofa and stared at the little boy on the tricycle, the plump little chap, with the dark brooding eyes.

There was a commotion outside and then she heard David shouting, furious. "Alex? Alex? Where are you? What the hell's all this? Did you arrange this? These bloody loonies again?"

She looked up at the mantelpiece and Fabian grinned back at her from his tricycle.

"David," she called, her voice scarcely louder than a whisper, and heard his voice, heated, in the distance.

"Can't you see—she's come here to get away from it. All you're going to do is bring it down here—whatever the hell it is. Why can't you just leave her alone? She'll be all right, she'll get over it; a few days of country air is what she needs."

"It's not that simple, Mr. Hightower. I wish it were." She recognized the singsong voice of Morgan Ford instantly.

"David."

There was a long silence.

May 4.

She shuddered.

"David."

She heard Ford's voice, gentle but firm. "I think we should start now."

"No," said David. "She doesn't want to."

"For both your sakes," said Ford.

No, she tried to say. *No.* But nothing came out.

"Your son's spirit is disturbed, Mr. Hightower. You cannot leave him like this. Until we have helped his spirit over, your wife will have no peace."

Don't let him, David, please don't let him.

"Couldn't you do this some other time? When she is stronger?"

"She won't get stronger while he is around. He's using her power all the time, draining her energy."

No. You've got it wrong. Can't you see? Oh God, can't you see?

"She's acting like a battery to him; he's taking all the time. We must put something back in—or free them from each other."

"What do you mean, a battery?"

"Spirits have no energy of their own, Mr. Hightower. They draw their energy from carnate beings."

"And you say he's drawing his energy from Alex?"

"Earthbound spirits live in a world of darkness, Mr. Hightower. Just as humans in darkness head toward any light they can see, spirits make for sources of energy. Grief is a strong source of energy. As is love. Your wife's grief is acting like a beacon to him. Her love for him is fueling the power of her grief."

There was a silence. "And that's your theory?"

"No, Mr. Hightower; it is not my theory. It is what I know."

"And if we do nothing, what will happen?"

"There is a danger that he could end up possessing her completely."

"I'd like to have a word with my wife in private."

"Yes, of course. There is an important consideration. You see, she must understand that she may be responsible."

She heard David's voice rise. "Responsible?"

"We believe your son's spirit is still on the earth

plane," said Ford, very matter-of-fact. "But we do not
know whether that is because he did not depart from it, or
whether he has been brought back. You see, if Mrs. Hightower had ignored his manifestations, his signals, and
hadn't come to see me . . . they may have just been his
way of saying goodbye. Nothing more might have happened. Often spirits don't want to return—they are summoned unwillingly, like Samuel when Saul consulted a medium. And sometimes it is the power of the grief or the
love of a bereaved one that pulls the spirit back."

There was another silence.

"I just wanted to make that point, Mr. Hightower. It
is important."

"So it's all my wife's fault, is it?"

"Not necessarily, Mr. Hightower. Not necessarily at
all. But it is a possibility."

There was a long silence. Then she heard David
shouting, "Alex? Alex!"

She looked around.

"Where the hell is she?"

She heard footsteps, then his voice again.

"Here you are! Have you gone deaf—I've been looking all over the place for you!"

She said nothing.

She heard the door close.

"Your damned medium friend is here—and that
bloody loony Sandy—and the rest of them. Why the hell
did you ask them down?"

"I didn't."

"What?"

"I didn't."

"So who the hell did then?"

"Fabian," she said simply.

She heard the click of his tobacco tin, the rustling of
paper, and then silence again.

"What do you mean?"

She stared at the child on the tricycle: her child,

whom she had brought into the world. Her infant crying in
the night. Her infant crying for the light. She shuddered.
The smiling child on the tricycle was out there in the darkness, confused and frightened.

"Help me, Mother."

How?

"I don't know. I don't know what I mean."

"What do you want to do?"

"Help me, Mother."

She heard a click, saw a brief flash of light, then
smelled the sweet smoke of his cigarette.

"Morgan Ford upset you last time."

"Help me, Mother."

"It's my fault," she said, trembling. "It's all my
fault."

"Of course it's not."

May 4.

The door opened.

"Shall we begin?" said Ford.

Alex turned around. The young man with a gold earring carried a wooden chair into the room, bashing the
doorway with it in the process. He looked down at her and
nodded. The slicked-back hair; the creepy face. Orme, she
remembered. Orme.

The tall meek man in a brown suit followed him in,
also carrying a chair. He held it off the ground and looked
around apologetically, as if waiting for someone to tell him
he could put it down. The postman.

David stood silently, frowning, uncertain, his anger
abated.

Morgan Ford was standing over her. Gray suit, gray
shirt, gray tie, gray hair, all perfectly color-coordinated.
He gave her a firm, assured smile. She saw the glint of the
rhinestone ring and looked up at his face, at the black
haystack of Sandy's hair, at Orme's gold earring, at Milsom's brown polyester suit; at the reluctant nod of David's
head and the strange look of anxiety in his eyes.

She heard the sound of the curtains being pulled, and the room went dark suddenly. There was a click of the light switch, and she blinked against the sudden brightness. She heard the screech of tape, and watched Orme sealing the curtains.

No. Don't let them, David. Oh God, don't let them.

"There is so much power here," said Ford. "So much power."

Don't let them, David.

"Let her stay there," said Ford. "She's fine like that. Let her be comfortable."

No. Please. No.

"The process of releasing the spirit can sometimes be a little distressing," said Ford gently, looking at David then Alex. "Sometimes the spirit will relive those last few moments of his carnate existence."

The light went out.

I have to do this on my own. Please. Don't let them, David. Don't let them give him any more power.

"Dear God, we pray to you that you will look after our circle and that we shall come to no harm."

Don't you realize what's going to happen?

There was a click and she heard Vivaldi, light, airy, sad.

"Feel the grass soft and springy; it's good to walk on. You see a white gate ahead of you. Go through the gate and you can see a river."

Stop them. Please, David, Stop them.

"You can see people on the far side, standing there. Your friends, waiting to greet you. Cross over the bridge now, go to them, greet them, hug them, spend time with them. Don't be afraid, go, enjoy, be happy with them."

She stared across the river, to the far side of the old stone bridge, and saw Ford, standing in his immaculate gray suit, waving at her, beckoning. Behind him were more people, grouped around, chatting as if they were at a cocktail party. Sandy, Orme, Milsom and David.

I'm here. Over here.

She put a foot on the bridge, but they all turned away, ignoring her.

I'm here.

She tried to step on to the bridge, but a pair of hands gripped her arms, held her back.

Let me go.

You'll drown; it's a trap; the bridge isn't safe.

Who are you?

There was a click, then silence; complete silence. She opened her eyes and stared, terrified, around the dark room.

"It's started," said Ford. "He is impatient. He is not willing to wait for us to finish our meditation."

She felt icy air swirling around her.

A car roared past outside the window, followed by a heavy truck. The room shook with the vibration. She stared wildly around. Impossible. There was no road. No road, she thought again. Had David heard it? Had they all heard it?

"Mother!" A gruff, rasping whisper, scarcely louder than the silence. It was coming from the postman.

"What is your name?" said Ford in a plain business-like tone, as if he were answering a telephone call.

There was another long silence.

It's a con. That's not his voice. Don't you realize it's a con?

"Will you please tell us your name? If not, kindly leave the medium at once."

Alex heard breathing, right beside her, halting erratic breathing, deep gulps, then long pauses.

"Are you Fabian Hightower?"

There was a sharp smell of gas. She heard others sniffing; they could smell it too.

"Are you Fabian Hightower?"

The smell increased suddenly and the fumes stung her eyes.

"We're going to help you, Fabian."

She couldn't breathe.

"To help you go over to the other side."

It was as if a mask had been pressed over her face. The harder she tried to breathe, the closer she sucked the mask into her face. The breathing beside her was becoming calmer, more rhythmic, like the breathing of a diver.

No.

She was beginning to shake. *Give me some, don't take it all; oh God, don't take it all. Air. Oh God, give me some air.*

She fought with the vacuum around her face, tried to push it away, to duck under it, to turn away from it. Her chest was aching.

The fumes; the fumes had taken the air.

Then she noticed. The breathing beside her. Rhythmic, contented.

No.

She rocked violently backward and forward, shaking, more and more.

The fumes. Gas. It was going to explode.

Let me breathe, darling. Give me air. Please give me air.

Something was moving inside her; something cold, bitterly cold. A cold hand brushed her forehead, gently pushed her hair back from her forehead, squeezed her shoulders. She heard the sofa shaking, rattling, clattering in the silence, as she shuddered, fighting for breath. There was something cold inside her ear now, seeping into her head like liquid.

And then, suddenly, she felt strong. Stronger than she had ever felt before. So strong, she no longer even needed to breathe. *No. Please no. Please no.*

Another car hurtled past outside and into the distance. Suddenly there was a slithering sound, a desperate, frightening sound, which seemed to go on forever. *No.* She tried to stand up, but an immense force pushed her back on to the sofa. She tried again, and a hand tugged her back, insistent. Who's? David's? Ford's? She tore it free, and stood up again. Something tried to push her back, some huge force like a falling wall. She pushed against it, with all her new strength, and felt the floor rise up sharply in front of her. She went on to her hands and knees, and slowly inched her way across, tugging at the strands of carpet with her fingers; she reached the door and clung to the handle, which took all her weight, clung to it to prevent herself falling backward into the dark room.

Still the slithering sound continued, eerily, a car with locked wheels sliding across a damp road.

She forced the door open then tumbled through it suddenly, rolled over and over across to the kitchen wall and hit the sink with a thump that jarred her.

Her lungs were bursting. She gulped down air ravenously, long deep breaths, then lay there for a moment, exhausted, staring fearfully at the door to the drawing room, the door she had just come through that had closed behind her. Were they sitting there, still? In the dark room? Had they noticed she had gone? She felt a cold prickling down the back of her neck, climbed unsteadily to her feet and listened. But she could hear nothing. She stared at the key hanging on the nail, and at the cupboard with the flashlight. *Time. Was there time?* The key felt cold, rough, heavy. *Was there time?*

The key turned easily, too easily. The lock had been oiled. The door was harder to open; it was warped and sagging on its hinges. She had to push hard to make a gap big enough to go in, then she closed it behind her.

She turned to face the darkness, breathing in the dank, lifeless smell, and heard the scrape of her foot echo around her.

"I'm here, darling," she said, and heard her voice fall flatly away into the dark. She switched on the flashlight and saw the stone steps a few feet in front of her. Exactly as she had remembered.

She went down them and felt the air getting damper, and colder. At the bottom was a massive watertight steel door, with a huge round wheel on the front of it, like a submarine.

"If there's a leak and one of the sections has filled up, you'd be drowned if you opened the door."

She tested the handle and it rotated easily. She gave it six full turns before it stopped. She swallowed, then pushed the door. It swung open with no effort at all and just the merest groan from one of its hinges which echoed along the dark tunnel ahead like the cry of a wounded animal.

She shone her flashlight at the concrete floor then up around the curved walls. To her right was a series of valves, dominated by another huge wheel on the wall. "Never touch these," the estate agent had warned. "They would flood the tunnel." Dimly, at the end of the beam, she could see another door, like the one she had just opened. She shone the flashlight down at the floor again and a puddle glinted at her. Nervously she pointed the beam up at the ceiling. The plasterwork was mottled with fat brown blotches and flaking away.

A tiny blob of water launched itself from the center of the blotches with a faint plop. It smacked into the concrete floor. Plang. The sound echoed around her, and she shuddered, spun around and beamed her flashlight back where she had come from. She heard breathing, heavy breathing, and stiffened. She held her breath and the sound stopped. She breathed out again with relief, then stepped forward into the tunnel, deep under the silent black water of the lake, under the mist and the fish that jumped and the reeds like dead men's fingers.

There was slime on the floor and patches of mold on the walls. The beam of the flashlight threw streaks of light and long shadows all around her, and the dull echo of her footsteps followed her at first and then overtook her. The door was coming closer, the door to the ballroom. If the ballroom was flooded . . . If.

She stopped when she reached it, and looked behind her fearfully.

Plop. Plang. The noise echoed around like the slamming of a door. Oh Christ, no. She shone the beam back where she had come from, saw the prick of light dance on the roof, then on the floor. The door was still open.

Plop. Plang.

She rotated the wheel, and it turned silently, well oiled, six turns, exactly as the previous one.

Then her flashlight went out.

No. She shook it. *No.* She shook it again. No. She switched it on, off. Nothing; she shook it. Nothing. Please, she whimpered. Please. She shook it again, and she heard the faint tinkling of glass inside the lens. She closed her eyes, then opened them again. There was no difference. She held her breath and listened to the silence. She had never before heard such silence.

Plop. Plang.

And then silence again.

She pushed open the door. Light. There was light; so bright it startled her. She stared in wonder up at the domed roof, its thick panels of glass, coated in slime and limp strands of weed, exactly as she had remembered. The panels were so bright, almost as if they had lights behind them; it felt as if you could reach through them and touch the sky.

For a moment she was dazzled by the brightness, too dazzled to see anything in the green light that filtered down and around the room.

Then the stench hit her. A horrendous pungent stench that flooded through her nostrils, down her throat, deep into her stomach, unlike anything she had ever smelled before.

She pinched her nostrils together tightly with her fingers, felt her stomach heave and then gagged. Something banged into her shoulder, and she shrieked, then felt stupid. It was the wall, which she had backed into.

The stench hit her again; she cupped her hands over her nose and took a deep breath through her mouth.

And then she saw the person on the floor on the far side of the room watching her.

She froze.

Slowly, she felt her legs buckling. She tried to back out of the room, felt the jarring thump of the hard slimy wall. She pressed her hands against it, feeling her way, inching along. Where was the passage? Where was it? Where was it?

Someone had closed the door.

"No. No." She spun around and saw the wall right behind her. The door was still open, through to the blackness of the passageway, just a couple of feet to her right.

She looked over her shoulder. The person was laughing at her, laughing silently, motionless. The stench filled her nostrils again and she gagged.

"They're going to let me out today."

"Don't let him, Mrs. Hightower."

"Don't listen to the little bastard."

I want to get out. Please, God, I want to get out. She turned and looked down the tunnel, then back over her shoulder.

Plop. Plang.

She heard a cry; a single tiny whimper. Her own. It echoed around the room, came back at her.

"I'm sorry," she said. "I'm so sorry."

She felt the safety of the wall and began to walk across the room. A shadow flitted past her and she spun around. Nothing. The shadow flitted again; she looked up, and saw the dark silhouette of a fish nibbling at the weed on the outside of the glass.

She took another step forward, then another.

Move. Please move. Please say something.

The stench was getting worse.

There was a sharp crack, right underneath her. She screamed wildly, then again and again. Then her scream subsided into a whimper as she looked down and saw a plate, split in half by her foot.

She took another step forward and then she was close enough. She stared, shivering in horror, at the girl's face, shriveled like dried leather, at the eyes staring hopelessly ahead at the door she had opened far too late, and the twist of her mouth like a hideous laugh.

"No," Alex whimpered. "No." She stared at the chain around the girl's neck that trailed off to an anchorage somewhere beyond in the gloom. "No."

"He'd been coming down a lot, just lately." David's voice echoed through her head. *"Since around about Christmas. Really seemed to be taking an interest in the place. I used to watch him, sitting out there on the island, fishing, for hours on end. I used to wonder what he was thinking."*

"No."

She backed away slowly, desperately slowly, inching her way as if she were pushing against a huge force. She tried to look away, at the walls, at the ceiling, but she was drawn back, like a magnet, to the face: *"Hi Mum, This is a really friendly place, lots of things happening, met some great people. Will write again soon."*

I'm sorry. She mouthed the words, but nothing came out. I'm sorry; I'm so desperately . . .

There was a noise right behind her.

She froze, felt the terror surging. She looked down at the ground, unable to turn around, then back again at the face like leather.

A shadow moved; the shadow of the person who was standing behind her.

She shook her head. *Please no.*

The scrape of a foot.

Please no.

The rustle of a coat.

No.

She spun around.

Nothing.

Nothing but the black entrance of the tunnel.

Then she heard a noise behind her, from the girl.

Oh no. Oh Christ, no.

She turned around slowly, fearfully.

The girl was grinning. Grinning at her, grinning at her fear.

No. Please don't do that. Please don't.

"Admiring your son's handiwork, Mrs. Hightower?"

The voice ripped through her like an electric shock. She lost her balance and nearly fell on the girl. She blinked, felt a surge of nausea, lost focus for a moment.

Otto.

He was standing in the doorway, coat slung over his shoulders.

She began to shiver violently. Something in his expression; something terrible. She put her hand in front of her mouth, staring at the eyes. And then she realized. The eyes; the same expression in the eyes. Fabian on his tricycle. The portrait on the wall. Bosley. Otto.

She stepped back, trod on something which crunched under her foot, and jumped in fear. She spun around, saw the girl staring at her, stepped back, stared up at the ceiling, around at the walls and then back at Otto in the only doorway.

She tried to speak, but still nothing would come out. She spun around again, stared at the girl; the girl seemed to move. She tried to scream. Nothing. *Oh God help me.* She turned back. *Move, oh Christ, move! Say something.* She was shivering wildly; it was freezing in here now; as she breathed, her lungs hurt, and her breath hung in front of her like a cloud.

"What do you want?" She mouthed the words, her voice tight, cracking, faint, as if it were a long way away.

He smiled.

Say something; for God's sake, say something.

Otto continued to smile.

The air was going; it was getting harder to breathe. She started gulping, looking around wildly. Panic seized her.

"I—want—to—go—now—" she said, and began walking toward Otto, walking against a huge force that was pushing her back.

"Fabian will be here in a minute, Mrs. Hightower; aren't you going to wait for him?"

"Will you let me by, please, Otto." Her voice was calm suddenly, firm, normal.

Still smiling, Otto stepped out of the way. It took her what seemed like an eternity to reach the doorway. She stood there, staring fearfully at him, waiting for his move, waiting for him to grab her, but he just smiled, his expression unchanging.

"He'll be so disappointed to have missed you."

She turned away and ran, stumbling, down the tunnel.

Plang. The droplet of water hit her like a fist, knocked her sideways.

"No!"

She stumbled forward.

Another drop hit her on the forehead like a hammer. She reeled, crashed into the wall, fell on her face into the slime. Another drop hit her on the back of her neck like a kick. She picked herself up, stumbled forward. Which way was she going? The wrong way. No. She could see the light. The ballroom. *Oh God, help me.*

Another droplet smashed on to the bridge of her nose; her eyes watered. The ballroom disappeared and she stumbled forward, into the wall. A droplet smacked her scalp and stung like acid. She turned and staggered toward the dark; the dark that seemed to go on forever. "Help me, God, please help me."

A beam of light shone in her face, dazzling her.

Her scream echoed down the tunnel and came back at her from every direction at once.

Then she stood for a moment, frozen like an animal. Two arms closed around her.

She felt the rough denim of David's jacket, hugged it tight.

"Oh God." The emotion welled up inside her and burst over and she began to sob. She ran her hands up and down the jacket, up into the soft curly hair at the back of his neck. "Thank God, thank God." She felt his neck and the thick tangle of beard and sobbed uncontrollably. Then she heard his voice.

"It's all right, Mother, it's all right."

The shiver ran through her.

"It's going to be all right."

"No," she whispered, horrified, as she tried to back away.

She felt the grip on her arm like a pincer of iron.

"Chained her up in a cellar."

"David?"

"And left her?"

"David, please let me go."

The voice was gentle, soothing. "Don't worry, Mother."

She screamed, pulled herself away, tripped, fell over into the slime, rolled hysterically.

She stood up, saw the light at the end of the tunnel, saw a dark shape block it out suddenly. She turned again, ran, slipped and fell. She flailed around with her arms, slithering, scrambled back on to her feet and ran as fast as she could. Then she tripped and fell again hard, winded. *Door. Close door.* She climbed back on to her knees, trying not to pant, and cracked her head. She cried out in pain and put her hands up. Something round, cold. The door handle.

She stood up, seized the huge wheel with both hands. But it would not move. *Come on; come on.* She turned the wheel sharply, rotated it completely and pulled again. *Oh, come on, please;* she rotated it again; stiff, creaking, grating. *They'll hear; they'll hear. Christ, it wasn't stiff before.*

A fine spray of water hit her in the face.

She rotated it again and pulled. A jet of water hit her in the chest and flung her against something. The wall. She heard the hissing of the water, venomous, getting louder.

"Mother!" She heard Fabian's piercing scream.

"Never touch these; they would flood the tunnel"

The wrong wheel; that's why it would not move. *No, oh Christ, no.* She had turned the wheel of the valve, not the door.

The water stung her eyes like acid. She opened them, blinking against the pain. Where was the light? Which way? Water was spraying at her from every direction.

There was a creaking sound, faint at first, then a louder cracking, like the splintering of wood. It sounded as if someone were opening a gigantic packing case. The noise spread, surrounding her, deafening her. Then suddenly it stopped and for a moment there was no sound at all.

She stared wildly around in the dark, trying to orient herself, trying to find the way. But there was nothing but the black.

She heard a rumble, faint at first, like distant thunder. It turned into a raging bellow, right behind her. She spun around, and for an instant she saw it: the light, the ballroom. Then the wall of water.

No.

The wall of water that was hurtling at her.

The light went first. Then the sound. It was silent as the water scooped her up, enveloped her, swept her down.

Completely silent.

30

Everything was very white, soft, diffused, milky. White fingers glided noiselessly around her, leaving silent ripples in their wake. Consciousness was still only dimly registering. Pills, she thought. Pills that made her feel good, dream good dreams; they were hard to wake up from.

The stern gaze; fronds of mustache; steely blue eyes. How long had he been there?

"All right, girl?"

She smiled weakly.

"It's jolly stuffy—shall I open a window?"

She nodded. There was a sharp clack as the blind shot up and the room suddenly filled with bright light. The illusion was gone and reality had intruded again. Another day. Another day that would not matter.

"What's the date, Philip?"

"May 18."

Christ. She tried to sit up suddenly, but the pain in her shoulder prevented her.

"No change?"

"I think it's a little better."

They sat in silence for a few minutes. She watched Philip smoking, saw the flickering of his eyelashes, then tried to think again, fighting against the drugs that were meant to stop her from thinking.

"I killed them," she said suddenly.

"It was unsafe. Could have gone at any time. Should have been sealed off."

"I thought David was going to—I thought that he'd become Fabian, that he—that they were going to chain me —I opened the valve. I thought it was the door."

She stared at the blue of his eyes. Light danced on them like ponds. Medieval ponds. The shudder ran through her. "I killed them."

"No, gosh, good Lord no."

"I did."

"An accident, girl. An accident."

"I didn't even go to his funeral. I didn't go to my own husband's funeral." She watched as Philip stood up and walked over to the window. He leaned on the sill and looked out. "I should have gone to Otto's too. He came to Fabian's."

"Germany," Philip said gently. "I gather they took him back to Germany."

"So many funerals," she said.

There was another long silence. She shivered. "I didn't even send any flowers to Otto—or to the girl."

"The girl?"

"Carrie."

"Carrie?"

"The girl who—" She paused and stared at him. "You know. Who was there."

"Who was where?"

"Under the lake."

"What girl under the lake?"

"The one that Fabian—" She paused. Why wouldn't he talk about it? Why did he keep denying it?

He walked back over and sat down beside the bed. "The lake was drained." He pulled out another cigarette. "There was just Otto and David. No one else."

"But—I—I saw—Philip?"

He shook his head firmly.

"In the ballroom," she said, lowering her voice.

"Rubble," he said. "All rubble. Whole thing imploded. Extraordinary piece of engineering." He stood up again and walked back toward the window.

"She's under there," Alex said softly.

He stared out of the window again. "It's what saved you," he said.

"What do you mean?"

"The engineering. Stressed in sections. You must have been pushed out like toothpaste."

"Why didn't it save them?"

He stared out the window in silence.

"Philip—she was there."

He continued to stare out the window, for a long time. "There's a balance," he said softly, without turning around. "Always a balance. Two bits of dust; positive and negative; meeting in a void; bang. One without the other would have been useless—no life; nothing." He turned and stared at her. "The sun's out there." He nodded toward the window. "Can you imagine going there? Hell. The inferno. Hell, girl. But we need it; we need it to exist. Do you understand?"

The door opened and a nurse walked in dressed in white. She lifted her arm and looked at her watch. "I'm afraid it's time for your—" She looked at Philip.

He stood up awkwardly and blushed. "Righty-ho—I'll er—tomorrow?"

Alex listened for the click of the door closing. The new routine of life. Easy; so easy; sometimes she wished she could stay here forever.

31

The moving van arrived at nine. She could see it without looking up: a great blue shadow across the window. She heard the rattle of the engine, the slamming of doors, voices.

"They 'ere, Missy Eyetoya, they 'ere."

"Let them in, Mimsa."

Mimsa stared at her wide-eyed, uncertain.

"Go on." She nodded, smiling.

They carried the packing cases out first, then the furniture. She watched the house, now already bare, being gutted. Cleansed, she thought to herself, walking around the rooms, checking. God, they looked small suddenly. Tiny.

She stood on the pavement and watched the van reverse away. Eighteen years. Eighteen years and she wasn't sure what her next door neighbor looked like. They wouldn't miss her; the street wouldn't miss her; there was no sentiment here. Only inside her own heart.

As she climbed into her Mercedes, she saw the young couple arrive in their blue BMW and park opposite her. He was smart, trendy, in a Paul Smith suit; she was a willowy blonde. He lifted a small boy out of a car seat and plunked him on the pavement. Then the three stood, looking at the house.

"I think red for the front door," she heard her say.

"Or black," he said. "Black would be smart. Look, there, 46, that's black."

The same conversation they had had, she thought, a tear rolling slowly down her cheek; eighteen years ago; they had stood on that pavement, the three of them; David in his Tom Gilbey suit, herself and their son. Fabian. The thrill. The hope, the dreams, the plans. Plans. She sighed, and started the engine.

A new beginning. It was a bright day for it, a fine August morning. She felt a twinge of pain in her shoulder as she turned the wheel. They told her it would still hurt for a while to come. But it was healing; all the wounds were healing, both the physical and the mental. It was the memories that would last the longest. She wished it were as easy to empty her mind as it had been her house.

The moving van was already at Cheyne Walk and they were piling her furniture on to the pavement.

She climbed the stairs to the top floor and walked around the huge empty apartment. She felt free suddenly, free of so many things. She hardly noticed the moving men bringing everything in; there seemed to be no effort, no effort at all. Even the huge bouquet of flowers that arrived from Philip scarcely registered more than a gentle smile.

She slept well that night, without pills, without anything; slept well for the first time, she realized, since it had begun.

There was so much that had passed. So much for her to come to terms with. What darkness had twisted her beautiful son? What evil had lain dormant in him for so long that she had never seen? Something that had taken him over so completely that he was no longer really her son? And David? David had always seemed so good. So strong. Had the evil found a weakness? What weakness? *Evil will not enter a person who will not receive it.* Was that true, or just wishful thinking? Had her rejection of David soured him, begun to turn him evil? Or had the spirit made

a mistake, in thinking David would receive it? A terrible
mistake that had . . . ? Explanations. So many people
had attempted explanations. The chaplain of Broadmoor.
The psychiatrist at the hospital. But they could only ever
know part of the story. Without the body, Fabian had done
nothing wrong. Without the body that was buried under
the rubble at the bottom of the lake, buried under the
rubble of her mind. Without the body, it could all be a
product of her mind. And they believed it was. All of them
except Philip. Who knew.

It was Philip who had got her through the past
months. Philip, with his theories and explanations, who
had helped her peel away the layers. It was Philip who
dismissed the idea each time she thought of telling.

"If they did look . . . and found nothing? What
then, girl?"

That, she knew, would be the worst horror of all.

She stared out across the Thames streaked with the
morning sunlight, at the trees of the park on the far side, at
the rooftops of Battersea, Clapham, Wandsworth and beyond.

She smelled David suddenly, the musty vinous smell
of his denim jacket, felt the warmth of his body, the bristles of his mustache, and heard Fabian's voice calling out
from inside him and shivered. Conductors, conduits; re-
ceptors; the technical jargon; the explanations; Philip; the
chaplain; Morgan Ford; it sounded like something to do
with electricity, not with the . . . She stumbled on her
thoughts, trying to make some sense out of all the bits and
pieces of remembered conversations swirling around in her
mind.

> *"In a violent death, usually an accident or a
> murder, the spirit needs to be helped over. He may
> not be aware that he has died."*

"If a possessed person dies, what happens to the evil spirit?"

"It goes with him to Hell."

"Could someone bring it back?"

"Perhaps."

"If an exorcism is successful, where does the spirit—the demon, whatever it is that's driven out —go?"

"It has to find a new host."

"It was horrible, Philip. It was David, but he spoke with Fabian's voice."

"That happened before."

"This time it was different."

"Because the tunnel made you scared."

"No. It was Fabian. He had made David his host."

"Ford was wrong. He said David wasn't receptive. I knew he was."

"How?"

"I knew."

"No, girl. If David had been truly receptive, you wouldn't have got out of there."

"Evil will not enter a person who will not receive it."

"Do you think David had come down to find me? To help me?"

"Perhaps."

"The spirit wanted me. I wouldn't receive it so it tried to enter David."

"Perhaps."

"And he was fighting it too?"

"Perhaps."

"That's how I escaped? David's resisting sapped his strength to stop me?"

"Perhaps."
"Did David sacrifice his life?"

"Evil spirits can be very cunning. Good mimics. Take on a departed person's characteristics. Voices. Mannerisms. Appearance."

"The circle creates energy, like a beacon. He can find his way to the circle."
"Does evil have beacons too? Could Otto have been a beacon?"

"Mrs. Hightower, no clergyman who is a true believer can rule out the diabolical."

A lone jogger, in a tee shirt and shorts, was running across the Albert Bridge. Jogging, she thought. It had been a long time. Tomorrow she would jog again.

She felt a strange stillness and calm. David's dying had released her from something. She was sad, deeply sad, and sometimes she missed his phone calls and the glee in his voice when he talked about his wine, but in a strange way, in her grieving she was free.

It was as if the past had begun to exorcise itself.

She walked up the stairs to her office. She was looking forward once more to work. To the deals; to the piles of manuscripts. To concentrating on something different.

"How did it go?" said Julie.

"Fine; I thought it would be much worse. The flat is gorgeous—the view this morning was quite fantastic."

"I'd like a view," she said.

Alex smiled. "Anything happen yesterday?"

"Nothing urgent. Philip left a message—something about the theater on Thursday; he said your phone wasn't working yesterday."

Alex walked through into her office. It felt chilly after

the warm sunlight and she pulled up the blinds, opened the window and let the warm summer air soak in.

Her desk was stacked with letters, manuscripts, message slips. Challenges. God, she was so far behind, from her weeks in the hospital and from the preoccupation with moving. She stared around the room for a moment, collecting her thoughts, making a mental schedule for the day. Then she smiled to herself again. It was over. She stared out at the blue sky. The long slow climb had begun, back to where she had been once, back to somewhere that could never be the same. Sighing, she stretched out her arm and switched on her VDT.

Two green words stared back at her, bright, unflickering.

HELLO, MOTHER.

ABOUT THE AUTHOR

PETER JAMES was born in 1948 in England. After a film school training he moved to Canada and founded an independent film production company and made eight films, among them the award-winning *Dead of Night*. Returning to England in 1975, he founded Yellowbill Productions, which has produced a number of films and videos, including *Biggles,* which is scheduled for release in the United States in 1988. Turning to writing full-time in 1979, James went on to publish three thrillers. *Possession,* his fourth novel, is the result of his own experiences with the supernatural. Peter James and his wife live in Brighton, Sussex, where he is currently working on his next book, also a novel.